TI
SHACKLETONS
— *of* —
WHITEHAVEN

This copy is for you
Margaret.
I hope you enjoy it —
with best wishes.
Lorna.   Oct. 2022.

LORNA HUNTING

Published by Goldcrest Books International Ltd
www.goldcrestbooks.com
publish@goldcrestbooks.com

ISBN: 978-1-913719-63-0
eISBN: 978-1-913719-64-7

This book is dedicated to

Pippa
Arthur
Lottie
Annabelle
Nathaniel
and
Sophie.

Six little people who bring me great joy.

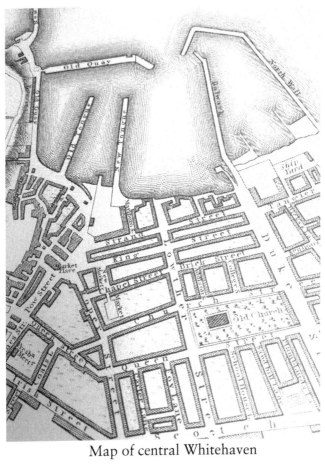

Map of central Whitehaven

CHAPTER ONE

Whitehaven Friday April 13th 1860

On his way to bid for the *Gregory Peat*, Fergus Shackleton heard the clock strike two. He had half an hour before the bidding book closed, allowing him plenty of time to walk the short distance from the company offices in Tangier Street to the Indian King Inn. It was a gloriously sunny April afternoon, with no breeze to speak of. It was good to be out and about, and all the more so for being unexpected. Had their office manager; Mr Craggs, not been 'out of sorts', Fergus would have been spending all day inside, sorting through invoices and ship manifests.

It had been a hectic week. The *Cheery Rose* had come in from Antigua the previous day and was tied up discharging her cargo. Three vessels were engaged taking on iron ore for Cardiff, Chester and Liverpool. When news came of Mr Craggs' absence, Fergus's father, Hector Shackleton, had stuck out his lower lip – an action he'd favoured as a boy when perplexed or crossed, and never grown out of.

'*You'll* have to go, Fergus,' he'd said. 'There's no one else. You've a £6,000 limit plus commission, which should be no more than £50, including other fees. And whatever you do, don't be late, or you'll not be able to bid and we'll lose her.'

Fergus's eyes had widened. His father sending him on such an important mission? The same man who, two days earlier, had described his son as 'barely a man, just out of university, spending all his time with his nose in a book'? It was proving quite a turnaround and he was still finding it hard to take on board.

Fergus was halfway along New Street when a cart passed by. It was going far too fast and one of the barrels in the back was rocking from side to side. As Fergus watched, it jumped out and, with a sickening thump, struck a young boy in its path. The boy cried out in pain and surprise. People began shouting and running in all directions – some to stop the carter, who appeared oblivious to the accident, and others to see to the boy. Fergus was the first to reach him. He looked no more than ten or maybe eleven years old. His eyes were open, his eyelids flickering, and he was looking around, alarm written all over his face. His breathing was shallow and raspy. The coal dust pitted in the creases of his face and limbs indicated he was a pit boy. Probably a trapper, cooped up all day or night, pulling a rope to open and shut a ventilation door in conditions no better than an underground dungeon. He was wearing the coarse woollen jacket all the pit boys wore.

As Fergus bent down, tears began snaking their way down the boy's face, mixing with the dust to create drunken pathways. The barrel had knocked him backwards and landed with full force on his right leg. With care, Fergus moved the boy's dark fringe back from his eyes – eyes that were full of pain, in a thin face white with shock. His top teeth were biting down hard on his bottom lip.

'What's your name?' asked Fergus. He wasn't going to ask the boy if he was all right. He could see he wasn't.

The boy's voice was weak and trembly. 'Rory. Rory Rooke. I'm on an errand for Mammy.'

'Well, Rory Rooke, you look like a brave boy. I want you to hold my hand as tight as you can while these gentlemen lift this barrel from your leg.' He indicated two men standing by. 'Can you do that, Rory Rooke?'

The boy nodded and took Fergus's outstretched hand. Fergus felt the dead skin scales in the pits and rough callouses of the boy's palm. He was certain by their depth that the splits and cracks generated pain, and that the boy must have been working down the pit for some time.

The two men lifted the barrel to reveal a bloody mess that began at Rory's knee and ended just above his ankle. His legs were painfully thin.

One of the men drew in his breath. 'T'lad needs to see a doctor, and quick.'

The boy was still on his back and couldn't see his leg, although from his eyes, the way he was clenching Fergus's hand and associated agitation, the pain was clearly increasing.

'Dr Lennagon's rooms are to our left, we can take him

there.' Fergus smiled at the boy. 'The doctor will sort you out, young man.'

The two men, with some difficulty, picked the boy up. He began screaming as they walked across the road.

The carter approached and laid a hand on Fergus's arm. He smelt of stale tobacco and onions.

'T'wasn't my fault. My horse got frit.'

Fergus turned to the man. 'You were going too fast. I saw the whole thing.'

'Your eyes deceived you.'

'Take my advice. There are several witnesses to this accident. When the constable interviews you, you should tell the truth. It will go better for you in the long term.'

'What's the truth, then?' The carter puffed out his chest and pulled his waistcoat down, preparing for confrontation.

'That you were going so fast an insecurely attached barrel leapt out and hit the boy. Mr Parkin, kindly let go of my arm so I may proceed with my business.'

The carter stepped back. 'How'd you know my name?'

'It's painted on the side of your cart.' *What a fool.*

Quitting the carter looking worried and scratching his head, Fergus saw the doctor's front door close on the men, leaving them still standing in the street, holding the boy. Blood was dripping from his leg onto the flagstones below.

'They won't have him,' one of the men said. 'The woman said to take him to the Infirmary.'

'Won't have him? Why not?'

The man turned his face from the boy and indicated to Fergus to draw near. When he spoke, it was in a whisper.

'My guess is it's because he's a pit boy. Coal dust, and all that.'

After nodding at the boy in what he hoped was an encouraging manner, Fergus took hold of the lion's head knocker on the doctor's door and gave it three loud bangs. After a moment a stout woman with thin hair in a tight bun appeared at the door.

'Yes?' She looked at Fergus sideways, with her chin held high and her arms folded tightly across an ample bosom.

'We've an injured boy here requires attention from the doctor.'

'I've already told them. He needs to go to the Infirmary.'

'That may be so, in due course, but it's obvious to me the boy needs attention right now, not least to stem the bleeding and something to relieve the pain.'

'To the Infirmary, the public subscription side, not the private side,' she said, and made to close the door.

Fergus put his foot against the door jamb. 'Kindly take a message to Dr Lennagon that Fergus Shackleton is at his door with an injured child.'

The woman looked at him. 'Won't make any difference.'

Fergus raised an eyebrow and held her gaze. 'Kindly do as I request.'

'All right then, but he'll not see him. He doesn't do charity work.'

She went to close the door again, but, finding Fergus's leather boot now firmly wedged over the threshold, abandoned the idea.

The two men and Fergus waited silently for the outcome,

listening to the pitiful sound of the boy calling for his mammy. His screams had subsided into sobs.

After a few minutes Dr Lennagon appeared.

'Fergus, delighted to see you.' They shook hands and the doctor looked at the boy, then patted him on the head. 'But under such sad circumstances.' He turned to his housekeeper, who was now standing behind him. 'Constance, this is Mr Shackleton, the shipper's son. You should have called me straightaway.'

Constance opened her mouth as if to defend herself then, wrinkling her nose, appeared to think better of it.

The two men carried the boy inside. Fergus remembered the auction. He pulled out his watch. It was twenty-five past two. He was going to be late.

He shouted at the doctor's retreating back. 'Send your account to me at Queen Street. I have urgent business.'

'I will. I know where you live,' the doctor replied. 'Your father and I are old friends.'

As he ran, Fergus thought of what his father would say if he missed the registration deadline. It would confirm everything his father thought of him: that he was a dreamer with his head in the clouds or else in a book. There would be a terrible row. Hector would make short shrift of his son's stopping to tend to a humble pit boy. He would pull faces, bang on his desk and shout about how the company must come first. This Fergus could bear – his father had a short temper and he was used to it – but Aunt Louisa, his father's sister, that was different. For some time now she'd been suggesting Hector give Fergus more responsibility within the company. If Fergus couldn't get this right then it would prove her wrong and his father correct. He couldn't let her down, not after all her support.

In his hurry to be in time to register, Fergus let the pub door slam behind him. The coloured glass in the top panels juddered. Inside it was noisy and crowded, and the smell of ale, sweat and smoke filled his nostrils. He turned to an elderly man sitting on a bench by the door, smoking a clay pipe and nursing a Jack Russell with spiky white whiskers and a blind eye.

'Where do we sign on for the auction?'

The dog pricked up its ears and lifted its head. The man studied Fergus for a moment then, using his pipe stem, pointed across the room. 'O'er yonder. See Becky, she'll sign you up.' He glanced at the clock over the bar. 'But best get a move on afore she shuts shop.'

A dark-haired girl, probably not yet twenty, with hair parted in the centre and drawn back over her ears into a loose bun, was sitting behind a small table. As Fergus made his way over, she rose and closed a large ledger. Now that she was standing, he could see she was tall, with long slim arms.

She looked him straight in the eye. 'If you're here to register, you're too late. It's gone half past and the bidding book's closed.'

Despite his agitation Fergus registered she had distinctive pale grey eyes set farther apart than was usual.

'I realise I'm a few minutes late and I apologise. Can you make an exception? Please?' His heart was sinking fast.

The girl shook her head. 'No exceptions.'

'Not even with an excellent reason?'

She shook her head again. This was the second member of the female sex who'd tried to thwart him in less than half an hour. He offered what he hoped was his most persuasive smile. 'I really do have a reason.'

'All right, try me,' she said.

'A young boy was hit by a falling barrel and I've been overseeing his visit to the doctor.' He might have imagined it, but he thought he saw a crack in her defence. The girl put her head on one side.

'An injured lad, that's a new one.'

Fergus pulled his jacket sleeve back to reveal his shirt cuff. 'See, the boy's blood is on my shirt.'

She studied the red streaks. 'It's still bright red, so it must be fresh.' She glanced at the clock, which was registering twenty-five to three, then looked around, before picking up the ledger and opening it. 'You're lucky, I haven't ruled the list off yet. What's your name?'

'Shackleton. Fergus Shackleton.'

She wrote his name in the ledger then looked up. 'One of *the* Shackletons?'

'I'm sorry?'

'One of the shipping Shackletons? From Tangier Street?'

'Yes. Is that a bad thing?'

Fergus thought he detected caution in her voice. ''Appen not. You've obviously a kindly heart to see to that lad. I'll put Shackleton and Co. in brackets.'

She entered the company's name in the bidding ledger. Her writing, while nowhere near that of a trained scribe, was clear and precise, and the figures were lined up neatly in their columns. She looked at the clock, which was now registering just before twenty to three, and in the column headed TIME wrote '2.29'.

'Now I think about it, the clock's a bit fast today,' she said, giving him a wide grin.

Fergus settled himself at a small table, with his back to the wall so he could survey the room during the bidding, and pulled a slim volume of Longfellow's poems from his pocket. When the auctioneer banged his gavel on the bar counter and the room fell silent he put the book down.

'Today we're offering for sale the 310-ton *Gregory Peat* of this port of Whitehaven. You've all seen this fine brig currently lying in the harbour and read her inventory. She's three years old and first-rate order, classed A1. What's more, she's ready to sail with crew and has a hold full of coal.' He looked around the room. 'I've several bids on the book. We start at £3,300. Who'll advance me on that?'

Bids came slowly, rising in increments of fifty, then one hundred pounds, but after a bid of £3,900 things began picking up. Fergus knew not to enter the bidding immediately so he waited and almost had to sit on his hand to stop himself raising it. He entered at £4,100 and found that, whereas he'd expected to find it exciting and a relief to enter the bidding, it was actually frightening. For one thing the auctioneer was now looking directly at him, encouraging participation, and secondly all the people in the room interested in the auction were also looking at him. He felt out on a limb. It wasn't as easy as he'd thought it would be. His toes were twitching in his boots and there was a pit in his stomach. He didn't like being the centre of attention and he was sweaty, whether from nerves or the heat in the room, he wasn't sure. He was quickly pushed up to £4,750. His opponent, who needed his whiskers trimming, was squashed into an old tweed jacket. He looked across at Fergus and raised his eyebrows.

He thinks my limit is £5,000, thought Fergus. When his opponent bid £5,000, there was just the trace of a smirk on his face. Fergus held back; he hadn't warranted a smirk just because he was bidding against the man. *Am I right to hold back? Should I bid again?* The auctioneer called for further bids and, to irritate the man he'd now nicknamed 'Tweedy' on account of his jacket, Fergus waited until the very last moment before he raised his hand. *You fool, you could have lost it. Don't do that again. Especially just to make a point.*

'£5,250 pounds,' he said, in a loud, clear voice that belied his nervousness.

Most people would have missed it, but Fergus saw the flicker of a frown pass over the man's face. *I've got you, Tweedy*, he thought, and assumed what he hoped was a bored expression. He began inspecting the nails of his left hand.

'£5,350,' said Tweedy.

This time Fergus put his bid in straight away. '£5,450.' And although he really wanted to, he held back from looking at Tweedy. Checking the opposition would make him appear anxious. Better to adopt a devil-may-care attitude. *If only I could calm down.*

Tweedy bid again. '£5,500.'

Fergus parried with '£5,580.'

He, and the rest of the room, waited for Tweedy to counter, and after what seemed an age to Fergus, the auctioneer brought his gavel down for the final time. Success was Fergus's and, never having regarded himself as particularly competitive, he was surprised how good it felt to win. It wasn't just the relief that he'd secured the ship, it was that he'd beaten the opposition.

'The *Gregory Peat,* sold this day for £5,580 to...' The auctioneer looked around the room then called out, 'Becky?'

'It's Shackleton's. He's the young Shackleton.'

On Fergus's nod, the auctioneer said, 'Sold for £5,580 to Mr Shackleton of Shackleton's.'

Fergus made his way over to the auctioneer to see to the paperwork. He was elated since his final bid was £420 short of his limit.

'You'll have an ale now won't you, Mr Shackleton?' It was Becky. She was standing in front of him, smiling. 'I think you owe us at least one purchase.'

Fergus laughed. 'I'll drink to that.'

'Sit yourself down when you've finished the business and I'll bring something over. What'll it be?'

'I'll have a brandy. I'm fired by a sense of occasion.'

'A brandy it'll be then, sir.'

Fergus signed off the paperwork, explained to the auctioneer why he was there instead of Mr Craggs, then returned to his place, where he put his papers face down on the table and set about inspecting his surroundings.

It was a hectic room. The walls were covered in landscape pictures and mirrors, both large and small, plain and decorative. High up behind the bar, Queen Victoria, in an ostentatious frame, took pride of place. Beneath her the mahogany shelves were crowded with bottles and tankards of varying sizes and colours. All the brassware shone, including an old ale muller to one side of the bar counter. A token fire burned in a cavernous fireplace, topped by an ancient blackened beam that had probably been salvaged from a shipwreck years ago. Fergus could imagine the fireplace stoked high with logs in the winter months. It was a cheery, welcoming room and it crossed his mind it was a lot friendlier than the Gentlemen's Club in the Lonsdale Hotel, where most of the people he knew met to drink, discuss business and generally hold court.

His thoughts were interrupted by the arrival of his brandy. He paid and gave Becky a penny for herself.

'Thank you, sir.' Her eyes traced his face. 'May I say I'm very pleased you got her?'

'Are you interested in ships?'

She assumed a conspiratorial tone. 'Not really, but it's put that Mr Todhunter in his place reet enough. Won't do him any harm not to win every time.'

'Mr Todhunter?'

'Jeremiah Todhunter. The man bidding against you. He and your Mr Craggs have fought it out here many a time.'

'Mr Craggs couldn't come today; he's out of sorts.'

'Let's hope he's out of sorts again, then,' she said, her eyes twinkling. 'Though not wishing him any harm, you understand.'

A mature female voice called out, 'Becky!'

'That's Mam. Everyone except me calls her Dolly.' Looking across at a plump, middle-aged woman with a friendly face who was standing behind the bar, Becky shouted, 'Coming,' and turned away.

Fergus tried to read for a while as he finished his brandy, but several times caught himself looking up to locate Becky. She was interesting, and the one person in the room who didn't seem to view him as an oddity. He'd seen her glance down at his book as if to see what he was reading. He remembered with a shudder what would have happened had she not bent the rules for him. His thoughts returned to the boy, young Rory Rooke. He wondered if he was going to be permanently crippled, and if so, what his family was going to do without his wage.

After he'd caught Becky's eye twice, and received two smiles in return, he left and went out into the street. When he arrived at the spot where the accident had taken place someone had cleaned up the flagstones and it was as if nothing had happened.

* * *

When Fergus left, Becky followed him with her eyes, wondering if she would see him again. He had strong features and when he'd spoken to her his gaze, which had sought to hold her own, had been bright and alert. When he laughed, his cheeks rose so his eyes almost closed completely. It was a wonder he could see out of them. She'd taken a big risk entering him in the book. It wasn't like her to bend the rules; she could have got herself into a lot of trouble if anyone had noticed, not least from Mam. Ship auctions brought in a lot of brass, and if word got round that they weren't straight and honest they'd lose business. Since Becky's father passed away three years ago it had been hard to keep things together, but they were on an even keel now.

There'd just been something about Fergus Shackleton. Something innocent? Kindly? No, that wasn't it. Exciting? Well, whatever it was, she hoped their paths would cross again.

Becky picked up his empty glass, then bent to pick up a piece of paper caught under one of the chair legs. It was resting on the sawdust they spread over the floor. She knew some people referred to the Indian King as a 'spit and sawdust', but it didn't stop them coming, and people through the door meant brass in the till.

She shook the paper and blew the sawdust from it. *Oh, no.* It was the consignment bill of sale for the *Gregory Peat.* She pursed her lips then took it over to her mam. 'I've found this. What'll we do? Shackleton and Co need it.'

Her mother scanned the paper. 'He'll be back for it, don't fret.'

'Shall I take it round?'

'Why would you want to do that?'

Becky knew why, but she wasn't going to tell her mam. 'He won't know where he's dropped it, and if I take it he won't have to retrace his steps looking for it.' She could see Dolly thinking it over. 'It's good service,' she added.

'Makes sense, but I need you to clear up after the bidders. If he hasn't come by when you've finished, you can drop it off.'

Becky hoped he wouldn't come back to the pub, since that might give her the opportunity to speak with him. She wondered what he looked like away from the pub's dim light, which was never that good at the best of times. They kept it that way because, being mostly colliers and sailors, and neither group liking bright light, the customers preferred it.

* * *

It was almost half past four when Fergus returned to the company offices. The shipping hall housed three large tables, with a senior clerk seated at each one, surrounded by papers and ledgers. Deep windows all the way along one side let in light, and the impression was of a place of industry, with maritime maps on the walls indicating the nature of the business. Three junior clerks were perched on high stools at tall writing desks with sloping lids.

Bill McRae, an old friend of Fergus's, greeted him as he entered. Bill was a well-proportioned, athletic-looking young man in his early twenties, sporting a fringe beard. As master of the *Arrow Lodge*, he had recently returned from Limerick.

'Been spending the company's profits wisely, Fergus?'

'Yes, indeed. A successful outcome.'

'Your father'll be pleased,' said Bill. 'He's always had an eye on her, at the right price.'

Hector's voice boomed down from the top of the stairs. 'Fergus, is that you?'

Fergus turned to Bill. 'I am summoned.'

Hector was sitting at his desk when Fergus entered.

'Well? How did it go?'

'We have a new brig.'

'At what price?'

Fergus knew this was the important question. The one his father would judge him by. '£5,580 plus costs.'

His father beamed. 'This *is* a surprise. Well done, indeed. Tell me about it.'

Fergus related the bidding, and when he mentioned Jeremiah Todhunter as the strong bidder against them, his father nodded.

'He's a professional bidder. I wonder who instructed him. It'll not have gone down well with whoever you outbid.'

'They should have given him a higher reserve.'

'I'll wager he set the price and advised his client.'

'That's unfortunate for him,' said Fergus.

'But, not for us my son.' In an uncharacteristic gesture, Hector stood up and came round to the front of his desk. He patted Fergus's arm. 'You've done well. Now let me have the bill of sale.' He put out his hand.

Fergus felt in his right-side breeches pocket and was rattled to find it empty. He couldn't remember where he'd put the paper and then, as his heart sank, he couldn't remember even picking it up from the table. He tried his other pocket, even though he knew it only held the book of poems. In what he knew to be a futile gesture, he opened the book and flicked the pages to see whether it was folded between them. His father frowned when he saw the slim volume emerge and returned to the other side of the desk. He was looking more and more disgruntled.

Fergus tried to calm himself, but his brain was shouting at him, *Oh no, you're in for it now.*

He swallowed and said, 'I must have left it at the Indian King.'

'What?' said Hector, dropping into his chair. 'You don't have the bill of sale?'

'No. I'll go back and get it right away.'

'Get it? A vital piece of information that seals our ownership?' Hector then voiced Fergus's worst fears. 'Are you sure it's there? That it hasn't fallen out of your pocket on the way back? That at this very moment some itinerant Irish tinker isn't using it to light his pipe?' His father's voice was getting louder and deeper, and with his bottom lip sticking out he had the air of a petulant child.

'I'm sure I can obtain a replacement document from the auctioneer,' Fergus said.

'I'm sure you can. However, what does it look like when the company representative cannot keep hold of a vital document?'

Fergus knew that although the staff would not be able to hear what his father was saying, they would know by the tone of his voice he was displeased, and that Fergus was receiving a dressing-down. All the pleasure of success he'd been enjoying a few minutes earlier had evaporated.

His father leaned forward. 'Was that brandy I smelt on your breath?'

Fergus nodded.

'That tells me everything I need to know. Find that bill of sale. Shackleton & Company do not deal with replacement documents.'

Fergus was out and onto Tangier Street in a trice. The paper could be anywhere. If he'd left it on the table, it might still be there. *Don't let someone have thought it rubbish and thrown it on the fire.* He walked with his head down checking his route, and would have bumped right into the girl from the Indian King if she hadn't called out his name.

'I think you may be looking for this,' she said, holding out the bill of sale.

Fergus took it from her. He could have scooped her up and kissed her. 'Thank you! Thank you very much.'

'It's no trouble,' she said, grinning at him.

Fergus put his hand in his pocket and brought out a penny.

Becky frowned. 'There's no need.'

'Take it. I've put you to trouble. It's a thank you.'

'You've already thanked me.'

Fergus considered pressing it upon her, but suddenly his offer seemed inappropriate to him, too. He put the penny back in his pocket.

'You should come and see us again some time. For a toff you were no trouble, and you seemed to enjoy yourself.'

A toff? Does she mean a dandy? No, more likely 'well-to-do'. Fergus put his head on one side. 'Invite me and I'll come.'

'There's an ale competition this Thursday the 19th. It'll be lively and I'll be there. You don't have to join in. You can watch if you want, although most of the men lay wagers.'

It sounds fun and she's said she'll be there. 'All right. I'll come.'

'I'll save you a table.'

Becky took her leave and was walking away when Fergus shouted out. 'Rebecca! Rebecca!' She kept on walking. He caught up with her. 'I was calling you.'

'Was that you? I'm Becky. Just plain Becky Moss.'

Fergus felt himself blush. He'd just assumed Becky was short for Rebecca. 'What time on Thursday?'

'Half past seven.'

'I'll be there.'

Fergus stood still as she disappeared. *I didn't imagine it,* he thought, *her eyes really are most distinctive.*

CHAPTER TWO

On Wednesday morning, Fergus was unexpectedly summoned to his father's office.

'I've invited Bill McRae to the Gentlemen's Club room at the Lonsdale for lunch,' his father told him. 'I've asked him to change ships and captain the *Gregory Peat*. He's trustworthy and I've known him since you were at school together. You can tell a lot about a man if you've watched the child grow. We have business to discuss before he goes. I'd like you to come along. It's time you began to learn a bit more about the business outside of the offices. Despite losing the paperwork, you secured the ship for us at a good price.'

Fergus knew that the loss of the bill of sale was a topic that was going to run and run.

'Yes, of course. What time?'

'One o'clock.' Hector looked at his son and then at the ornate wall clock over the fireplace. 'We have an hour. I've to speak with Mr Craggs and then we can leave together.'

✳ ✳ ✳

Upstairs at the Lonsdale Hotel, a discreet "Gentlemen Only" plaque marked the entrance to the Club. Inside, the room smelt of polished wood and expensive cigars.

'We'll take that one,' said Hector, addressing the chief steward, while indicating a round table to one side of a stained-glass window.

'I'm afraid it's already reserved, sir.'

Hector frowned. 'Reserved for whom?'

'I'm not at liberty to say, sir.'

'Not at liberty?' Hector lifted his chin and looked down his nose. '*We* are here and whoever *they* are, are not.'

Fergus stepped in, more in hope than the expectation of success. 'Father, we have confidential business to discuss. There's a quiet table over there with three seats.' He pointed over to his left, hoping his father wasn't going to make a fuss. It was in Hector's nature to do so when things weren't progressing as he wished. However, on this occasion, his father appeared to see the sense of his suggestion. They settled themselves in the ancient high-backed leather chairs.

Fergus had been in the Gentlemen's Club room several times and it was always the same. Genteel men of the town, mostly elderly, reading the newspaper, drinking, smoking, entertaining and sometimes napping. The atmosphere never changed, and it occurred to Fergus it was probably going to be the same for at least the next fifty years or more: gleaming mahogany woodwork; dark leather sofas with loose springs you sank into; the local newspapers neatly laid out on a large table pushed up against one of the walls; shelves filled from top to bottom with almanacs, directories and leather-bound books on travel to exotic places. The overall impression was of age, tradition and wealth.

Hector was just about to order two brandies when Bill McRae arrived, and so he made it three.

Fergus admired Bill's air of efficiency and the sound head he carried on his shoulders. 'So, it's Dublin tonight,' he said.

'Aye. I much prefer the shamrock run to the Lancaster-Liverpool one. The *Gregory Peat* is a fine ship and Dublin's such a vibrant city. The air is so often rank in Liverpool and the new steamships are making things worse down by the docks.'

'They have steamships in Dublin –' began Fergus.

Hector boomed out, 'Steamships are nothing but trouble. Just as you say, belching out smoke and smuts. Dreadful things. Noisy, too. And ugly.'

'I still can't interest Father in the new steamships,' said Fergus, an undertone of frustration in his voice.

Bill turned to Hector. 'They have the advantage of mechanical propulsion.'

'Exactly. They have lots of individual parts that can go wrong and which can't be put right at sea, unlike on a brig.'

Bill carried on, 'Their greatest asset is their speed. They're not dependent on the wind and –'

Hector, eyes wide and looking as if about to go into battle, fired another shot. 'They have no soul. Every ship needs a soul. It's like having a carriage without a horse. Think about that. Unimaginable.'

'Soul won't get your cargo into port on time,' said Fergus. 'How many ships lose a cargo they've reserved because they became becalmed, and an impatient agent's let it go to a competitor? Orders can be made with greater certainly when it's known exactly when a ship will arrive.'

'All you young men are interested in is doing everything quickly. And you think the world is going to become smaller with these steamships.' Hector lit a cigar and motioned to a waiter to refill his glass.

'Speaking as a captain,' said Bill, 'there is nothing more frustrating than waiting on wind.'

Fergus re-entered the fray. 'Another point is that steamships don't need to be secured with so many ropes and anchors because they don't drift as much, which makes them less controlled by tide or current, as well as by wind.'

Hector drew heavily on his cigar and tilted his head back, blowing out a long stream of smoke, then said, 'You're both forgetting the most important point.'

Fergus knew his father was about to play his trump steamship card. The one he always held in reserve whenever they were discussed.

'What's that?' asked Bill.

'Fire, that's what.' A triumphant look spread across his face. 'Fire.'

'There is that risk, I know –' began Bill.

Hector was now animated and his voice boomed out so loudly that other members turned their heads. 'Fire is a certainty. The boiler's in the heart of the ship. Don't tell me that's not dangerous. Any crack in the furnace wall will let out sparks and flames and start a fire.' He sat back in anticipation of victory and steepled his fingers. 'You don't think fire is a problem? I tell you it is. And there's the steam. That's dangerous too.'

Bill picked up the gauntlet. 'Fire's a problem on all ships, especially wooden ones. The new iron and wood combination ships perhaps less so.'

'It's far more threatening in a steamship, being embedded in the centre.'

'True, but steamships are everywhere now.' Bill turned to Fergus. 'I agree with you, it'll make the world a smaller place, because we'll be able to get to places faster. These steamships may not bring the future we're anticipating, but they're the future.'

Hector grunted. 'Well, that may be so, but I can tell you we're not buying any steamships. I'll not be responsible for our crew being burnt to cinders. You'll have to wait until I'm dead and gone.'

Fergus felt a wave of frustration pass through him. Why couldn't his father understand how ships that were never becalmed were revolutionising shipping? He wondered how long they'd be able to keep Bill in their employ if they didn't modernise. He had concerns for his own future, too. Somehow, and he had no idea how, they would have to convince his father they needed to modernise to survive.

Unexpectedly Hector's face lit up. 'I have a splendid idea. Bill, why not take my boy with you to Dublin this evening? Let him experience a ship's soul and he can meet our agent Flynn at the same time.'

'You don't know him, Fergus?' asked Bill. 'He's quite a character.'

'No, Father has kept me locked away in the office. He thinks I'm no sailor.'

Bill looked surprised. 'You've been to sea recently, surely?'

'No, I haven't.'

Hector began to bluster. 'I've been waiting for the right time. Always difficult. I'm thinking perhaps the time is right now, since he's not got his head buried in books as much as he used to. I think Oxford's influence is falling away. All that reading can't be good for the brain or the eyes.'

'Reading is what's required for an English Literature degree,' said Fergus. It was an old argument they'd gone over many times, and if anything, Fergus was finding solace in literature as much as, if not more than, ever.

'Surely education is never wasted?' said Bill.

'Ah, that old mantra. But English Literature, at university? All stuff and nonsense if you ask me. Except perhaps Thackeray,' Hector finished.

Bill laughed. 'Fergus with a book is nothing new.' He turned to his friend. 'I'll wager you've got one in your pocket right now. You've always had your nose in a book. Come with me tonight and we can discuss Dickens along the way. We've to be away by six, and all being well should be in Dublin by dawn the day after tomorrow – Friday. If there are no hold-ups with dispatching and loading, then we can be away again, leaving late the same day or the early hours of Saturday, and be back Sunday.'

Fergus smiled. 'I can do that,' he said, while thinking, *I can always visit the Indian King and see Becky Moss on my return.*

CHAPTER THREE

As the *Gregory Peat* cast off for Dublin under the captainship of Bill McRae, Fergus's eyes searched out Roper Street. The Indian King was too far along to be seen from the quay, and he wished he'd taken the time to send a note of apology explaining his absence from the ale competition. Becky would think him ill-mannered, but it was too late.

As they hit the open sea and the ship started to pitch, he began to feel slightly queasy. He moved amidships, grasped the rail with both hands and continued looking out. He didn't want the crew to think he was lacking in sea legs, even if it was true.

It was not the first time he'd travelled on a company ship, but this time he paid greater attention to her workings. He asked questions, and by the time they were halfway to Dublin he was enjoying himself, watching the men operate the sails and ropes. What's more, the nausea proved to be an initial response to the open water and passed when the wind freshened.

* * *

In Whitehaven, on Thursday evening, when the *Gregory Peat* was en route to Dublin, Becky was washing her hair. She then changed her skirt and chose the cream blouse with the embroidered cuffs. She'd designed and embroidered the decoration herself. She didn't have much spare time, but since her nan had taught her to be skilful with a needle, she liked to keep her hand in when she could.

At seven o'clock, she went up to her room and checked herself in her full-length mirror. She looked pale, but that was no surprise, since she was almost always working inside. She smoothed her hair and dabbed some scent behind her ears. Pinching her cheeks to colour them up and picking up a plaid shawl, she hurried downstairs with glowing eyes.

The bar was already crowded and business was brisk. She'd placed a reserved sign on the table that she now thought of as Fergus's – the one where he'd sat and read during the auction. When half past seven came and went, Becky was not unduly alarmed. She was sure she'd said half past, but maybe she'd said 'around' half past. She couldn't remember. When the clock struck eight and the competition began, she felt the first twinges of disappointment. She asked herself whether she'd really expected him to come. Perhaps he was just being polite when he'd shown interest. It was obvious he'd excellent manners. As time passed, she chastised herself for even thinking he wouldn't have better things to do, and in more well-to-do places. Even so, she couldn't stop herself checking the door when she heard the latch lift and the glass rattle, and each time when she saw it wasn't Fergus it was like a pinprick. At half past eight she took the reserved notice off the table.

Walking back to the bar she heard someone say 'Shackleton'. She looked around. Four men were playing cards. She moved closer and began clearing a nearby table.

'Aye, that's reet. 'Twas a Shackleton got the lad into the doc's house. They weren't going to take him, then Shackleton appeared and everything was suddenly all right.'

'Who told you?'

'Rory's mammy.'

'Amy?'

Becky's ears pricked up. *Was it Amy Rooke's boy? Rory? Was he the lad hit by the cask?*

'Aye, that's her. Lives on her own way up at New Houses. Course, he can't work as a trapper now. He's lame and can't get in the shaft bucket. He might even need a crutch. Looks like the slippery slope to the workhouse if she don't get wed soon.'

Becky felt sick. She knew Amy. They weren't best friends, but they'd shared the cake table a few times at the church fêtes and the Christmas bazaar. Poor Rory. She'd visit on Sunday after church. She continued listening in.

'That's terrible, she needs his pay. What happened?'

'A barrel landed on top of him. Leapt off the back of a cart and pinned him down. Anyway, Shackleton took off, said he was late for something, but not without saying he'd foot the bill.'

'This doesn't sound like the Shackleton I knows. He's a reet 'ornery old beast. Our Dick's brother-in-law works for him and says he's quick to lay men off and has a temper on him when things don't go his way, and even when they do.'

'No, it was the young one, not the crusty old man. He's got a funny Scottish name. I forget.'

Becky wanted to say, 'It's Fergus. Fergus Shackleton,' but then she'd have to explain how she knew, and more importantly they'd realise she'd been listening in, which was something they were not supposed to do. 'In the bar see nowt, hear nowt, and say nowt,' her father used to say.

So, Fergus did tell me the truth. Even though I saw the blood, I've wondered if he was blagging. Becky's mood lifted a little. Perhaps if he was a man of his word then he'd pay a return visit, as he'd said he would.

When she'd seen him outside, she'd liked him even more, and he'd seemed to like her. And after all, he'd encouraged her to invite him to the ale competition. She could picture his face quite clearly in her mind's eye. His high forehead, the tightness of the skin over his cheekbones and the strong jawline that contrasted with the delicate smattering of freckles sprinkled across the bridge of his nose. His eyebrows, whilst not bushy, almost met in the middle. His side whiskers and moustache were unobtrusive and neatly trimmed, which Becky liked. She'd noticed a few silver hairs nestling in his temples amongst the dark ones, even though he could only be early twenties at most. It wasn't just a physical attraction though – *a man who carries a book around with him and helps pit boys in the street can't be all bad, can he?*

* * *

Approaching the Irish coast just before dawn on Friday, they marked the Kish sandbank lightship. At Howth Hill, they caught the first twinkling of lights from Kingstown before moving up the river Liffey. The lights of Dublin City, at first sparse, gradually grew in number as lamps were lit in homes and businesses. The nearer they drew, the brighter the city became, until it seemed to glow in welcome.

On arrival, their towline was expertly caught by a steam tug belching out its gritty black smoke. The tug manoeuvred the brig into position, where she tied up. She'd made good time and, after discharging their coal and leaving a skeleton crew on board, the remainder of the men rushed to get ashore to sample the inns and alehouses. Bill and Fergus saw to the ship's papers and settled the harbour fees at the Excise Office, before returning to the ship and settling down to a late breakfast on board of ham pie, cheese and bread.

All business on board attended to, the two men walked along the quay in the shadow of the tall ships, taking in the sights, sounds and smells of the busy dockside, and commenting on the growing number of steamships – not just steam tugs and other service ships, but also larger seagoing cargo and passenger vessels.

'The port is much bigger than I expected and far busier,' said Fergus. 'All the bond stores and warehouses remind me of home. Everything is so familiar, but on a much larger scale than in Whitehaven.'

A cart loaded with bolts of cloth cut across their path and they stopped while it trundled by. The carter doffed his cap and they nodded in acknowledgement.

'We'll see the agent first, then I have to see to a tariff refund from my last trip here. How will you fill your time?'

'Deliver me to the biggest bookshop in the city and I'll be happy,' said Fergus. He was hoping to purchase *A Tale of Two Cities* and maybe some more poetry volumes.

'It's Hodges Figgis you want. It's been going a long time.'

A gull swooped down and Bill ducked to avoid it. 'Pesky thing,' he said batting it away. 'You'll soon see there's two things Dublin has aplenty and that's gulls and the destitute.'

'It looks prosperous enough to me.'

'It's not unlike Liverpool. On the outside it's prosperous, aye. It's a very busy port, and some of the architecture is splendid. It brews good ale, distils very drinkable whiskey and bakes excellent biscuits. But, with all the people having fled the countryside because of the famine, the city is full to bursting and accommodation poor. You'll see what I mean about the poverty soon enough when we walk to the agent's. It's not far.'

As they walked, Fergus realised Bill had been preparing him. The shops and offices they passed were well-maintained and smart horse-drawn carriages passed by, but everywhere, in amongst the well-heeled and fashionable, there were poorly dressed people with drawn faces and hungry, oversized staring eyes, standing in doorways or sitting on the pavements. Children in bare feet, dressed in ill-fitting rags, darted in and out between men in smart coats and women in fine dresses.

Fergus and Bill turned down a side street and stopped outside a once fine three-storey house that had been converted into offices. The words 'Messrs Flynn & Brady' had been flamboyantly etched into the glass on the door. Bill rang the bell and it was answered by a stern doorman in a bright red uniform with gold braid epaulettes.

'Captain McRae, you are most welcome.' He admitted them into an imposing entrance hall, looking at Fergus then back to Bill.

'This is Mr Shackleton Junior of Shackleton & Company,' said Bill.

The doorman looked Fergus over with increased interest, then said, 'Mr Flynn is expecting you, Captain.'

He led them up a fine staircase and Fergus noticed the carpet was an expensive one, held in place by recently polished brass stair-rods. Clearly their agent was running a most profitable business. Fergus wondered how a shipping agent could afford such pretentious premises and why he would want to put on such a show.

Flynn greeted Bill warmly. He was a balding, late-middle-aged man, with a bulbous nose and rosy cheeks, upon both of which there were a great many broken veins. He was wearing a gaudy red waistcoat decorated with a scrolling pattern of peacock feathers. *Just the thing for the popinjay he appears to be*, thought Fergus. *I'll wager he's the sort of man who wears snakeskin slippers.*

Flynn turned his attention to Fergus. 'You're the helper today, are you?'

Bill shook his head. 'Mr Flynn, may I introduce Fergus Shackleton, Hector Shackleton's son.'

Flynn, who initially appeared to have been only mildly interested in Bill's companion, now gave Fergus his full attention. 'I'm pleased to meet you, sir, indeed, I am.' He held out a hand.

Fergus accepted the handshake and was surprised to find Flynn had an unexpectedly limp grip for such a showy individual.

'What brings you to our fair city?' asked Flynn.

'Mr Shackleton Senior is eager for Fergus to expand his interest in the company,' said Bill.

'Excellent, excellent,' said Flynn, finally releasing Fergus's hand.

Fergus thought for a moment, then said, 'I'm just wondering, would it not be more appropriate for you to meet the ship on the quay, rather than have the captains visit you here?'

Flynn looked puzzled. 'Why is that now?'

'All the paperwork would be to hand; the risk that anything might be forgotten or mislaid would be avoided. You could sort any queries with the Excise men on the spot.' Fergus saw Bill was looking at him with his head on one side and wondered if his questioning was appearing more aggressive than he meant it to be.

Flynn swallowed and his Adam's apple bobbed up and down. 'I could do that, but usually there is confidential business to discuss, and whichever captain is here we retire to a nearby hostelry.'

'A hostelry? You discuss private company business in a public place? Really? At whose expense?'

Flynn ran a finger over his lips and seemed about to reply when Bill butted in. 'I should say that in my experience with other representatives, we discuss the business details in the agent's office then retire to a hostelry. It's normal practice for the agent to cover the expense.'

'With Shackleton petty cash?' asked Fergus, knowing he was splitting hairs in order to make Flynn wriggle, but there was something about him he didn't like and, more importantly, he didn't trust him.

'Yes, I suppose you could put it like that.' Flynn's attempt at a smile resulted in an awkward grimace.

Fergus could see he'd caught their agent on his back foot.

'Let's see to the paperwork and adjourn to a hostelry,' said Bill, handing over a sheaf of papers.

When the business had been dealt with, Flynn collected his top hat from a mahogany hat stand by the door. Fergus wasn't surprised to see it was a showy one made from imported Canadian beaver felt. Everything about the man was expensive and gaudy. Fergus's business instincts were on high alert.

Flynn placed a light hand on Fergus's elbow and steered him in the direction of the door. 'Have you tried any of our dark stout, Fergus? I recommend it not only as a drink, but for its medicinal qualities too.'

Fergus would have preferred to be addressed as Mr Shackleton, since the agent was in their employ, but he knew it would appear petty to say so.

As they left the office, Flynn turned to Bill. 'You must tell me all about this new ship you have. What is it? The something *Peat*?'

Leaving Flynn's offices and walking at a brisk pace, the three men bypassed several lively hostelries until they arrived at the Green Man, which was busy, but where they were able to secure a table.

'You'll try our Guinness dark stout now, won't you?' asked Flynn, in a voice that anticipated agreement.

'I'm looking forward to it,' Fergus lied, knowing it would be ungentlemanly not to partake of the local brew.

'And you too, Captain McRae?'

Fergus felt irritation. *He addresses Bill as Captain yet calls me by my Christian name. He underestimates me.*

'It's true I've a liking for the local stout,' said Bill.

When they were seated and the ale ordered, Fergus asked, 'Tell me, Mr Flynn, as our agent, what is it you actually do?'

Flynn looked momentarily baffled, but recovered quickly. 'I manage all the business for your company here in Dublin. Isn't that right, Captain McRae?'

Bill nodded.

'When you dock, the first thing you must undertake is to provide a customs manifest,' Flynn went on. 'That lists all the bills of lading. I then see to all the duties, oversee the unloading of the ship and the loading of the return cargo. In between times I source cargo for the company to buy or transport and sort out any problems that may arise.'

Fergus noticed there were beads of sweat on the man's brow. He was visibly uncomfortable.

'That seems most comprehensive,' Fergus said. He knew better than most what an agent did – after all, he'd worked in the company offices since coming down from Oxford. He'd not phrased the question correctly and now, unhelpfully, he'd irritated Flynn. The pulsating vein rising in the man's temple indicated that.

Flynn added, 'Think of me as the company's Dublin lungs. I keep the company breathing.'

A pretty girl with thick dark hair that hung down to her waist brought three stouts to the table and set them down. Flynn put his hand around the back of the girl's dress. She jumped and gave a little shriek. Flynn chuckled. 'Good job I waited until your tray was empty, eh?'

The girl giggled. 'Mr Flynn, sir, that was naughty, but since it's you I'll let you off.' She walked back to the bar counter, Flynn following her with his eyes. Fergus imagined her thinking, '*What an old fool*,' while raising her eyes skywards to the other servers. Although he'd often witnessed such brashness before, he was horrified and wanted to apologise to the girl for his companion's lewd behaviour. Then a thought entered his mind as if from a shafted arrow as it occurred to him men might treat Becky the same way. When he'd been at the Indian King, he'd not seen anything untoward, but it was now a worry.

He brought the dark medicinal smelling stout up to his lips and tried it. He was not surprised when he found it not to his liking. It was bitter and thick on his tongue, but as it was drinkable, he would finish it so as not to cause offence. His mind was filling up with worrying scenarios featuring Becky that could have persisted and increased in their imagined dreadfulness had his thoughts not been interrupted by a stranger approaching their table, nursing a pewter tankard. The man's face had bidden farewell to youth while his bearing was that of a much younger man.

'Ah, Flynn,' he said. 'You've guests, I see.'

Flynn sighed. 'That's right, Conran, we're talking business.' His apparent reluctance to greet their unexpected visitor was reinforced by a lack of eagerness to introduce his two drinking companions. However since the man, who had a carefree cheerfulness about him, had pulled up a stool and sat down, Flynn had no choice. After the introductions and some small talk about Dublin on a Saturday being too crowded, Conran turned to Fergus.

'You're a Whitehaven Shackleton then?'

'Yes,'

'Sure, I knew your father. A while back. We did business.'

'No longer?'

'Best ask your father.' He upended his tankard and looked at Flynn.

'You'll be wanting another, will you, or you've business elsewhere to go to?' Flynn asked, with what sounded like hope for the latter.

Fergus, with dark thoughts in his head towards Flynn, gave Conran one of his widest smiles. 'You must join us in another round. A brandy this time, perhaps? An old associate of my father's is welcome at this Shackleton & Company table.'

Flynn tried unsuccessfully to smother a frown. 'What about you, Captain?' he asked.

Bill stood up. 'I must keep an appointment I mentioned earlier, and since it concerns payment, I cannot be late. You must forgive me.' He spoke directly to Fergus. 'In the meantime, I'm sure Mr Flynn will be more than happy to direct or escort you to Hodges Figgis for your books.'

With Bill departed, and the brandies delivered, Fergus made a point of engaging Conran in conversation. Flynn volunteered a few lacklustre comments then excused himself from the table to 'go out the back'. As soon as he'd left, Conran leaned forward, took Fergus's hand in his and placed what looked like a coin in his palm.

'Here, take this, It's my merchant's token. Flynn's not the only agent in Dublin. I may have had a falling out with your father, but I like you. You may have need of me regarding future business.'

Fergus looked down at the coin-shaped token in his hand. It resembled a penny, being the same size and brown, although it was lighter in weight and probably brass. Lettering ran around the edges and in the centre were the words: PADRAIG CONRAN, BUSINESSMAN & SHIPPING AGENT. Fergus turned it over. More lettering encircled the head of a woman with a Grecian hairstyle. IMPORTER OF WHOLESALE & RETAIL FRENCH & ENGLISH CLOTH – DUBLIN.

'Quick now, slip it deep into your pocket,' Conran said. 'For sure Flynn won't take kindly to my poaching on his patch.' Keeping his eye on the door through which Flynn had disappeared, he handed Fergus an envelope. 'Take this too. Look later. I've something you might like to be setting your mind to carrying. It's special and new to the market –'

He broke off mid-sentence, and out of the corner of his eye Fergus saw Flynn bearing down on them. By the time he'd made his way back to their table everything was just as it had been when he'd left, and the envelope and token were safely stowed away. Conran was leaning back in his seat, cupping his brandy glass, engrossed in conversation with Fergus. Ten minutes later, after Conran had left, Flynn put Fergus into a cab, directing the driver to take him to Hodges Figgis.

On arrival at the bookshop, Fergus made straight for the antiquarian department. He'd high hopes they might have some illuminated manuscripts for sale. Whilst he liked to buy poetry and modern literature to read, his real love was vellum and parchment. Others of his acquaintance of a similar age spent their money on fine wines and fancy clothes. Fergus enjoyed spending some of his not insignificant salary on manuscripts. As well as satisfying his aesthetic tastes, he knew they were a good investment. They contained everything he loved: the decorative writing; the elongated, gold-leaf embossed capital letters; the paintings; the strange, sometimes comical, figures. On the trip over he'd wondered about finding time to visit the Book of Kells at the university, but their arriving at dawn and aiming to depart the same day late in the evening did not allow such a luxury.

Disappointingly, Hodges Figgis had no manuscripts, so Fergus gravitated to the recently published fiction counter, where he was shown an attractively bound volume of *A Tale of Two Cities*. He was about to pay for it when it occurred to him, on a whim, that perhaps he could buy something small for Becky as well, as an apology for missing the ale competition. The longer he'd been away, the worse he'd felt about not having sent a note.

He was directed to a pile of second-hand books on a table towards the back of the shop. He looked through several then saw one with a tooled leather spine, with the title *Forget Me Not* and *1825* inscribed on it. He picked it up and on opening it saw the end-papers were marbled, and that it contained a selection of stories, poems and engraved illustrations. It was small and obviously meant for a lady's hand. The book was exactly what he'd hoped to find, although he had no idea whether Becky liked to read or, if she did, what books she enjoyed. There had just been something in the way she'd looked at his book of Longfellow poems at the auction. Something in her eyes had suggested she'd wanted to pick it up and look at it. Since he had this feeling that she too had an affinity with the printed word, he felt emboldened to take an impulsive gamble on his instincts.

As he was walking out of the shop, a voice in his head asked him whether it really mattered if she thought him unreliable. *Oh yes,* he replied to the voice. *I think it matters a great deal.*

* * *

Just after eight o'clock on Sunday morning, the *Gregory Peat*'s look-out shouted, 'We're home, lads,' and those on deck turned their heads and looked into the distance, seeking Whitehaven's most famous feature, the Wellington mine candlestick chimney. A loud cheer went up and several of the crew mouthed prayers and crossed themselves. By ten o'clock, Fergus was almost home.

* * *

Up at St James' Church, on the north side of town, the Sunday sermon was proving long and dreary, and Becky's stockings were new and itchy. There was no sign of Amy Rooke. If it wasn't raining when the service was over, she would call and see her.

Coming out to bright sunshine with no hint of rain, Becky bade her mother goodbye and went in search of Amy. Walking down the valley side into town from St James' then climbing up the other side to New Houses made her sweat, even though there was not much heat radiating from the sun. Halfway up she began questioning the wisdom of her decision, but it was too late to turn back. She stopped to catch her breath and rolled up her sleeves.

The dwellings making up New Houses had been built in three rows, one behind the other, into the hillside. Usually it was an area bustling with colliers coming and going on and off stint, small children running loose in packs, and women standing at the water pumps, gossiping and passing the time of day. On Sundays, being the Lord's Day, it was much quieter. The only advantageous feature about the New Houses area of Whitehaven was the view over the town. The elegant terraced houses below, the ships in the harbour, the view out to sea, they combined to form one of the best views Whitehaven could offer. Although the disagreeable odours of New Houses' tightly packed communal living and the factory and foundry smoke rising from the valley had to be set to one side.

The Rookes' home was to the eastern end of the middle row. Becky noticed the doorstep was clean, although the windows were mud-streaked. Everywhere around there were indicators of poverty and want: homes badly in need of repair; barefoot children dressed in hand-me-down clothes that were either too small or swamped their skinny bodies; the boys wearing their caps pulled down over their foreheads to hold them fast, mimicking their fathers, even on the sunniest of days. Becky thought the caps were some sort of symbol – boys doing men's jobs in the mine. She knew the children in New Houses didn't have much of a childhood, but she'd not been up there for a while and she'd buried the hopelessness of it all.

Amy answered her door holding a threaded needle. Being petite in height and figure she gave the impression of fragility. Her dark hair was tied back loosely and a few strands had escaped and were hanging down. When she saw who it was, she smiled, pushed the stray strands behind her ears, and motioned to Becky to follow her. What struck Becky at once was the lack of decoration and the musty smell emanating from the stamped earth floor. The room was bare apart from an old low-lying chest, a three-legged table and two chairs. A kettle rested on the range beside a round pan, with a lid that was bigger than it needed to be.

Amy gathered up a pile of clothes from one of the chairs and put them on the table. 'It's nice to see you,' she said. 'Sit down, I'm doing some sewing. How's your mammy?' She spoke as if she was seeing to household mending, but it was clear to Becky she was taking in paid mending, since the clothes she'd moved onto the table were of a far higher quality than any she could afford.

'I missed you at church,' Becky said. 'I've come to see how Rory is after his accident. They were talking in the pub and I overheard.'

'I meant to go, but I lost track of the time and anyways, I needs to get through this.' She pointed at the pile of clothes.

Becky considered offering to help with the mending, but sensed Amy might see it as a charitable gesture and be offended.

'Is Rory still in the Infirmary?'

'Aye. He doesn't like it much as he's the only bairn, but I can't have him here yet. Anyways, you heard what happened?'

'Aye, I know. Fergus Shackleton took him to Dr Lennagon's.'

Becky told Amy how Fergus had been at the auction and how she'd returned the bill of sale. She omitted the part where he'd said he would come to the ale competition and then let her down.

Amy put her sewing to one side. 'For a Shackleton he sounds very thoughtful, and it's so good what he did for my Rory. It could have been a lot worse if the doctor hadn't got to him so quick. As it is, he's going to have a gammy leg for ever, but they told me he could have lost it. It's odd, I've always heard working for Shackleton's is hard, since you can be sacked for any minor mistake.'

'Fergus Shackleton brought a book with him to the auction.'

'A book to read?'

'Aye, sat all by himself and read it, waiting for the

auction. We don't get much of that sort of thing in the Indian King.' Becky didn't say it, but she'd like it if they did have more of it.

'What kind of book?'

'I'd have liked to have asked him and taken a look, but it seemed a bit rude at the time. We've spoken in the street since and he was so polite, even perhaps pleased to see me, so I could ask him another time.'

CHAPTER FOUR

When Fergus arrived home from Dublin, his parents and Aunt Louisa were still at Matins at St Nicholas' Church. Samuel, their butler, handed Fergus his post. Amongst it was a note of Dr Lennagon's charges for Rory. The boy's address was given as 8 New Houses. Fergus checked the grandfather clock in the hall. If he was quick, he'd enough time to get there, check on the boy and return in time for luncheon. If he waited, it would probably be another week before he could go.

There being no numbers on the houses, and no one close enough to ask, when he reached the street Fergus counted up from one end and arrived at what he thought might be number 8. Standing at the front door he heard voices. He paused for a moment then knocked. At least there was someone in who could direct him if he had the wrong house. The door was opened by a young woman.

'Good morning, I'm looking for Mrs Rooke.'

'I'm Amy Rooke.' The woman crossed her arms in a defensive action.

He smiled. 'I'm Fergus Shackleton. I'm calling to enquire about your son Rory.'

Enlightenment dawned. Amy smiled and invited him in.

Once inside, Fergus almost gasped out loud when he saw Becky holding her bonnet. For a moment he was so surprised at seeing her he forgot about the reason for his visit. All he could see was Becky standing up to greet him, looking surprised to see him too.

'Mr Shackleton.'

Is she pleased to see me? She was looking at him with the same expression she'd had when he'd first tried to get her to reopen the bidding book. He stepped forward. 'Miss Moss, I owe you an apology.'

'An apology?'

'For not attending the ale competition.'

'Oh, that. There was nothing definite, was there?'

Fergus felt put out. *I thought there was.*

Amy cut into his thoughts. 'Will you take some refreshment?'

'Thank you, but no.' Remembering the purpose of his visit Fergus asked after Rory.

'He's still in the Infirmary. He may need a crutch, but the doctors say he'll be able to walk. That's thanks to you, sir, getting him help so quickly.'

'I was only too happy to help. I left for Dublin unexpectedly or I would have called sooner. I'll settle the doctor's account tomorrow, and please refer the Infirmary charges to me too.'

'Thank you again, sir, but he's in the part you don't have to pay for. It's for the public, he's not in the gentlefolk bit.' She pointed to her chair. 'Will you take a seat?'

'Thank you, but I have luncheon waiting. I just wanted to say if I can help in any other way, please let me know. You can contact me at the company offices in Tangier Street.' A thought occurred to him, and he took a florin from his pocket and placed it on the table. Amy's eyes went straight to it like a jackdaw's to polished silver.

'I'd like to reward Rory for his bravery. I had some toy soldiers I used to play with and perhaps he may like some too.' He was about to ask whether Rory already had some, but judging by the paucity of furniture and general air of poverty thought it safe to assume he didn't. 'He will be able to entertain himself with them until he gets better. Can you buy some for him?'

Fergus could see her wrestling with the idea of taking the money. He picked it up and handed it to her. 'I'm sure he'd like some and you can perhaps take him with you to choose them.'

Amy's fingers closed around the coin. 'Oh sir, that's too kind of you. I'll get him some and tell him you said he was brave. Thank you. Thank you very much.'

Fergus smiled; he was relieved she'd accepted his gesture. He knew the soldiers would cost less than the amount he had given her, so she could buy something else as well.

'I must take my leave,' he said, looking across at Becky.

Amy thanked him again before saying, 'Becky is leaving too. She was just putting on her bonnet when you knocked. Perhaps you'd walk her back?'

Fergus looked at Becky. 'Is that agreeable?'

She nodded and, picking up her gloves from the table, said, 'Thank you. Your company will make the walk seem shorter.'

When they were outside Fergus turned back to Amy, who was standing in her doorway. 'I almost forgot. I saw the accident and you have a clear case for compensation. I will be happy to make a statement on your behalf.'

'The constable came to see us at the Infirmary. He told me the carter is going to pay so he doesn't have to go before the justices.'

'Excellent news. Remember, call on me if there's a problem.'

*** * ***

As the sun had risen in the sky it was far more taxing for both of them walking down the hill than it had been walking up. Becky would have liked to have taken her gloves off, but it was Sunday. The few people about were looking at them curiously. She wondered if Fergus realised he was a novelty; toffs didn't make it up to New Houses very often, especially not on a Sunday.

Fergus apologised again about missing the ale competition, and this time Becky was more accepting. Going to Dublin at short notice was beginning to seem a good enough reason for not having been able to keep his word. He told her about the city and how much he'd enjoyed being on the ship, and she was content to just listen, walking beside him, enjoying the timbre of his voice. He spoke beautifully, with animation and enthusiasm.

She smiled as she thought about Amy manoeuvring them both into walking together. She hadn't said anything to Amy about liking him. *Is it obvious I like him? Perhaps more likely Amy thought it a practical arrangement for us both, and nothing more.*

Some boulders had fallen from a low wall onto the path. Fergus took her elbow and guided her around them. It was the first time he'd deliberately touched her, and to her surprise she found it exhilarating. She was so caught up in the excitement of it, she was caught off guard when he asked, 'What do you do when you're not working?'

'My time off?'

'Yes.'

'I do embroidery, I make clothes and sometimes I play chess with visitors, like our guests. We take in overnight paying guests. Just bed and breakfast.' Then almost as an afterthought she added, 'And I read.'

He turned to look at her. 'I read too. A lot.'

'What were you reading at the auction?'

'Longfellow poems.'

'He wrote *Hiawatha*, didn't he?' She may have imagined it, but she thought he looked surprised.

'Yes. *Song of Hiawatha*. Have you read it?' He was looking at her intently. So much so he almost lost his footing when he tripped over a stone in their path.

'Not all of it.'

'I can lend you my copy, if you'd like that?'

'Aye, I would.'

Neither of them spoke for a few moments, then Becky said, 'I like to read poetry too.'

Fergus's eyes widened. 'We could read some together. Or perhaps you could read one to me.'

'I don't know you well enough.'

'Or not well enough yet?'

She knitted her brow. 'You could say that. Aye, not well enough yet.'

'I look forward to the day when you do,' he said, holding her gaze again and smiling.

Becky felt herself blush.

They'd reached the junction of Queen and Roper Streets, where their paths were to separate.

'I'll walk you to the Indian King,' he said.

'It's not far, there's no need. We can see it from here.'

'Then I'll wait here until I see you are safely home.'

As she walked away, Becky felt awkward knowing he was watching her, but in a pleasant way. Arriving at the Indian King she turned to see him and he waved. She waved back with a joyful heart. *I think he likes me.*

✤ ✤ ✤

At luncheon Fergus, wondering what sort of mood his father was in, watched his father stride into the dining room and take his place at the head of the table.

'All well in Dublin Fergus?'

'We hit some rough water about an hour out on the return trip, but nothing serious. We've despatched the crew.'

Hector nodded. 'And you made the acquaintance of our agent?'

'Flynn? Yes.' Fergus waited for his father to continue the conversation, but he turned his attention to his beef broth. 'I have to say I was surprised at the grandeur of Flynn's offices,' Fergus went on. 'Does he have private means?'

Hector halted, his spoon 'twixt bowl and mouth, and looked at Fergus through half-closed eyes. 'What do you mean?'

'A doorman in fine livery with golden thread epaulettes, expensive carpets, Shackleton petty cash used to treat our captains and Flynn to refreshments in local hostelries. Something doesn't seem quite right to me.'

'Are you suggesting he's not to be trusted?'

'I'm not sure. I'm just wondering whether they're overpricing. I'd like to go through his invoices from the last few months and check them against other invoices. Perhaps it's time we thought about sounding out another agent in Dublin.'

'Don't be ridiculous. You can spend your time far more profitably, and besides, I've been using Flynn for the last twenty years.'

That's probably the problem, thought Fergus. 'Surely it won't do any harm. Even a quick check could show up any irregularities or inflated charges. It's possible he feels too secure with our business. At the very least, the threat of a little competition might bring his charges down.'

'Are you questioning my judgement?' Hector dropped his spoon in his bowl with such force that the soup splashed out onto the tablecloth, creating a nasty brown stain that was going to be difficult to get out.

'I'm just mindful that a fresh pair of eyes may see things more clearly. And how long is it since you were in Dublin?'

Side-stepping the question, Hector said, 'So you're saying I'm dim of eye now, are you?'

It was Fergus's Aunt Louisa, his father's sister, older and taller than her brother, who broke the uncomfortable silence that followed. She and Fergus shared the same gold-flecked hazel eyes. 'Tell me, Fergus, did you enjoy yourself in Dublin?'

'Yes, I did, very much.'

Louisa sighed. 'I've always wanted to go. I hear it's a very fashionable place. I imagine the ladies' shops are full of interesting fabrics.' She turned to her sister-in-law. 'We've been saying for years we should go.'

Elizabeth, Fergus's mother, was a plump lady, not yet fifty, but close to it. Her hair was neatly arranged in the side curls more usually favoured by younger women. She raised her eyebrows at the suggestion of visiting Dublin. 'I hardly think so, my dear. I've heard it's a place of drunkards and pickpockets.'

'I think you're both right,' said Fergus. 'I found it a city of contrasts. The architecture is outstanding and some of the ladies are very fashionably dressed, yet there is much poverty.'

'That's all very well,' said Hector, wiping his mouth with his napkin, 'but I hope your mind was focused upon business. Dublin's brought us a lot of trade. Coal to Dublin and iron ore to Cardiff have been the jewels in our crown. My father started out with post-boats for our shamrock connection.'

'Now it's your turn, Fergus,' said Aunt Louisa.

Fergus smiled at his aunt; she was always on his side

and he loved her for it. He thought once again how close he'd come to letting her down and how Becky had saved the day.

'It's not yet his turn,' said Hector. 'I was well into my thirties when I took over from father.'

'Hector, don't be so sour.' Aunt Louisa was one of the few people not in awe of her brother and prepared to put him in his place. 'I'm sure Fergus has a good business brain like our father, if only you'd let him show it.'

'And *I* don't? Is that what you're implying?'

Aunt Louisa straightened her cutlery.

'Anyway, I *am* giving him a chance. I sent him to Dublin. You know that, but there's a lot of truth in that saying – clogs to clogs in three generations.'

'I don't understand,' said Elizabeth, dabbing the corners of her mouth with her napkin.

'The first generation has children who are hungry. They have clogs and sometimes may not even have any shoes at all. The founder of the company works all day and night to feed them. The second generation remember the hard times, the poverty and being hungry, and they don't want to go back to that, so they continue working. They pass from clogs to leather shoes. The third generation is born with no experience of hardship, is brought up with luxury, and doesn't value it as the previous generations did. They are born into leather shoes. As a result, they don't work as hard and tend to take unnecessary risks, losing everything and having to revert to wearing clogs.'

Aunt Louisa smiled at her nephew. 'I can't see Fergus taking unnecessary risks.'

'Hopefully not when he's properly trained, but who can tell what the future brings? It pays to be prudent. We only have to look at Nathan Shipping.' Hector turned his attention to Samuel, who was carving a large joint of beef that was sitting in state on an elaborate trolley on wheels. 'Another slice for me, Samuel. A thick one.'

'Oh yes, Nathan Shipping.' Elizabeth's face took on a solemn expression. 'The old man turned to drink.'

'I heard they lost everything,' said Fergus.

'Yes, everything. We picked up two of their brigs cheaply, so it was helpful to us.'

'You can't build strong foundations on another's unhappiness,' said Aunt Louisa.

'That may be so, but if a financial opportunity comes his way, a sound businessman such as myself does not shy away from it,' said Hector. 'It wasn't our fault the man couldn't hold his liquor. Too many evenings spent in the Indian King settling wagers and playing cards with his men. He should have maintained a distance from them. Too much familiarity breeds disciplinary problems.'

When Fergus heard 'the Indian King' he began paying more attention.

'Exactly,' said Aunt Louisa. 'Crewmen who have nowhere to go when they land ashore fall into the clutches of the crimps and end up in bars and houses of ill repute.'

'Louisa!' said Elizabeth. 'Not at the luncheon table please, especially on the Lord's Day.'

Aunt Louisa ignored her. 'Some of those men get off the ships with ten months' pay. That's why we fund the Seamen's Haven to protect them. The difficult part is getting them inside the door.' She turned to Fergus. 'That reminds me, I've been meaning to ask if you can help me there.'

'What can I do?'

'We've a trustees' meeting on Thursday evening and we usually have some entertainment from the warden, but he's to be in Carlisle visiting his sister. I wondered if you'd be able to give a short lecture. Just twenty minutes or so on one of those books you're always reading.'

Fergus smiled. *I can still go to the Indian King on Friday.* 'For you, Aunt Louisa, I'll be happy to.'

'I suppose that's one way of putting all that book-learning to good use, speaking to do-gooders and sober seamen,' said Hector.

❋ ❋ ❋

Thursday came quickly, and after the Seamen's Haven lecture Fergus settled Aunt Louisa in her favourite chair in their first-floor drawing room with a small sherry and some sweet biscuits. He thought it a soulless room, full of items on display as though they were exhibits. Everything had its prescribed place, and all that was lacking was the descriptive labels found in museums. Immediately opposite the expensively draped windows looking out over Queen Street was a large mahogany bookcase, the middle shelves of which held a selection of travel books in pristine condition. Never to be looked at, only dusted, they were for show only. On the higher shelves, three silver swans had been placed alongside two blue-and-white Chinese dragon vases.

He sought out his father and found him in his oak-panelled study at his desk. The room always held the lingering odour of expensive cigar smoke and reminded Fergus of the Gentlemen's Club. Most evenings Hector retired to his study to 'contemplate worldly affairs' with a large port.

Hector drew on his cigar until the end glistened. 'How was your lecture?' he asked.

'It went well. I spoke on *David Copperfield*, took some questions, and that was it.'

'Oh yes, "Barkus is willing.".' Hector laughed. 'He's the best damn character in the whole book.'

Fergus cringed; how could his father be so shallow? The book was a masterpiece, with a host of captivating characters. 'I think Aunt Louisa was happy with my effort.'

'She does a lot of good work with the Seamen's Haven.' Hector cleared his throat. 'I have a proposition to make. I think it a good idea for you to take on some more voyages.'

Fergus was surprised and pleased. He beamed. 'Thank you.'

'Don't get any ideas of running the business, or me retiring, it's just that I think it a good idea for you to meet the agents face to face. I've been thinking about what you said about Flynn. I have no doubts about him, he's a good man, but some of those London and Glaswegian agents might need a look over. You can be my eyes and ears. I had a lot of trouble with a chap called Conran in Dublin a few years ago. I let him have too free a rein.'

When they'd first talked about the Dublin trip, some inner caution had warned Fergus it would be unwise to mention he'd come across Padraig Conran, and now he was doubly glad he hadn't mentioned him. There was a story there, and he'd no doubt that in good time it would come out.

'I'm happy to visit our agents.' It wasn't much, but at last his father really was giving him responsibility, or at least noticing him.

'I'll speak to Mr Craggs. Although I dare say the crews will think you're there to spy on them. Agents are a different breed to crewmen. Ask around, see what you can sniff out. No harm in making a few enquiries and seeing the whites of their eyes.'

CHAPTER FIVE

After several weeks travelling, Fergus found that what had previously passed across his desk as cargo receipts, harbour toll invoices and agents' commission sheets now represented real activities, and he became completely wrapped up in them. Names became faces, and the quays had custom halls and alehouses and inns he could now visualise. Every day he gained in confidence and expertise.

If he'd thought being away from Whitehaven would purge his thoughts of Becky Moss, he was mistaken. Sometimes she came to him in his dreams, like the spectre at the feast, hovering, watching him, unseen by others. In one dream she berated him for 'leaving her on the quayside', which he felt rather unfair, since this time he'd sent her a note to say he was going to be away.

During a particularly bad storm on their way back to Whitehaven from Cardiff, when there had been a terrible wind and he'd thought his life might end, he'd decided he must visit the Indian King and lay the spectre to rest. When dawn broke to a clear sky and all were safe and well, and he realised he still felt the same way, he knew he must seek Becky Moss out the very night his feet landed on the quay.

* * *

The Indian King was packed, but Fergus saw Becky immediately. She was sitting exactly where he'd first set eyes upon her. She even had ledger-books open in front of her, just as she had on that first day, but this time a long line of men was queuing to speak with her; it was pay day. As he watched, he saw her check each man's name in a ledger then hand over some coins. Some employers issued their wages through a third party and often at a public house, but Shackleton's crew came to the office and queued at their wage window. Fergus's mother had seen to that, saying it was preposterous to pay men in a place where they doled out alcoholic beverages, since the men would drink their wages on the spot. Fergus knew his mother was wasting her breath, since he'd seen their men pocket their wages and make their way to the nearest inn or alehouse. It didn't matter where they sourced their wages, it usually ended up slipping down their throats.

The same old gentleman was sitting on the bench by the door, smoking his clay pipe, with his one-eyed Jack Russell by his side. He nodded at Fergus.

'You're back, I see. There's no ship to buy today.' He patted the bench. 'Get yourself a drink and I'll shift Molly then there'll be room for you.' He scratched behind the dog's ears.

When he'd returned, and Molly had been transferred to the old man's knee, Fergus settled himself. For the next half an hour his eyes were drawn to Becky, unbidden by any conscious instruction on his part. It was as if they had their own agenda and couldn't get enough of her. They travelled her face, taking in its shape and her ever-changing expressions as she greeted each new individual and calculated the amount owing.

The old man nudged him. 'She'll be a while yet.'

'She?'

'I can see where your eyes are fixed.' He nodded towards Becky. 'I may be long in the tooth, but I'll wager I know what brings you back here when there's no ship auction.'

Fergus opened his mouth to protest, then thought better of insulting the man by lying to him. He was being friendly, and besides, there was not another spare seat in the house.

'I've been away at sea.'

'I can tell that by the tanning on your face. That's sea wind given you that colour.'

Dolly, serving behind the counter, looked at him, then across at Becky. Now he knew her better Fergus could see the family resemblance in the way mother and daughter smiled and moved. They shared the same colouring, although Becky was a good three inches taller and didn't have her mother's V-shaped widow's peak. He swung back to find Becky had her head down and her brow creased in concentration. She was still doling out wages, although the queue had dwindled to half a dozen men.

After she'd seen to the last man, Becky closed the ledgers and put them on the bar counter along with the cash box. Her mother took the box and said something to her. Becky looked around and saw Fergus. She raised her eyebrows in what he judged to be happy surprise. He smiled broadly, willing her to come over and speak to him. She gave a half smile, then turned her attention to some empty glasses on a nearby table.

Fergus didn't know what to think. *Is she keeping her distance because she's embarrassed in front of everyone, or is it because it's pay-day Friday and she's busy? Perhaps I've made a mistake coming, but I had to come, if only to stop the dreams.* All these thoughts were running through his mind when he saw she was making her way over to him. He downed the remains of his drink. The least he could do was ask her for another.

Becky picked up his empty glass. 'Brandy?'

'Thank you.' He looked right into her grey eyes. 'I'm back.'

Becky laughed. 'I can see that for myself.'

He suddenly felt awkward and tongue-tied. He counted out the correct change and handed it to her. Becky took the glass and reappeared with what he thought was a generous measure. 'Here.' She put the glass down on the table before leaning over and petting the dog. She was close enough for Fergus to draw in her perfume. It was new to him, fresh and lemony, and he liked it.

She addressed the old man. 'Now then, Sergeant Adams, can I get you another or have you had your two?'

He smiled at her and held out his glass. 'I'm ready for a top up, thank you.'

'Allow me,' said Fergus, putting his hand in his pocket and bringing out some change.

'Nay, I can't have that,' said Sergeant Adams. 'I always pays my own way.'

'You've given up your seat for me and I'm sure we owe an old soldier a drink on a Friday night, don't we?' Fergus looked to Becky for confirmation.

'It was Molly gave up her seat,' said Becky. 'I'll bring her a bowl and a bit of sausage.'

When Sergeant Adams had been served with his top-up and Molly with her sausage, Becky spoke to Fergus. 'If you came looking for entertainment, tonight's no good. Come tomorrow, there's something special. We've a tin-whistler from Dublin and there'll be a lot of Irish in. It'll be noisy though, because they sing.'

'I'll be here,' said Fergus, luxuriating in the comfortable feeling he enjoyed when he was with her.

'I've heard that afore,' said Becky, raising an eyebrow.

Fergus made a mock show of cringing. 'I know and I apologise again for the time I let you down.' From his pocket he pulled out the *Forget Me Not* book he'd bought in Dublin. 'This is a gift, by way of an apology.'

Becky's eyes lit up. As he'd thought, it fitted perfectly in her hand, and he could see she was pleased by the way she held it. She opened it, looked at some of the pages, then leaned over and touched his hand, saying, 'Thank you. Thank you very much.' Then she was away and back to her work.

* * *

After they'd closed, Becky was collecting up the glasses when Dolly called her name. She turned to see her mother behind the bar, juggling three lemons. 'I think we can make up some lemonade jugs with these. If you see to it now, they'll steep overnight.'

'I'll do it,' said Becky. She took the lemons and went into the back kitchen. It was a cosy room. On the mantelpiece were two straight-backed blue-and-white Staffordshire pottery figures of a cowherd and shepherdess. Linen, neatly folded, was airing on a wooden drying rack hanging from the ceiling. An old spindle-backed oak carver was to one side of the range, matched by a smaller rocker on the other side. In the centre of the room was a well-scrubbed pine table with a chopping board that had seen a thousand cuts, and it was on this that Becky began quartering the lemons. She put them in a pan with some sugar and added boiling water.

Then she sat down in what had been her da's chair and thought through the evening. She'd heard Shackleton's drove a hard bargain, yet Fergus appeared generous and kindly. Paying for Doctor Lennagon, calling to see how Rory was, buying a drink for an old soldier, bringing her the lovely book. However, it was easy to be generous when you had money, and it was obvious to everyone that he had plenty by the way he dressed, from the fact that he lived in a big house on Queen Street, and because he was the Shackleton son and heir.

✳ ✳ ✳

The next evening the tin-whistler was in full flow, and with the Indian King's windows open, Fergus and Bill heard the sounds from halfway down Roper Street. Inside, people were clapping along and tapping their feet. Customers were seated at tables playing cards, and the click-clack of domino-shuffling greeted Bill and Fergus's ears as they joined the throng.

'You were right,' said Bill, looking around. 'This place *is* lively.'

'They've good ale too.'

Bill put his head to one side and laughed. 'If that's all that brings you here, then what do you need me for?'

'Well, that's not exactly all. You'll see.'

'My money's on a lady.'

'Am I so transparent?'

'If it's not just for the good liquor, and it's not business, then I don't see what else it can be. Unless there's a bookshop hidden away in a back room.'

Fergus laughed. 'Put it like this, if you weren't happily married then I wouldn't dream of bringing you along with me. I don't want any competition.'

'Ah, it's an opinion you want?'

Fergus studied his friend's face. 'Maybe. Tell me if I'm madcap or not, but there *is* a girl.'

'And you can't get her out of your head?'

'Something like that.'

Bill looked over Fergus's shoulder. 'And it's my guess it's the dark-haired beauty with the striking eyes.'

Fergus swung round. Becky was talking to two men working behind the bar while loading a tray with ale pots.

'Yes. Am I ridiculous or not?' He tried to read Bill's face for his honest opinion. He saw neither approval nor disapproval.

'I see the attraction, but does *she* like *you*?'

'I think she might.'

'Well, if she's not spoken for already, why not? She's a beauty, that's for sure.'

'Father and Mother won't sanction it if they find out. They're both so worried about what other people think and a publican's daughter is probably not what they have in mind for me. Mother only ever refers to her Yorkshire origins and never mentions our distant line of Shackleton Irish blood. She said once she didn't want people thinking we were "Irish tinkers".'

Bill laughed. 'As if. We're talking of a fling though, are we not? If not, I think you're rushing things.'

'All I'm sure of is I want to get to know her better. There's something about her that's haunting me in an exciting way. I can't express it exactly, except I'll admit to being fascinated by her.'

'Well, while you think about it, let's get some ale in. I've to be home by half past nine.'

The tin-whistler was a professional entertainer, well used to holding a pub audience in the palm of his hand. When the singing threatened to become too raucous, he skilfully directed them to *Molly Malone*. By the time he reached the part where 'she died of a fever' there was hardly a dry eye in the house, and he had to sing it twice more before his audience was satisfied.

Not long after that, Fergus began feeling light-headed

and slightly tipsy. He'd seen Becky look their way several times and he decided to stay on after Bill left. Sergeant Adams and some of the older patrons were replaced by a younger crowd. An hour after that, still not having spoken to Becky, Fergus was standing up to leave when a fellow drinker won at dominoes and there was a sudden whoop of delight. It made Fergus jump and he whirled round to see where the shout had come from. As he did so he collided with a youth holding a full jug of ale. The sharp crack of breaking pottery as the jug hit the floor was followed by the splattering of the ale, lapping up its newfound freedom. Fergus looked down to see the sawdust soaking up the liquid and churning it into a sodden heap.

'Eejit,' said the young man taking a step towards him 'that's our whole jug gone.'

'I'll replace it,' said Fergus, stepping back from the mess.

The youth looked him up and down then back at the floor. 'We've not only lost our jug. Look at the mess on the floor. How about we make it a bottle of our favourite grog? That should see us to rights.' The youth was sneering, challenging him making Fergus feel threatened.

Fergus hesitated, but stood his ground. He knew he was being taken advantage of, but he *had* cost the four lads their ale. He sighed. 'Name your tipple.'

The youth punched the air with a closed fist before shouting across to Becky. 'A bottle of your best brandy.' Then, turning his back on Fergus, he sat down and slapped his palms on his thighs. 'Time to get supping, lads.' The other youths thundered their approval, clapping their hands and banging on the table. Other drinkers were looking over at them, seeking the source of the disturbance.

'The best'd be wasted on you lot,' shouted Becky over their voices. 'It's a replacement jug of ale, or nothing.' She spoke jovially but, standing hands on hips, she looked irritated as, thought Fergus, she had every right to be, since he assumed it was going to be her job to clear up the spill.

Placing a full jug of ale on the table, then nodding towards the bar, she said to Fergus, 'You'll be better off standing over there than in the middle of this rowdy lot.'

He followed her to the bar counter, paid for the ale and apologised for the mess and the broken jug.

'I'm sorry,' she said. 'I think you were set up there. I'll get Mam to sort them out after I've cleaned it up.'

'Please don't. I'm the visitor. They can do it once, but I'll not let it happen again.' He glanced back at the young men. 'Besides, you've been busy all evening and it's given me a chance to speak with you before I leave.'

Becky's cheeks began to flush.

He bade her good night and left with joy in his heart, striding out with a light step, his mind mulling over the evening's events. He'd not gone far along the street when he felt a blow to the centre of his back so forceful it pushed him forward. He lost his footing, slipped off the kerb and fell into the road. Before he could recover his balance, a man hurled a harsh punch that caught him just under his left eye, sending him sprawling over the cobbles. He felt a cruel kick, then another. A hand began searching through his pockets and he heard the sound of jingling coins landing beside him. The man leaned over him, scooped them up and ran off.

✽ ✽ ✽

When Becky heard that 'the toff' was lying in the road outside, she flew out of the door. Fergus was flat on his back surrounded by the four youths who'd taken advantage of him earlier.

'He doesn't deserve this,' said one of them.

'Seems like a decent gent,' said another. 'He took our jape in good spirits.'

'Did you do this?' asked Becky, kneeling down beside him.

'No,' said all four in unison.

The one who'd dropped the jug of ale said, 'D'you think we'd be standing around if we had? What reason did we have to do this, after he stood us the ale in good humour?'

Fergus, who'd been stunned and silent, began groaning. He put his hands up to his face. When he took them away, he stared at the blood on his fingers.

'I hope your nose isn't cracked,' said Becky, leaning over him.

Dolly appeared at the pub door and looked anxiously up and down the street. 'Quick, bring him in and take him into the kitchen. We'll clean him up there.'

The youths helped Fergus to his feet. He was looking around with wandering eyes, as if trying to get his bearings. The drink and the beating combined seemed to make it hard for him to focus. He accepted the youths' help, and

Dolly and Becky settled him in the spindle-backed chair. He was shaking and blood was pouring from his nose.

Becky pulled a cloth down from the laundry airer, soaked it in cold water and handed it to him. 'Press this on the bridge of your nose and put your head back.'

Dolly thanked the four youths and sent them on their way, promising them a drink on the house the next time they passed by. Then she turned to Becky. 'Ask one of the barmen to bring in a large brandy.'

Becky hurried off, returning a few minutes later, with a brimming glass.

'Who did this to you?' asked Dolly, as she handed Fergus the brandy.

'A man just came at me.'

'Did he say anything?'

'No.'

'What did he look like?' Becky asked.

'I don't know, he came from behind.'

Becky looked to her mother. 'We should call the constable. I heard the same happened at the Dog and Duck a few days ago. Likely a rogue seaman between voyages, spent his wages and now sparse on brass.'

Shaking her head and looking alarmed, Dolly said, 'No, we mustn't involve the constable.'

Fergus nodded. 'It won't do your business any good if it gets round town a Shackleton was set upon at the Indian King.'

'But it wasn't in the pub, it was outside,' said Becky.

'Aye, but he's reet,' said Dolly. 'The paper'll say after drinking in the Indian King he received a beating. People'll think he was drunk and that the Indian King is a rowdy house. I'm sorry, sir, and thankful for your thoughtfulness on this.'

Fergus, who was regaining some of his colour, waved her apology away with a lift of his hand and a smile. 'I'll live.'

Becky watched him look round the room. Their kitchen must be very different to the one in his own home which probably had shiny brass saucepans for the servants to polish. *What's he thinking? That it's pokey? Is he looking down on us or just taking in his surroundings?*

After almost an hour, during which Becky and Dolly cleaned his face up and brushed the road dirt from his jacket, Fergus was looking a lot better. Feeling steady enough to leave, he refused an offer of help from one of the barmen and thanked everyone profusely. As the door closed behind him Becky turned to her mother and said, 'I don't suppose we'll see *him* again.'

* * *

By the time Fergus arrived home he had a shocking headache and bruises were forming, but his heart was happy. He'd felt so comfortable in the Indian King kitchen, with its warm range and cosy furnishings. He thought of their own kitchen with its brass pans shelved in regimented rows, cold stone sinks and scrubbed tables.

When he looked in the mirror in his bedroom, he found his nose and top lip were swollen and the skin stretched and shiny, although the bleeding had stopped. He was still feeling shaky, but it was more the shock of being set upon than pain from the injuries he'd sustained.

The next morning he underplayed it, telling his family he'd had a run-in with a drunken sailor who'd landed a single blow to his face then disappeared. It wasn't an unusual occurrence in Whitehaven on a Saturday night. The bruises that were going to develop on his body could easily be hidden. He was careful not to mention he'd been in the vicinity of the Indian King and turned down the family's concerns about informing the constabulary. He decided to stay away from the Indian King until all traces of the attack had gone. It was going to go round quickly enough that he'd been set upon. No need to parade the evidence. He would send another note so there was no misunderstanding, since the last thing he wanted was to upset Becky's mother. He suspected she was wary of him as it was.

CHAPTER SIX

Thursday the 7th of June, market day, was the day before Aunt Louisa's birthday. Fergus looked through the window and saw the sun shining. He'd a pile of papers strewn over his desk, but the thought of feeling the sun's rays on his face was too tempting, and he'd an errand to run.

He made his way to the market, where he was pleased to see the confectioner in his usual pitch.

'I'll take a large box of your sugared almonds, and please tie a velvet ribbon around it,' he said.

A voice came from behind him. 'I didn't realise you'd a sweet tooth.'

Fergus jumped. He'd been concentrating on watching the confectioner, who had exceptionally thick fingers, wrestling with the ribbon.

It was Becky, holding a wicker basket with a puppy inside.

'These are for my aunt's birthday tomorrow. She loves sugared almonds.' Then, looking down at the puppy, which was curled up in a tight ball fast asleep on a blanket, he asked, 'Who's this little fellow then?'

'Charlie. I've just collected him. He's coming to live with us. We're so sorry about what happened.' She scanned his face. 'The bruises are almost gone, so you'll be able to come back soon if you want to.'

Her eyes are a deeper grey than I remember. 'I'd like to. I'm completely recovered.' He paid the confectioner, and they moved into a gap between two stalls. There was an awkward pause before Fergus said, 'Have you any more entertainment evenings organised?'

'Nowt this week, but you're welcome to drop by any time, and I don't think those lads will try it on again. You were such a gent and stood them that ale. They're not a bad lot really.'

He pulled out his pocket-watch and checked the time. 'I'd like to stay, but I have to return to the offices now for an appointment. I'll see you shortly.' If he could have skipped the appointment he would have done, but he'd only left the office to buy his aunt's present.

Becky hesitated for a moment, then said, 'Well, when you do visit us again, you can entertain Charlie. I can see you like puppies by the way you're looking at him.' She stroked Charlie's head then darted off, and had soon disappeared.

Suddenly the prospect of dealing with the bills and invoices in the office and talking with the customers didn't seem so dispiriting. Seeing Becky again had raised Fergus's spirits more than he could have imagined. He had a smile on his face and whistled tunefully as he made his way back.

His buoyant mood didn't last long. Upon his return he was greeted with the news he was to leave in two days to meet more agents in Glasgow and Edinburgh. He wouldn't be back until the 20th of June, which was almost two weeks. He couldn't visit the Indian King the next day, as they had guests coming to celebrate Aunt Louisa's birthday. He'd said he'd see Becky shortly. How long was 'shortly'? He wasn't sure, but he did know the fates seemed determined to bring them together only to torment them by separating them.

Becky was tying the week's newspapers into a bundle. They rented them out for one penny an hour, and after two weeks she crumpled them up to light the fires. Her da had taught her how to light a fire and he praised her if she only used one match. She thought about him every time she did so.

A week had passed since she'd bumped into Fergus at the market. He'd said he'd call 'shortly'. Was that a week? Ten days? On her afternoon off she'd wandered down to Shackleton's offices and watched from a distance as the clerks and managers left at the end of the day. She hadn't seen him, which was a disappointment, but a sensible voice in her head said, '*he's probably gone to sea again.*' She allowed herself a few minutes to wonder what it would be like to be married to Fergus before reprimanding herself. A Moss girl take up with a Shackleton? Not likely. All the fancy town ladies would be appalled. Still, she was sure he liked her. His eyes had lit up when she bumped into him in the market and he'd held her gaze all the time they were speaking.

✳ ✳ ✳

Fergus's arrival in Edinburgh couldn't have been more different to his arrival in Glasgow. He'd set foot on the quay there under a depressing, cloud-filled sky, whereas Edinburgh was welcoming him with cloudless blue and bright sunshine. He decided against taking the train, thinking he would see more of the countryside by coach. He was dropped off near Clipstons Close in the Grassmarket.

Waiting for his luggage, Fergus looked up at the forbidding castle perched on its rocky crag, then surveyed his surroundings. It was an unusually wide-open space for the centre of a city. A host of fully laden merchants' carts, waiting for horses, seemed to have been haphazardly abandoned, their goods hidden beneath hessian sheets. Carriers huddled in tight groups, drawing on their pipes, gossiping and playing cards. Larger covered wagons were lined up waiting for business. A sign written in an untidy, sloping script was attached to one of the wagons: '*Inside the Black Bull Inn. Competitive terms. Ask for Reliable Jack.*' Fergus looked across at the inn. To one side of it was the spirit merchant J. K. McKenzie's premises, and on the other J. Wilson & Sons, tobacco and snuff manufacturers. A North American Indian wooden figurehead, with a pipe in his mouth and a skirt of tobacco leaves, had been fixed over the latter's door.

Children ran around laughing and calling out to each other, in contrast to a troop of soldiers who passed through in silence, rifles on their shoulders, boots clicking in unison upon the cobbles.

Fergus took out his handkerchief and wiped his brow. The church clock struck three. He was being collected by their agent, Mr Cameron, at four, allowing him an hour to wander around. Leaving his luggage in the charge of the Black Bull's porter, he set off walking westwards, thinking he might find a stationer's or a bookshop. He'd gone about a hundred yards when he came upon a jeweller's. For want of nothing better to do he glanced in the window. In the centre, taking pride of place, was a large emerald and diamond necklace. However, what caught his eye was a drop pearl resting on black velvet, within a leather box with a tooled gold border. In Glasgow he'd been regretting not telling Becky he was going away and that his 'shortly' was going to be longer than he'd intended. Perhaps he should buy her another gift. She'd really appreciated the *Forget Me Not* volume and had mentioned it several times. Now, as he looked in the shop window, the idea was taking root.

A bell jingled as he opened the door and a small stout man with untidy hair appeared. He was dressed in a dark suit that looked uncomfortable on him, as if it had been his brother's or perhaps an uncle's. A blue-and-green tartan cravat was draped around his neck, the ends tucked inside a white linen shirt.

'Good afternoon, sir,' he said, readjusting his shirt collar. 'How may I be of service?'

Fergus felt his financial circumstances being appraised. He was glad he was somewhat dishevelled after his long coach ride and somewhat dusty.

'I see you have a pearl in your window.'

'I have several. Which one were you thinking of?'

The man moved towards a black wooden screen and unlocked a small door so he could gain access to the window.

'I'll show you.'

From outside, with much pointing and gesticulating, Fergus managed to indicate which pearl he was talking about. Back inside he saw the jeweller had taken three from the window display and had lined them up on his counter.

'Each of these is of a very high quality. You will see they are each of slightly different hue. May I ask the colouring of the lady? I assume it is for a wife, or perhaps a sweetheart?'

Fergus hadn't thought of Becky as his 'sweetheart', but if she wasn't, it was not from want of wishing on his part. 'The lady in question has dark hair.'

'And her eyes?'

Fergus recalled Becky's eyes, so vibrant, so alive. 'They're grey. Unusual and sometimes a bit misty.'

The jeweller put two of the pearls to one side and moved the remaining one closer to Fergus. 'Then may I suggest this darker pearl?'

Fergus hesitated; it wasn't the one he'd noticed in the window. Now he wasn't sure.

'Sir, my daughter is as you describe – dark-haired. Might I call upon her to demonstrate for you?'

'If it's convenient.'

The jeweller rang a bell and after a few moments a

young girl entered. She was indeed dark and pretty, although she had dark brown eyes and, in Fergus's mind, was not as breathtakingly pretty as his Becky. Each pearl was taken out of its box and held against the daughter's cheek. The jeweller was right; he knew his trade. Next to the girl's skin the dark pearl seemed to have greater luminosity than the creamier ones. This pearl was also the biggest and therefore, Fergus thought, the most expensive.

'Would you like some restorative refreshment sir?' asked the jeweller.

Fergus thought it an excellent idea and the daughter disappeared, to return with a bottle of Scottish whisky and two glasses.

'Are you resident in the city?' asked the jeweller.

'No, I've just arrived on the stagecoach from Glasgow.'

'Then welcome to Edinburgh. You'll be needing a chain. Do you think the lady would prefer gold or silver?'

Fergus didn't know, but he preferred silver. When he'd entered, he'd seen that the jeweller was wearing a large gold ring and he'd thought it rather vulgar. No, silver it must be. He didn't want to think about the jeweller's hands every time Becky wore the necklace.

After they'd gone through the size of silver chain-links he required and finished their whisky, they arrived at the question of price. To Fergus's surprise, the jeweller took the box in which the pearl had been displayed and lifted up the velvet. Underneath was a price ticket and that said two guineas. His appearance was not going to determine the price, it was fixed, and this gave him greater confidence to purchase. The jeweller put the price tag on the counter. The chain had a small ticket, attached by a piece of cotton. On it was written one guinea.

'That's three guineas, sir.'

Fergus hesitated for a moment, then said, 'Can we say three pounds?'

The jeweller pursed his lips. 'Well, since it's your first visit to Edinburgh I'll make it three pounds exactly, including the box.'

Fergus was neither surprised nor delighted with the price, since he had no idea how much jewellery cost. He'd already decided it would be what it was going to be, although had he stopped to think about it in terms of his usual purchases, a great many books could be had for three pounds. What he did know was that he could well afford it; his personal finances were healthy. He had few expenses and could indulge himself if he felt like it.

Several clocks struck the third quarter and Fergus handed over the money, saying, 'I must be away. I've an appointment at four.'

The jeweller put the box in a drawstring bag. Fergus was elated and couldn't wait to get back and place it around Becky's neck. He knew it would look glorious.

Arriving at the Black Bull with five minutes to spare, Fergus found Mr Cameron waiting for him in the entrance. They walked the few streets to his office, where it took Fergus only half an hour to decide Mr Cameron was an able businessman who was looking after their interests.

Back in Glasgow, as before, the city seemed grey, and Fergus's mood fell. However, when he reached the agent's office Bill McRae was there. They retired to a nearby coffee house.

'When do we sail?' asked Fergus.

'We're loading liquor today and waiting on cloth from the Northern Islands. It should have been here yesterday. Hopefully tomorrow.'

'If not tomorrow?'

'Then the next.'

'We could be held up for a couple of days then?'

'Unlikely, but possible.' Bill laughed. 'Missing your sweetheart?'

Fergus felt his cheeks redden, 'Maybe I am and maybe I'm just not happy about spending time in Glasgow.'

'That's because you don't know where to go. Trust me, I can show us a good time.'

'As long as you can find me an interesting bookshop, I'll be happy. I'll wager they have the latest editions here from London.'

'Didn't you find a bookshop in Edinburgh?'

'I did make a purchase, but not for myself, and it wasn't a book.'

'Going to show me?'

Fergus hesitated. Now he half wished he hadn't mentioned it, but he was excited about the necklace. 'It's for a lady.'

'Ah, a love token then?'

'No. Yes. Well, maybe.' Fergus extracted the box from the drawstring bag and opened it.

Bill drew in his breath. 'She's a lucky girl. I take it it's for the lovely Becky?'

Fergus nodded. 'Do you think she'll like it?'

Bill put his head on one side. 'There's no doubt she'll

like it. It looks expensive. I'll wager you could have bought a small library with what that cost.'

Fergus ignored Bill's last comment and put the necklace away. By showing it to him he felt he'd made a declaration to the world that he was seriously interested in Becky.

'She's different,' he said. 'When I'm with her I feel happy. I'm more alive. Do you feel like that about Mary?'

'When I was in Leith, sitting my exams for chief officer, I always felt part of me was back in Whitehaven, and I couldn't wait to get back.'

'What about when you were in America? Was it the same then?'

'No, that was when I was only a second officer. I had lady friends, it's true, but I never felt the pull back to them as I did with Mary. You had acquaintances in Oxford; you've mentioned them. What happened to those?'

'They were mostly the sisters of fellow students who came visiting. They were delightful, full of fun and a pleasure to be with, but there was no one I wanted to give my name to.'

'Don't tell me – they didn't read fine literature?'

'You mock me. Although if I'm honest, that could have been part of it.'

'I tease in jest, I assure you.' Bill slapped Fergus good-naturedly on the arm.

'I know. Becky reads poetry, which at the very least indicates to me she has a feeling for words.'

'Really? She sounds perfect for you. I'll try and get us back to Whitehaven as soon as I can.' He stood up. 'And sitting here will not get the job done.'

They were away by mid-afternoon. Back at his office desk on Wednesday afternoon, the 20th of June, Fergus wrote a note, folded it and closed it with sealing wax. Then he called one of the clerks over and asked him to deliver it to the Indian King.

CHAPTER SEVEN

Becky took delivery of the note and was surprised to see it addressed to herself. She turned it over and her heart leapt. The red wax seal was imprinted with the words 'Shackleton & Company'. It must be from Fergus. She put it in her pocket. The bar was busy; it would be a while before she could be alone and savour the moment.

Her chance came when Dolly, who'd fallen behind with the guest breakfasts and was hurrying to catch up, called her over and asked her to fetch clean glass cloths. When Becky entered the kitchen, the puppy stepped out of his basket by the range and came forward to greet her. She picked him up.

'Not now Charlie, I'm busy.' She cuddled him and put him back, then broke the seal and opened the note. It *was* from Fergus – short and to the point.

Dear Becky,
If it would please you, I would like to invite you to take a stroll

tomorrow, Thursday afternoon. I have something for you. Unless I hear to the contrary, I shall call for you at half past four.

Cordially,

Fergus

Becky was suddenly all of a dither. *He's got something for me? What can it be? Should I have something for him in return?*

Hearing nothing, Fergus spent the day in a state of nervous anticipation. He mixed up the names of the Glasgow and Edinburgh agents on some documents and had to add up a column of figures three times. The wall clock seemed to be scorning him, its hands taking forever to pass through the hours. At four o'clock he put his pens away and left the company offices. He tried to walk slowly, but even so he arrived at the Indian King with fifteen minutes to spare. He turned away, walked back to Dr Lennagon's, paused to read the brass plaque beside the door, then retraced his steps.

Becky was waiting outside when he approached. He waved and she began making her way towards him, her wide skirt swaying with each step. As she drew near, he found himself checking her for jewellery. An oval brooch with a green stone was pinned to the left side of her jacket, but he could see no necklace.

'Let's go down to the harbour,' said Fergus. He was so pleased to be in her company, he wanted to give her his arm, but thought it perhaps too forward.

They began walking. Fergus placed himself between her and the road. The pavement was narrow, so her skirt brushed against his breeches with each step. He was close enough to smell her perfume again; breathing it in made him feel light-headed, in a good way. His mind wandered into what it would be like to kiss her. Two gulls paid them some attention then, seeming to realise they had no food to offer, flew off, cawing loudly to each other.

Becky was just as pretty as he remembered her, even more so out of the confines of the bar. Her hair was arranged in a loose plait finished off with a bright yellow bow, a ray of sunshine tumbling down her back.

'You've been away?'

'To Glasgow and Edinburgh. I only returned yesterday.' He knew she deserved an apology and he was anxious to explain. 'My work means I'm often called away at short notice to meet agents in other ports. I check that the people we depend on are working well for us.'

'You're a spy?' she said, laughing.

'Not really. It sounds like it, but the people know who I am and so it's not a deception. Mostly I'm learning the running of the business.'

'The ropes?'

Fergus laughed. 'Yes, being at sea on a brig I suppose you could say that.'

'Will you go to foreign places like America?'

'There are no plans for me to be away for months at a time. The present arrangement is a temporary one. Once I've visited the ports we do the most business with, then I'll be working from the offices here again.'

'How many more've you to visit? Have you been to London? I've always wanted to go there. I've only been to Workington, St Bees, and once to Cockerm'uth for a cousin's wedding.'

'I've been to London several times. When I was at the university in Oxford I would visit with fellow students, but the next time I go it will be to the docks to meet our agents and suppliers again, in a different part of the city.'

'Is this what you want to do? Be in the shipping business?'

'I've been raised for it and I'm enjoying it more than I used to.'

'And if you didn't have the family business, what do you think you'd be doing?'

'I'd have opened a bookshop somewhere, like Callander & Dixon's in Market Place.'

'So's you could sit around and read all day, looking at book covers?'

He grinned. 'Something like that. It would just be so stimulating to be surrounded by books. I like books for what they are and how they feel in my hands, as much as to read.'

'Old books, like the one you gave me?'

'Yes, especially old books with thick leather bindings. Illuminated manuscripts, that sort of thing.'

'Illuminated what?'

'Illuminated manuscripts. Books written by monks in abbeys and churches for patrons and for the glory of God. The individual letters are decorated, sometimes with gold leaf, and so are the margins, with flowers and mythical animals. They're even decorated with people sometimes.'

'Are they prayer books?'

'Exactly, and they also illuminate the Gospels. However, it seems I'm destined to be with Shackleton's, keeping the family business afloat.' He made the movement of a fish swimming through water with his hand.

Becky laughed.

They arrived at the harbour just as a three-masted barque was going out and they stood and watched her leave.

'Soon all the ships in this harbour will be powered by steam,' Fergus said. He turned to face her. 'Here I am talking ships again, but steam is the future.'

'Living here it's impossible not to talk ships and shipping. How many steamships do you have?'

'None, I'm ashamed to say. My father thinks they're death traps likely to blow up at any moment. Some of our competitors have them and it's costing us business in contracts. However, we're not here to talk about business. I've a gift for you.' He drew the black leather box from his pocket and held it out to her. 'I bought it in Edinburgh.'

'For me?'

'Yes, especially for you. Think of it as an apology for going away again and having to send notes all the time.'

Becky took the box and ran her fingers over the gold tooling on the lid before opening it. She lifted the black velvet cover. 'It's beautiful.' She touched the pearl lightly with her forefinger. 'I don't know what to say.'

'Thank you?' he suggested, laughing.

'A big thank you, but I can't possibly accept it.' She closed the box and made as if to hand it back to him.

Fergus put his hands behind his back. 'Why not?'

'It's so beautiful, it has to be expensive. Really expensive. I mean, look at the quality of the box.'

'It's a gift, and you should never question the price of a gift. Accept it. Please, I saw it and thought of you.'

'I can't. Really, I can't. For a start I've nowt to give you and I could never afford anything of this quality.'

'There's no need to give me anything. You haven't been away or let me down and had to send notes.'

'I don't feel easy about it.' When she held out the box, Fergus took it back.

It was too much too soon; Fergus could see that by Becky's face, which was now registering agitation. It was almost as if he'd behaved indecently. She had interlocked her fingers and was twisting her palms together. It was a slight movement of unease, but enough for him to register her discomfort.

Fergus looked away over the harbour wall, gazing into the distance for a moment or two, before turning back to face her. 'I've a proposition. I'll look after the necklace for you and when you bring me what I'm about to ask you for, then you can accept my gift.'

'What can I give you?'

'Bring me a poem and read it to me.'

'Any poem?'

'A favourite one, or one that means something to you.'

'I said before, I don't feel I know you well enough to talk about poetry yet. It's a private thing. I mean, only Mam's seen me reading poetry, and other folks'll laugh if they find out.' She was still looking uncomfortable.

'Then when you do know me well enough, as I hope

you soon will, we'll exchange the poem for the necklace. Are we agreed?'

He could see she was thinking it through. He was cross with himself. He'd got carried away. *I've overwhelmed her. What to me is a simple gift that I can well afford is, judging by her reaction, almost an insult, as if I'm trying to buy her. I've frightened her and it's too late now.*

He held out his hand. 'If you take my hand, then we have an agreement. When you're ready, and only then, we'll exchange a poetry reading for a necklace. Or to put it another way, wisdom for a pearl.'

Becky put her hand in his. He hadn't anticipated the surge that rushed through him when her skin touched his. There was a connection that had not been there before. It was as if all his senses were centred on their hands. She was blushing. *Does she feel the same way?* He'd expected her to withdraw her hand straightaway, but she didn't. He felt giddy.

Becky broke the moment. 'Wisdom, is that what you said?' She laughed. 'Wisdom? You can't expect a young lass like me to read in an old man's voice. I'm no sage.'

Fergus knew in that moment that he was right. Here was a girl who thought as he did, who understood his wordplay and who he found irresistibly attractive in every way, mentally and physically. Here was a girl he could not only love, but was already falling in love with. He wanted to shout it out and tell the world.

They headed back along West Strand, taking a short cut through Hamilton Lane to reach Quay Street, where, halfway down, a young boy was sitting beside the road, with what looked like slates spread out before him. One leg was stretched out in front of him, the other tucked underneath. He looked as if he hadn't seen a bathtub for a while, and his clothes, ill-fitting and patched, also needed a good wash, but his eyes were lively, and he gave them a cheery smile as they approached. They stopped and looked at the slates. Each one was decorated with a different type of ship.

'Hello,' said Becky, smiling at the boy. 'Did you do these?'

He nodded and looked at them from underneath long, dark lashes. 'They're all Whitehaven ships and they're for sale.' He picked one up and held it out for them to see. 'I only do ships, not folk.'

'These are very good. You have talent.' Fergus took the slate and turned it over in his hands. 'Where do you get them?'

'I gets them from the beach and I paints them back home.' He gestured in the direction of New Houses.

There was something familiar about the boy. Fergus looked more closely. 'Don't I know you?'

'I don't think so, sir, but I know you,' he said to Becky looking at her with a grin. 'I've seen you in church, haven't I?'

'Yes, I'm your mam's friend.' Becky grinned at the two of them. 'I can't hold out any longer, you do both know each other, you're just not realising it.'

Fergus looked more closely. The boy had pointed towards New Houses, where he'd been to see Amy Rooke. 'Is it Rory?'

The boy's head shot up. 'How'd you know that?' He suddenly looked fearful and began biting his bottom lip, just as he had done when lying on the ground, after his accident. Fergus thought he might try to bolt, although it would be obvious to anyone watching that he couldn't run very far, or fast, with his bad leg which, now he specifically looked at it, Fergus could see it was damaged.

'Don't worry. I'm Fergus Shackleton. I saw to you when the carter's barrel hit you. I didn't recognise you straightaway because the last time I saw you, you were in pain and upset.'

Rory stopped biting his lip, thought for a moment, then smiled. 'Thank you, sir. My apologies for not seeing you for the same gentleman.'

'How many ships have you sold today?' asked Becky.

'I came out with eight.'

He still had eight slates laid out. 'So, you haven't sold any at all?' asked Becky.

'Not yet, but I'm hopeful *you'll* buy one.' Rory grinned at her.

'How much are they?' asked Fergus. He felt sorry for the boy, out in the world trying to earn a few pennies. Despite his aura of poverty, and his clothes needing a scrub, his hair was clean and he had good white teeth. There was a cheeky manner about him that Fergus liked.

'They're fourpence each or two for sevenpence.'

'I'll take two,' said Becky.

'And I'll take six,' said Fergus.

Behind the boy's beaming smile and profuse thanks, Fergus could see relief. Was it relief at having made pocket money, or relief at not having to carry the stones back home? Or perhaps it made the difference between them having, or not having, a proper meal the next day.

Rory wrapped the slates in an old newspaper and they handed over the coppers.

'I'm sorry I didn't recognise you, sir,' Rory said again.

'I'm not surprised. You were in shock when we met last time. And your leg?'

'It's keeping me out of the mine, so I makes brass this way, with my painted slates.'

'That's a good idea. I hope you do well,' said Fergus.

Becky placed her hand lightly on Fergus's arm, which he interpreted as a gesture to keep silent.

'I'm thinking, now you can't go down the mine, have you another job?' Becky asked.

The boy shook his head. 'Who'll take on a crippled boy with a gammy leg?'

Fergus couldn't contain himself and had to speak. 'What about the carter? Did he give you any money?'

'A man in a big top hat called to see Mammy two days ago and gave her three pounds and she signed a paper. I think they called it an agreement.'

Fergus shook his head, but kept his silence. That's what he'd paid for Becky's necklace.

'What does the doctor say?' asked Becky.

'That I'm to exercise my leg or I'll need a crutch, so I walk down here every day and then back home. Can I go now, sir? Mammy waits for me.'

Fergus watched the boy walk away, leaning to one side dragging his foot. He was mobile, but not fit for any kind of labouring job, and not schooled enough for an office position. He seemed bright, though. He'd speedily worked out how much they owed him for the slates with cumulative discount.

Becky interrupted his thoughts. 'There's a hopelessness about him, and no wonder, as I don't suppose he has many friends. All the boys his age'll be working, and the girls too. Even if they're free to play I'm thinking they'll probably run around and tease him; children can be cruel over an infirmity. Some men in the pub were talking about him, saying how he and Amy could end up in the workhouse if she doesn't remarry.'

They walked a little way in silence until Fergus said, 'I feel I ought to do something to help Rory, but how, and what?'

'I understand. It's like you and he have a bond.'

'I feel that. I'll see if I can find someone to employ him.'

''Appen there *is* something he could do. He's able to walk, and the puppy needs to be exercised. Why don't I ask Mam to get him to walk Charlie? He's only a pup, doesn't need to go far, and the lad'll enjoy the company, I'm sure of that. It'll give him some brass coming in regularly.'

'Do you think your mother will agree?'

'If I explain his circumstances, she might. Although she'll say it's a waste of money, but I can pay. It won't be much.'

'I'll pay for it,' said Fergus.

'There's no need. Really, I'll see to it.'

'It's a splendid idea. A way of helping him without it being charity, and it gives us time to find him something permanent.'

'Time's on our side,' said Becky. 'He's coming up eleven, and when he's grown a bit, then he'll be more employable. He can certainly draw. Perhaps we can find him something connected with that. Sign-writing?'

Fergus noticed Becky's use of 'we'. It shouted out to him she regarded them as paired, although in what way he wasn't yet sure. Friends or more than that? Either way, she was uniting them in a cause they both felt worthwhile. Fergus would find something for young Rory Rooke; he'd a feeling he was going to be part of his and Becky's lives, but in what way?

CHAPTER EIGHT

The next morning, Becky decided she'd better not say anything about the necklace to her mother, but she did mention Rory and the dog-walking idea.

'What do you think? He seems a nice lad and he's making an effort. Look at these slate paintings.'

'He's talent. I've no bone to pick over him taking Charlie out, but I need to make it clear that as far as engaging him in any other capacity, we can't. I need strong lads and men to change the casks. Even Da used to say it was sometimes too much for him, and you remember how strong he was afore he got sick.'

'I've thought of something else too. Do we have a space we could put some of these slates in? Folk might buy one.'

'If we start that, everybody'll want to use us to display their wares. No, I don't think that's a good idea.'

Becky persisted. 'There's a little space by the fireplace. That square shelf. There's nothing on there and they'd brighten that bit up.'

'Why all this for Rory Rooke? There's plenty more like him. Are you going to employ them all?'

Becky sighed. 'His prospects are so poor with his gammy leg and he's such a bright lad, with intelligent eyes. He's had bad luck and he'll struggle to find a job until he's older, and maybe not even then. If he and his mam end up in the workhouse they'll separate them, label them debtors, and he'll never be able to make anything of himself.'

'Nothing to do with Fergus Shackleton, then? You need to be cautious there.'

'I know Fergus has the lad's interests at heart, like me, and for them only to have been given three pounds as compensation, that's a scandal. Why would his mam accept it?'

'Because having three pounds in her hand that day was better than waiting six months for ten. I'll say it again, I think you should be cautious.'

'What do you mean?'

'I'm just saying, a young man like him, with money, is usually seen walking out with a girl from a similar background.'

'You mean I'm not good enough for him?'

'Nay, I don't mean that at all. I mean he's from a different world. Just be mindful of the differences, and be watchful. Also, of what people may think. You're the most precious thing in my world. I'm keeping a watch out for you, as any mam would.'

'He's behaved exactly as a gentleman towards me at all times.'

'He's to prove himself to me that he's got the best of intentions towards my lass and when he's done that, then – and only then – will I trust him.' Dolly began clearing the breakfast dishes away. 'Why don't you go and see Amy about Rory's little job?'

'Now?'

'It'll be quiet for a while, so it's a good time. But a word of warning. We both know Amy's a good mam and keeps a tidy house as best she can up there. She loves that lad, but he's fatherless, as she's never given word who his da might be. Although he'll not be the only one who may never learn where his father's buried for lack of his name. If there's any whiff of charity about him walking Charlie, she'll turn you down flat.'

✳ ✳ ✳

Amy was busy with her mending again when Becky arrived.

'Is Rory about?'

'I've sent him out. He's to walk out every day, the doctor says.'

'Fergus and I saw him selling his paintings yesterday.'

'Aye.' She smiled. ''Twas a good day for him. He said he sold all seven of them to Miss Becky, and the man who helped him when he had his accident. He thinks you're a pretty lass.'

Becky was going to correct her, to say that it had been eight paintings, not seven, then, just in time, it occurred to her Rory was probably keeping a few pence for himself. *And why not?* she thought. It was *his* handiwork.

'Rory told us about walking every day to help his leg, and I thought he might walk our puppy as a little job at the same time. We're so busy in the summer and we don't have time to give him all the exercise he needs.'

Becky waited for Amy's reaction. She saw relief roll over her face, as if she realised Rory had done nothing wrong. Then a wariness descended.

'Why Rory?'

'He passes by the Indian King on his walk to the harbour, so why not call and collect our puppy?'

'Won't he pull Rory over now he's got his bad leg?'

'Charlie's just a baby.' Becky indicated his size with her hands. 'He still fits in my basket.'

'I'd have to ask him. I'm not sure.'

'Well, tell him there's tuppence and a glass of lemonade each time if he wants the job.'

'You'd pay him?'

'Oh, aye. It's not charity.' Becky cursed herself. She'd said the dreaded word, and it was now whirling around the room, bouncing off the mud-streaked windows.

'We couldn't be doing with that. Nay, we've always paid our way.'

For a moment Becky thought Amy was going to cry. She went quite red in the face and, with her head down, rubbed a finger over an imaginary mark on the table top.

'It's not charity or a poor handout; it's a fair wage for a fair job. He'll be expected to treat it as he would any other job. I'll leave tuppence here on the table in advance for tomorrow. If he decides he doesn't want it, then he can return it when he passes next. That's fair, isn't it?'

Amy nodded. 'I'll tell him.'

'You needn't worry. We'll look after him.'

On the way home, not for the first time, Becky mulled over the consequences of the Rookes ending up in the workhouse. The first thing they'd do was shave Rory's head and put him in one of those dreadful uniforms.

❊ ❊ ❊

In the Indian King, Becky found her mother changing the sheets in one of the guestrooms upstairs.

'I saw Amy.'

'What did she say?'

'I think she'll encourage him to do it. They don't have much by way of belongings and she's taking in mending.'

'Is she still bonny? She was a good-looking lass last time I saw her.'

'Aye, she is, but you can see she's worn out and in need of a good meal.'

'I'll wager she keeps a clean doorstep.'

Becky nodded. How strange it was that a clean doorstep should be such an important indicator of a well-kept home. And it always seemed to her the cleaner the doorstep, the poorer the home.

'We'll see Rory tomorrow, I'm sure of it,' she said, gathering up the dirty pillowslips. 'She'll do anything to keep him out of the workhouse.'

'Aye, let's hope she doesn't have her head turned by a cocky young lad with a velvet tongue and a few coins in his hand.'

'Oh no, I can't see Amy resorting to...that.'

'I've seen it happen. A young widow desperate not to be separated from her bairns by the workhouse will sell anything she has to hand, and I don't mean the furniture or her jewellery.'

'We must make sure it doesn't come to that. Have you thought any more about Rory's paintings?'

'Aye, you can put a couple out, but heed my words – only for his as a special case, no one else's.'

Becky stood up, spread her arms and gave her mam a hug. 'Thanks, Mam.'

CHAPTER NINE

On Tuesday afternoon, Rory called for the puppy and Becky waved them off, just as a messenger arrived with another note from Fergus. This time Becky opened it in front of her mother.

'It's an invitation.'

'What for?'

'A concert in St Nicholas' Church. He would like me to "accompany" him. He's very polite, isn't he?'

'Aye, he does have good manners and a nice way of speaking, that's fair to say. When?'

'A week on Wednesday, at six o'clock.'

'Thursday would be better, but if you want to go you can have that afternoon off, instead of Thursday.'

Becky thanked her mother with a wide grin. 'I must reply. It's from the Queen Street address.'

'Nice houses with carriages and servants.'

'I'd like someone to do my washing and make the beds,

but having someone around watching me all the time, no, I wouldn't want that. I've been thinking about what you said, and I know we're from different backgrounds, but I enjoy his company and he treats me as an equal.'

'Just don't get your hopes up too high, and be careful. A broken heart is painful and takes a long time to heal. Sometimes, you know, they never do.'

❈ ❈ ❈

On his way to deliver some documents, Fergus saw Bill walking towards him.

'Did the lovely Becky reply? Is she coming?'

'Yes, she's coming.'

'Excellent. It's not every day Mary has a solo. She's been rehearsing for weeks. To be truthful I'll be relieved when it's over. I could take her place, I know the tune so well.'

Fergus laughed. He knew Bill was secretly proud of his wife's musical prowess.

'After the concert there's a bit of a "do", but it's for singers and spouses only, I'm afraid, so you can't join us.'

Fergus was disappointed. He'd hoped Mary and Becky could be properly introduced after the concert. He wanted Becky to be accepted by his friends.

When the day of the concert arrived, they met outside the church.

Fergus offered his arm. 'Bill's inside saving seats. You'll recognise him; he came with me to the Indian King one evening. His wife is singing a solo.'

They had only walked a few paces inside when Fergus heard a familiar voice.

'Fergus, you didn't tell me you were coming, my dear. And who is your friend?' Aunt Louisa was looking at Becky in a kindly, interested way. Fergus had been wondering when his parents were going to learn about his friendship with Becky and who was going to tell them. Now he knew.

Embracing the *fait accompli* moment with one of the big smiles that almost closed his eyes, Fergus said, 'Aunt Louisa, may I introduce my friend Miss Moss. Miss Moss, my aunt, Miss Louisa Shackleton.'

Aunt Louisa extended a hand encased in a kid leather glove.

Becky smiled. 'I'm pleased to meet you.'

Fergus caught an amused half-smile pass across his aunt's face when Becky gave a little bob curtsey.

'And I am pleased to meet you too, my dear,' she said. She gave a teasing smile. 'Do you have a Christian name?'

'Becky. It's Becky.'

'That's a pretty name for a pretty girl. Is it a family name?'

'Nay. Mam's called Dorothy. Well, she's Dolly, really, and my gran was Eliza, and we called her Lizzie.'

'You must come to tea one afternoon.' She smiled at Becky again then, before making her way to her seat, she said to Fergus, 'It's so nice to meet one of your friends.'

When she was out of earshot, Becky said, 'She's very nice. You have the same eyes.'

'Yes, so I'm told. She's wonderful. She does a lot of work with sailors at the Seamen's Haven. It's her life, really.'

Fergus was pleased and relieved he'd had the opportunity to introduce Becky, especially as Aunt Louisa had seemed genuinely interested to meet her. Becky was looking particularly lovely, and he was proud to have her on his arm. Perhaps he was fearing needlessly about any potential parental doubts over his relationship with her.

The church was still only half full and they quickly found Bill chatting with a group of people in the central aisle. A string quartet was arranged at the front in a semi-circle. Exactly on cue, as the church clock struck six, the conductor bowed to the audience and lifted his baton.

For the next hour, all Fergus could think about was how physically close he was to Becky. He was aware of every fold of her skirt, every slight movement of her foot and how her hands lay at rest on her lap. Her hair was freshly washed and plaited, fastened at the end with a generous cherry red bow. Her nails were clean, cut short and shaped neatly, giving no indication she lit fires, or that she polished and frequently washed glasses and tankards. He breathed in her perfume, and knew he would always think of her now if he smelt it anywhere. Twice he looked sideways at her and she caught his eye and smiled. He'd no idea whether she was enjoying the programme, but she showed no signs of boredom. When it came to Mary's solo, Fergus gave her a slight nudge and Bill looked across at them both, all smiles.

After the concert they bade Bill goodbye and waved to Aunt Louisa, who smiled and waved back.

Once outside Fergus offered Becky his arm. 'Shall we walk?'

'Would you like to come back to the Indian King?' asked Becky.

'Escort you home?'

'Not exactly. I thought we could sit together in the kitchen for a short while, since it's not usually that busy on a Wednesday evening. Mam'll be behind the bar.'

Fergus agreed and when he was settled in the kitchen Becky left, to reappear a few minutes later holding a slim volume with a green marbled cover and worn leather spine. She held it out to him.

Fergus read the title aloud. '*Cumberland Poems,* by John Rayson.' He opened the volume and looked inside. 'Didn't he die recently?'

'Aye, last year. The bookshop had a small display to commemorate him and I bought this. I'm not ready to read a poem to you yet, but would you like to borrow this in advance?'

'I'd like that very much...' He paused and then, feeling suddenly emboldened, he continued with, '...but only if we can seal the borrowing with a kiss.'

As soon as he'd said it he wished he hadn't. *I've been too forward too soon.*

Becky looked momentarily surprised. He could see her thinking about it then, looking up into his eyes, she gave a half-smile. 'All right, just one as a thank you for this evening.'

Fergus put his arms around her and leaned forward. Afterwards, when thinking about it, he recalled the moment as a brief, sweet kiss, probably Becky's first, but he knew it was much more than just any kiss; it was a most important one. They had crossed a threshold and were now more than just friends.

* * *

Fergus arrived home at Queen Street to be informed by Samuel that the family was gathered in the drawing room. This was not particularly unusual; it was the way Samuel looked at Fergus as he told him that alerted him something was amiss. He hoped his father wasn't in one of his haranguing moods, and that no crisis had befallen one of their ships. But he had a fair idea of what might be coming and he was prepared. Standing outside the drawing room door he took a deep breath, blew the air out slowly, ran his fingers through his hair, then opened the door.

His father was standing warming himself in front of the ornate fireplace, while his mother was sitting in a large upholstered chair with an embroidered back. To her left was a small mahogany table upon which sat an open sewing-box.

Aunt Louisa, who was semi-reclining on a chaise-longue to the right of the fireplace, looked up when he entered. She put her book down and took up a small glass of sherry from a card table close by.

His father broke the silence. 'We understand you have a young lady friend.'

It was as Fergus had anticipated. He was ready. 'Yes, I have a friend.'

Aunt Louisa said, 'I've been telling them about Becky, the pretty girl you introduced me to at the concert.'

His mother closed her sewing-box. 'We're planning a musical soirée and Louisa has suggested we invite her as your guest.'

'I'll be happy to invite her.'

There was a pause, then his mother asked, 'Is she a gentlewoman of good background?'

Fergus took a deep breath. 'She's called Becky. Becky Moss. She's eighteen and her family have owned the Indian King for two generations. It's a well-run house worthy of its licence. Her mother is a widow. By gentlewoman, if you mean born into wealth and privilege then no, she's not, but as a person she's honest and true.' He stopped speaking and waited for a response. His parents seemed to be struck dumb.

Aunt Louisa held up her empty sherry glass. 'She's very pretty, with dark hair and captivating eyes.' She looked at the decanter on the sideboard. In the silence that followed, Fergus collected her glass and refilled it for her.

Of his parents, Hector was the first to gather himself. 'Is she of Irish stock?' he asked. 'A lot of Irish keep alehouses and...' His voice trailed off.

His mother had turned quite pale and seemed lost for words. Fergus could imagine what was going on in her head. *An Irish publican's daughter? My son frequenting a common public house?*

'No, she's not Irish, but it wouldn't matter to me if she was.'

'How long has this been going on?' asked Hector.

'If by "going on" you mean how long has she been my friend, we met at the auction for the *Gregory Peat*. She was in charge of the bidding book.'

111

His mother found her voice. 'That was in April, three months ago, and you've said nothing to us about her.'

'Do you have an attachment to this girl?' Hector asked. 'Do you hold loyalties towards her? Is there an understanding between you?'

Fergus hadn't noticed it earlier, but his shirt collar was now too tight. He put up a hand and readjusted it. 'She is my friend and I have always aimed to be loyal to my friends.'

'Your failure to introduce us to this girl speaks volumes.' Hector sucked in his cheeks. 'It is as if you are ashamed of her.'

'I most certainly am not. I was delighted to have her on my arm today and proud to introduce her to Aunt Louisa.'

'Do you feel sorry for her?' asked his mother.

'Sorry for her? Why would I feel that?'

'The circumstances of her home and life.' His mother's eyes travelled the room. 'It must be very different from here. Rather lowly I expect.'

'She comes from a loving home. She and her mother work hard and they're honest, God-fearing people. Thank you for the invitation to the musical soirée. I would like to bring her here to meet you.'

Hector moved away from the fire. 'That will not now be possible. Allow me to give you some advice. While you live in this house you may spend your money as you wish, you may associate outside this house and the company offices with whomever you wish, but you may not bring a licensed publican's daughter into our home.'

'Father, you're forgetting we're nothing more than

merchants ourselves, which many would describe as "trade".'

Hector frowned. 'I will remind you this is my house and you live under my roof.' He was attempting to stare Fergus down, but Fergus held his gaze steadily. His father went on, 'This is a prudent moment to let you know that if you marry someone your mother and I regard as unseemly, in any way and for whatever reason, then you will not be welcome here, and I will instruct my solicitor to draw up a new will from which you will be excluded.'

Louisa gasped. 'You can't do that.' She paused as if to compose herself then continued in a quiet, low voice, shaking with emotion. 'You ruined my chances of a love marriage; you must not blight Fergus's future as you did mine.'

Fergus was shocked. He knew there was some low-level tension between his father and aunt, but he hadn't realised the roots of it lay in Aunt Louisa's marriage prospects.

Elizabeth sighed loudly. 'Oh, not that again, Louisa.'

Hector gave a dismissive wave in Louisa's direction and stood up. 'Enough of all this. I have made myself perfectly clear to Fergus that we will not be entertaining his friend in this house, and now I wish you all a good night.' He turned to his wife. 'Come, Elizabeth, it is time to retire.'

Fergus and Aunt Louisa found themselves alone.

'I'm sorry, I really am,' she said. 'I should have thought before I said anything. I like her and she seems to have nice manners.'

'Don't worry. It's for the best it's out in the open. I seem to have fallen out of Father's favour once more.'

'Follow your heart. I was prevented from following mine, and I was young, and there was no one to take my side.'

Fergus waited for her to continue, but it seemed as if his aunt now regretted her words. 'I'll say no more this evening because now is not the right time. Too much has been said already.' She put out her hand. 'Come help me out of my chair. I may not yet be sixty, but my bones are beginning to creak.'

'There's plenty of life and spirit in you,' said Fergus with a smile.

She laughed. 'You've grown, and now you're too tall for me to ruffle your hair like I did when you were little, but I can see you've not lost your boyish spirit. Hold onto it, Fergus. Don't let the older generation beat you down and mould you to their ways. I'm sure your father will see sense in due course.'

Fergus was not so sure. It was not like his father to back down once he'd made a stand, but one thing Fergus *was* sure of – he was not going to say anything to Becky about what had just transpired.

CHAPTER TEN

It was the 14th of July, Bastille Day, and the French sailors in port were celebrating. Their companions needed little encouragement to join in, and the town's streets were crowded and spirits high.

Taking her arm, Fergus introduced Becky to Mary. They smiled at each other and Becky complimented Mary on her concert performance. She judged Mary to be a little older than herself, or perhaps it was just that her face was fuller. Maybe she was twenty, which would make her two years older. She was smaller than Becky and rounder in girth.

Bill led the way through the stalls. They ate gingerbread biscuits, and bought toffee for later. The disorganised pressure of the eager throng carried them past the skittles and the children's swing boats. They were walking towards the hoopla when Becky saw Rory and Amy.

'Amy, it's a treat to see you out and about,' she said. After introducing her companions, she went on, 'And you, Rory, are you enjoying yourself?'

'We're just here to look,' he began, before Amy stepped in with, 'Can I take the time to thank you again, Mr Shackleton, for helping Rory?'

Fergus batted away her thanks, but Becky could see he was pleased to receive them again. She'd noticed immediately how Amy looked thinner and was paler and more drawn than when she'd last seen her.

Rory tugged on his mother's sleeve. 'Mammy wanted to buy some...' He looked up at her. 'What's it called?'

'Nay, I just said I was thinking on it.' Amy looked embarrassed.

'You said you wanted to buy it to make you better.'

'Hush, Rory. We're delaying these good people.' She began apologising for Rory's persistence, but he cut her off.

'Elixir,' he shouted, with a satisfied smile on his face. 'I've remembered. From the man over there.' He pointed to where a quack doctor, sharp-featured and square-chinned, wearing a cheap top hat, was surrounded by potions and bottles of cure-all health elixir. *He doesn't inspire confidence*, Becky thought.

'Mammy's not been well,' said Rory, as if he felt they needed an explanation.

'Have you seen the doctor?' asked Mary.

Amy shook her head.' No need, I'm just a little tired.'

Becky didn't believe her. *She hasn't seen a doctor because she can't afford one.*

Rory looked up at Fergus. 'Mr Shackleton, sir, can she see the doctor I saw?'

'If she'd like to, then of course,' said Fergus, looking across at Becky.

'Hush, Rory, there's no need for that.' It was no surprise to any of them when, looking a little teary and blotchy, Amy seized hold of Rory's hand and began pulling him away. They'd only taken a few steps when Rory looked back and said, 'Thank you for the soldiers, Mr Shackleton. They came in their own special tin.'

❊ ❊ ❊

The next day, after church, when an early morning sea-fret had lifted, Becky called on Amy. She found her, as she usually did, alone, surrounded by a pile of other people's mending. Becky pulled a bottle of dark ale from her bag and held it out to her.

'This is for you,' she said. 'It stimulates the appetite.' She half expected Amy to decline it, but she took it and put it on the table.

'Thank you.' Amy looked at Becky expectantly.

How am I going to approach this? 'Did you enjoy the fair?' Becky asked.

'It made a change. Rory enjoyed it. The bright lights and the noise. We walked around for a while then came home.' She paused then added, 'I didn't buy any of that elixir.'

Thank goodness. 'I think you made a wise decision. I don't see how one medicine can cure all ills.'

Amy indicated to Becky to sit down. 'Would you like something to drink?'

Becky shook her head. 'I've called to say Mr Shackleton says if you would like to see the doctor he'll pay.'

'Why would he do that?'

'Because he's a kind man and he's fond of Rory.'

'Nay. I'm sure he means well, but we've already charity enough from him over Rory's accident and the tin soldiers.'

'But if you're not well?'

'I'm not that sick.'

'I'm not so sure and other folk can see it.' There was an awkward pause. 'It's clear to me you need to see a doctor.'

Amy began protesting again and Becky put her hand up, palm outwards, to stop her. 'If you don't want to see Mr Shackleton's doctor that's your choice, but why don't you go to the Infirmary?'

'I don't need to.'

'Aye, but you do. If you get sicker, who'll look after Rory?'

Amy turned away from Becky's gaze.

'What if I came with you?' Becky persisted.

Amy rubbed two fingers along her brow. 'D'you have to pay?' she asked.

'Nay, it's covered by the poor rates. You could have something wrong with you or nothing, and if it's something, then better to find out for Rory's sake.'

Amy picked up the bottle of ale and moved it to a shelf by the hearth. When she turned around Becky could see her eyes had filled with tears.

'I've a lump,' she said. 'A lump here.' She put a hand on her left breast.

'Women get lumps all the time, especially around the month time.'

'It's not like those, it's the same as Mammy's was. They called it a tumour.'

'It's probably just a normal lump. Like I say, lots of women get them. You need to get it seen by a doctor to put your mind at rest.'

Amy continued as if Becky hadn't spoken. 'Mammy had one that started like a pea. Then it got bigger and she started losing weight and then...' She put her hand out and fiddled with the collar of a shirt in the mending pile. 'Then it went bad and she passed away.' She began sobbing.

Becky went over and put her arms around her. 'Now, you don't know it's anything like your mam's.'

'But what if it is? It's getting bigger all the time.'

'We can face that if it comes to it, not before.'

'We?'

'Aye, we. You'll accept my friendship, won't you? Rory's told me you don't have any kin close by.'

Amy nodded, took out a handkerchief and blew her nose. 'I'm scared.'

And you've every right to be. For a split second, in her mind's eye, Becky had an unwelcome flash of Amy laid out in the manner of an alabaster tomb found in churches: cold and white, eyes closed, hands together as if in prayer, feet pointing upwards. She shook her head to rid herself of it.

Before she left, she made arrangements to accompany Amy to the Infirmary the following Thursday afternoon.

CHAPTER ELEVEN

On the same Thursday as Amy's Infirmary visit, Fergus was surprised to be called away from his desk to see Mr Craggs.

'I've exciting news for you, Fergus.' He was beaming. 'It seems a good time for us to strengthen our business relations with Madeira.'

'That makes sense. Madeira has goods we can transport.'

'Your father has instructed me to inform you he would like you to oversee the operation. If I was younger, I'd be volunteering myself. The climate, I understand, is most agreeable, and from what I've heard at the Gentlemen's Club the agents and managers have an interesting social life. I'm sure you'll enjoy it there.'

'Enjoy it there?'

'Yes, I expect it will take about four months to have everything up and running, then you can oversee operations until the end of next year.'

Oh no, I'm not standing for this. 'Thank you, Mr Craggs. Thank you for informing me of father's plans, but I think it best I hear them from his own lips.'

Mr Craggs looked at Fergus with surprised eyes. 'Don't you want to go? It's a wonderful opportunity.'

'Indeed, it is, but for someone else.' He stood up, leaving Mr Craggs open-mouthed, and made his way to his father's office. Hector looked up as he strode in without knocking.

'You've not been very fair to Mr Craggs asking him to tell me you want to send me away.'

'Ah,' said Hector. 'Your mother and I are united in the opinion that you will benefit from travel. You have much to learn about the world, and a change of country will be beneficial. You're just the person to reinforce our Madeira links.'

'That's nonsense. You want to separate me from Becky. You've both made a decision about her without having even met her.'

'I won't deny a change of companionship was one element in our decision.'

'I thank you for the opportunity, but I have no desire to leave Whitehaven at this time.'

Hector sighed. 'That's all very well, but you're forgetting you're an employee in this company. It's within my power both to promote and to let go. I'm sure you have expectations. You're my only child, my only son. You're expecting the company to pass to you when I die. This is a reasonable expectation and one I held regarding my own father, so I fully understand your feelings on this. My intention is to make you a full director of the company upon your return, in what I expect will be just over a year's time. The company will then be listed as Shackleton & Son.'

'And if I don't want to go?'

'I would think you a foolish and wayward employee whose loyalties lie elsewhere.'

'What exactly are you saying?'

'I'm saying if you do not go then there will be no place for you within Shackleton & Company. You will have to find new employment.'

'You'd let me go?' Fergus was astonished. He felt his throat close up.

'No, you'd be choosing to resign. I'm offering you a more than reasonable task within the company, one that most men would leap at, even without the rich reward at the end that I'm able to offer you as my son. Should you decide not to take up this position, you will effectively be resigning from the company.'

Fergus felt nauseous. No father should treat his son in such a shabby way, and for it to be his own father behaving towards him in such a way should have been unthinkable. The Madeira trip was more than a dismissal from Whitehaven for a year: it was a loyalty test and a bribe. He would be trading Becky for a directorship, and that was verging on obscene.

His father, red in the face and beginning to wheeze, was scrutinising him with pursed lips.

'I will not go to Madeira and I will not have my actions dictated by anyone. If I must, I will leave the company, which means I will have no option but to also vacate Queen Street.'

'Leave home? Upset your mother and your aunt?' Hector smothered a smile. 'Where will you go? To the Indian King? I doubt they'll welcome you there when they learn you're jobless and no longer living in Queen Street.'

The implication that Becky was only interested in his financial stability infuriated Fergus and served only to strengthen his resolve. 'When you return home this evening, I regret to say you will find I am no longer there. You have given me no choice.'

'Indeed?' His father brushed his upper lip with his fingernail. 'Then I look forward to your return when you've realised the error of your ways.'

Fergus felt belittled. He was being treated as if he were a five-year-old, standing in a hall holding a suitcase filled with toys, waiting for someone to reach up and turn the door handle so he could run away.

'Where is your heart, Father? It seems you ruined Aunt Louisa's life. Why should I let you ruin mine?'

At the mention of Louisa, Hector paled and his wheezing grew worse. 'Confound you. Go then, and spend your life reading books and keeping bad company. I used to think you were like your aunt, not only in looks, but also in respecting filial responsibilities. She showed commendable duty looking after our father, your grandfather.'

'Yes, and I'm guessing you ruined all chances she had of marrying so she was imprisoned at home to do just that.'

Hector stood up, pushing his chair back so forcibly it made a terrible grating noise on the floor before tipping over and landing with a clatter behind him. 'Get out!' he shouted, waving his arms. 'Get out.' The wheezing turned into a coughing fit and, unable to speak further, he motioned with his hand towards the door.

Fergus knew everyone could hear his father shouting, which gave him the determination he needed to remain calm and not shout back. It had been a most unpleasant encounter, but one that he'd had to go through. He went straight to his desk and asked for a box so he could gather his personal pens and books. He collected his coat and, without looking directly at anyone, left and went straight to the Indian King. He had to see Becky. He had no doubts she cared for him. *Even if she turns me away, I won't go back to Shackleton's. Not now.*

* * *

Becky was taking bottles down from the shelves behind the bar and dusting them when Fergus arrived with his box. She pointed to a single table in one of the corners, then served two customers before joining him.

'There's been an upset,' Fergus said. 'Well, more than that. My father and I have had a dreadful argument. Father's given me a choice: go to Madeira for over a year to oversee and widen operations there, or leave the company.'

Becky's eyes widened. 'Why?'

'There was an argument earlier in the week, Aunt Louisa mentioned she'd met you and one thing led to another and – '

'And they don't like the idea of you walking out with

me?' *I've been waiting for this,* thought Becky, suddenly feeling nervous. *That which I feared has come about.*

'I won't lie. They are prejudiced. They question your suitability, yet refuse to even meet you. Aunt Louisa gave you a glowing report, if you can call it that. She likes you. Anyway, I told him I wasn't going, and he said as a result I'd effectively dismissed myself, which has left me no other option than to look outside the company and Queen Street for my livelihood.'

'Really? You didn't mean it, did you? What about your mam and aunt? How will they feel about it?'

'I'm not leaving Whitehaven, so I can still see them, although Mother was involved with the Madeira suggestion. She would see sending me away as a solution, but I'm sure she wouldn't want Father to dismiss me. I've never been close to him because his temperament has never allowed it, but...' He shrugged and changed the subject. 'The first thing I must organise is somewhere to live.'

'Are you sure everything is as drastic as you think it is? Things may seem different tomorrow.'

'Having seen my father's face and heard his words, I know he won't be changing his mind.'

'You seem so calm.'

'I *am* calm. Since leaving the company offices it's come to me I can make my own decisions now; I can plot my own path, and there's something liberating about that. I could even say exciting. What's happened has happened, and I must grab it by the horns and run with it.'

'You can come here. We've rooms, you know that. I'll ask Mam.'

'Don't. I think it seemlier if I find rooms elsewhere, otherwise tongues will wag.'

'What about?'

'About you and me being under the same roof,' replied Fergus.

Becky blushed. 'Oh, well, yes... it could be a little awkward.' She thought for a moment. 'There's always Mrs Williamson's on Irish Street. Number 8. A big house, near the white one with the double doors. She's a widow and she's fussy about who she takes in – no vagrants, ruffians, or dubious characters, and as her terms are also higher than most, she's not always full. She has captains and visitors from the cities. I understand her rooms are well-furnished and the meals of good quality. We could ask.'

'It sounds admirable if she'll have me.' Fergus stood up and picked up his box of belongings from the floor.

'A Shackleton?' Becky said. 'She'll be delighted to have you. Leave your box, we can go right now. I'll take you.'

As Becky had predicted, Mrs Williamson was only too happy to welcome a Shackleton lodger. She led the way upstairs and Becky could hear her explaining the house rules before moving onto the cost. She wished she'd thought to tell Fergus to indicate he could be there for some time, in order to get a better rate. Although the room might be nothing like he was used to, she was relieved to see him looking happy enough when he re-joined her.

'It's settled,' he said. 'I'll come back with you, collect my box and arrange for delivery of my other items.'

On the way back to the Indian King, Fergus's preoccupation was almost tangible. Becky tried to imagine what was going through his mind. Shock? Excitement? Without doubt surely sadness at the way he was being treated. Perhaps all of these things. Whatever it was he was not giving any of his inner thoughts away. He was walking purposefully with a strong stride, head down, fists clenched. She would have asked him to slow down but shied away from interrupting his thoughts.

After being advised of the situation, Dolly insisted Fergus have something to eat before venturing out again. Becky set to making toast.

'Have you any idea what you'll do?' she asked. The act of eating seemed to have unlocked Fergus's reticence and she sensed he now wanted to talk.

'Yes,' he said, loading his knife with butter. 'I'm going to run my own ship. It's in my blood, what I'm trained for and what I know. I'll be my own master.'

'But you haven't got a ship.'

'I'll buy one.'

Becky stared at him. 'It's not like buying a horse and buggy. There's a lot to it. You'll need to think hard on it.'

'I know, that's what my thoughts are full of.'

'I'm sorry, of course you know that, more than any of us. I'd like to stay and talk, but I've to leave you with your thoughts. I'm seeing Amy Rooke at three and I've chores to see to before then.'

'Forgive me, you're busy. I must go and organise the collection of my things from Queen Street. Father will still be at the office, so I can speak with Aunt Louisa and Mother.'

✻ ✻ ✻

It was a short walk for Amy from New Houses to the Infirmary in Howgill Street. She and Becky met, as agreed, and were dismayed to see that half an hour before the doors opened there was already a long queue outside.

'It'll be hours before I'm seen,' said Amy. 'I've things to do.'

'We're here now,' said Becky. 'Let's at least wait until the doors open.'

At twenty-five to four, when the door had still not opened, Becky could sense Amy was becoming restless so when she heard bolts being pulled back, she gave a silent prayer of thanks.

Just after four o'clock, they'd moved far enough up the queue to be standing in front of a stout nurse with grubby, hard-bitten fingernails, who was sitting at a table strewn with papers. She seemed surprised to see two of them standing there.

'Are you together?'

'Yes,' said Becky.

The nurse turned to Amy. 'I can see *you're* sick,' she said. 'And you?' she asked Becky. 'Are you sick too?'

'Nay.'

'Then what are you doing here clogging things up?'

Becky was taken aback. 'I'm her chaperone.'

'Hmm, well I suppose that's all right, as long as you don't take a seat.' She took Amy's details then pointed to a half-open door. 'In there. You'll be called when the doctor's ready.'

Inside the waiting room there were several empty chairs so Becky, taking care she couldn't be seen by the nurse, sat down. Amy sat next to her. They waited in silence, listening to the coughing and wheezing of their fellow patients. Eventually they were called through to the doctor and, as there was only one chair, Becky remained standing. The doctor ignored her.

'What ails you?' he asked Amy.

'I've a lump.' She put her hand to her left breast.

'Fever?'

'Sometimes I sweat, but not like a real fever. Just a bit hot.' She fanned herself with her hand.

'Hmm. I need to examine you.'

He turned away and waited as Amy handed her shawl to Becky before loosening her bodice. After a few minutes, he turned back and went over to her. Becky, still standing behind Amy, was glad she couldn't see; it would have been an invasion of Amy's privacy.

The doctor peered over his spectacles. 'How long have you had this?'

'A year, maybe longer.'

He asked her more questions and made notes as she revealed she had additional pain in her back, didn't sleep well and lacked appetite. A recent development was pain in her arm. When he'd finished, he returned to his desk and waited until Amy had finished dressing.

'I'm sorry to tell that it is my opinion have a tumour, and the pain in your back makes me think it has spread.' He apologised again. 'We could have removed it had you come earlier, but I'm afraid it's too late now.'

Amy was matter of fact in her reply. 'They did that to Mammy. The time doesn't matter. I'd never have let you cut me open. You see it made no difference to her and she suffered dreadfully.'

'When was that?'

'Eight years past. I'm going to die sooner than I should, but can you tell me how long? So's I can make arrangements, you understand.'

The doctor nodded. 'You've family?'

'I've a young lad.'

'And your child's father?'

'He's dead a while.'

Becky wondered if this was a convenient lie or whether Rory's father really was dead. She wished she'd been able to leave the room before the doctor began giving his diagnosis. She felt awkward being party to such a private conversation, although neither the doctor nor Amy were paying her any attention, and she was thankful for that.

The doctor cast a glance at the wall clock over the fireplace. 'I can't tell you the exact progress of your disease as tumour growth is unpredictable. They can become dormant for a while or speed up. We have no way of knowing, but I can help you in the journey you have to make. I've a medicine that will improve your appetite which will build up your strength so you feel better. I expect you're in pain or you wouldn't be here.'

Amy nodded.

'I can help you with that.' He began writing.

'Thank you.' Amy seemed to remember Becky was with her for she turned round and gave a sad smile. Although she was receiving what amounted to a death sentence she seemed neither to be about to break down nor shed a tear.

She must be in shock, Amy thought. *He's telling her to go away and die and she's not taking the information in.*

'Here.' The doctor handed Amy a piece of paper. 'Take this to the apothecary on King Street. There's no charge.'

Amy took the paper. 'Is it months? Years?'

'As I said, it's difficult, but I would suggest more than a few months. Take the medicine I'm prescribing and abstain from fat, oily and spicy foods, and no liquor. Stewed rhubarb is ideal. It's a wholesome food for the insides and you can add liquorice. Sweeten your tea with honey. I will order you some.'

Amy thanked him and they left. Outside in the street she said, 'It must be dreadful for him.'

'Who?' asked Becky, relieved to be out in the fresh air.

'The doctor. Seeing people like me all day and not being able to do anything. I expect he's hardened to it, but his manner was kindly to me.'

Becky caught her breath. Of all the things she thought Amy would say immediately after the consultation, it had not occurred to her it would be to express sympathy for the doctor.

Amy handed the piece of paper to Becky. 'What does it say?'

'"All items to be dispensed monthly as required." There are three things. "Stomach balsam elixir to be taken before meals thrice a day, a large jar of honey and an anodyne draught to be taken as needed.".'

'What's that?'

Becky, suddenly lacking the courage she needed to tell the truth, lied. 'I'm not sure. You can ask the apothecary.'

She knew it was laudanum for pain. Her father had used it. He'd begun with a small amount and by the end he'd called for it whenever the pain surfaced enough to drag him back into consciousness.

When they reached the Indian King, Amy insisted Becky go home and not accompany her to King Street to collect the medicines.

'Are you sure you can manage?' asked Becky.

'Aye, really, I am. The doctor just told me what I already knew. It's God's will for me. Don't say anything to Rory, will you?'

'Of course not. What plans have you for him?'

'It needs thinking on.'

On a sudden impulse, Becky, holding back tears, embraced Amy. Only when she was almost out of sight did she allow her tears to fall.

CHAPTER TWELVE

Aunt Louisa was taking her afternoon nap on the chaise-longue in the drawing room and his mother was out when Fergus arrived. He asked Samuel to arrange for two men to bring his travelling trunk down from the attic, then went up to his room. Nothing in it belonged to him apart from his books and clothes. Waiting for his trunk, he felt underneath the bed and pulled out a small suitcase. He put it on an oak table by the window then opened it to reveal three parcels. He unwrapped the first and brought out an old book. It was heavy and creaked when he laid it on the table and opened it. The volume was an illuminated manuscript of St Sebastian's Chapel Gospel, written in precise italic lettering on vellum. The first word of each sentence was in gold and beautifully embellished. The side margins were bursting with scrolling flora and painted animals, many of them mythical.

A knock announced the arrival of his trunk. He put the

book back in the box. *I bought wisely, but can I bear to part with them?*

'Are you going away, sir?' asked one of the men.

'Yes, I will be sending someone for my trunk later this afternoon.' The smaller man eyed the suitcase on the table. 'I'll take the case with me. That'll be all.'

With the men gone, Fergus began filling the trunk. After half an hour everything was packed. He had the trunk, the suitcase containing the manuscripts, two round hat boxes and two more rectangular boxes filled with books and his university notes. It wasn't a great deal to have collected over twenty-one years. He picked up the suitcase and a small bag with his toiletries and went in search of Aunt Louisa.

'I can't believe it,' she said. 'He would turn you out?'

'Father says I've dismissed myself.'

'And your mother is complicit in this?'

'Yes. You knew nothing of it?'

'No, not a whisper to me. They've been plotting silently. But do you have to leave your home too? It's all happening so fast; you should slow down.' Tears formed in her eyes. 'You haven't had time to think.'

'It's impossible for me to stay in such an atmosphere. You can see that?'

'I can see it might be difficult, but how can you settle your differences if you're not here? Your father is a blusterer and a bully sometimes. He can be loud and unpleasant, but as with most bullies it's a front. Despite his manner, he's not the businessman he likes people to think he is, and I think he's aware of it. Certainly, he doesn't have the business brain of our father, your grandfather. I'm not saying he's bad for the business, but I'm not sure he's good for it, either. I've noticed my dividend income on the company shares has been falling over the last five years, despite your father saying business has never been better. Not falling by a great deal, just enough to notice less income each year. Your father is a fool for alienating you when the business needs new ideas.' She came to a halt and apologised. 'I've spoken ill of your father and I should not have done so. Forgive me.'

'You're right about him not liking new ideas,' Fergus said. 'I would introduce steamships.'

His aunt sighed. 'Maybe it will all blow over. Where are you going?'

Fergus began to speak, but she stopped him. 'No, wait, let me guess. To the Indian King?'

'No, I've found rooms in Irish Street.'

'You will meet with me often in town so I can see you are well, won't you? And bring your young lady? Are you very fond of her?'

'Yes, I am. She understands me.'

'I will miss you dreadfully. You're starting a new life, Fergus. It's a big step. There will be stumbles and falls along the way, but I have faith God will protect you and that you will do well, whichever road you choose to take. I will pray for you, and you must promise you will return if the situation changes.'

'Give my love to Mother. I had hoped to see her, but…'

'I will tell her, but will you not wait to see her and tell her yourself?'

'No, I am angry with her. It's probably for the best she's not here.'

Fergus embraced his aunt, kissed her on the cheek and promised again he would meet with her often. After leaving, he walked with purpose to his lodgings in Irish Street. Only a short distance separated them from Queen Street, but the two places were worlds apart.

By early evening, Fergus had paid off the carrier and everything had been moved upstairs to his new room without mishap. His belongings seemed oddly out of place in their new surroundings.

It was beginning to drizzle as he made his way to the Indian King. He ordered an ale from Dolly and, as he settled himself, he heard her instruct one of the barmen to deliver the ale to 'Shackleton's table'. The thought flashed through his mind that his mother would be appalled to know he had his own table in a public house.

'I still have a mind to set out on my own,' he said when Becky came to sit with him.

'Over the last three months I've made working contacts with agents all over, from London to Cardiff, Dublin and Scotland. Many's the time I've come back after a trip thinking I could do this on my own, but with my loyalties rooted in Shackleton & Company I've never seriously considered it. With everything different now, and my ties with the company in shreds, this is my opportunity.'

'Not a bookshop, then?'

'No.'

'But you'll need ships.'

'My grandfather began with one ship and so will I. You've got the *Whitehaven News,* haven't you?'

'It's behind the bar.'

'Right, let's look for a ship, and tomorrow I'm going to London to secure funds. I'll sell my illuminated manuscripts, cash in some bonds and call in some favours.'

'Must you go so soon? You might wake in a few days and choose to do something else, or even change your mind and go back. You're angry and upset.'

'I won't.'

Becky made no comment. Fergus noticed a crease on her brow, and she'd left the glass of lemonade in front of her untouched. It gradually dawned on him that he was so wrapped up with his own problems he could be overlooking that Becky had problems of her own. Then he remembered she'd said she was going up to New Houses.

'How was Amy?'

It was as if he'd opened a floodgate. All the events of the afternoon came pouring out.

'She's so resigned to it. It's almost as if she welcomes it.'

'If she's in excessive pain, then perhaps she sees death as a release.'

'She's a strong Christian; she thinks it's God's will, but she's worrying about what to do about Rory.'

'There must be family who can keep him. Relatives?'

'She arrived from Cockerm'uth way with her mam when Rory was a tiny bairn. Her mam died eight years since. Gossip has it his father was a married man, but today she said he was dead. One thing's certain – she's never going to tell.'

'Maybe she will now Rory needs someone to look after him.'

'Aye, maybe, but ten years or more is a long time to keep a lad hidden from his da. Maybe he's never known there is a Rory.'

✻ ✻ ✻

Fergus returned from London with £3,000 to his name. He'd called in the debts relating to his student days, liquidated his savings and sold his illuminated manuscripts for £650. It was a little less than he'd hoped, but a fair price, and most importantly he needed the money.

With Bill away, Fergus and Becky spent a great deal of time together over the next nine days discussing the essentials of buying a ship. There were times when Fergus seemed a little different, when he assumed a serious business-like air. It was a side of him Becky had not seen before.

'What will you do for crew?' she asked.

'I've no worries on that score. One will either come with the ship or I can engage a fresh one. There's experienced crew on every street corner.'

'And a master? You'll need someone reliable.'

'I know. I'll travel myself to conduct the business side, but there's one person I would very much like to engage.'

'Bill McRae?'

'Yes. We've been friends a long while; he's loyal and knows everybody and everything about the waters around here.'

'He's a master, isn't he?'

'He earned his certificate two years ago from Leith.'

'But you can't expect him to leave his secure position

with your father's company, especially to come and work for you the way things are.'

'I agree it's not an obvious decision for him to make, but that doesn't mean I can't speak to him about it or make it worth his while when he's back in Whitehaven.' He drummed his fingers on the table top. 'I wonder if my father has offered him the Madeira position? If so, that could work in our favour, as I doubt very much it will appeal to him. I'll meet with him.'

'What about cargo? What will you carry?'

'Likely coal, iron ore or lime. Maybe even grain. That's what's common now going out.'

'What's coming in?'

'Mainly produce from the West Indies, America, the Baltic and the Mediterranean, but we won't be concerned with those places, not yet. I'll probably begin with my own shamrock triangle: Whitehaven to Cardiff, then Dublin, and back again. There's never enough transport available for that run.' Fergus was conscious the words coming out of his mouth indicated a higher level of confidence than he was feeling. He knew he would be all right once revenue started coming in, but until then things would be difficult.

'I really must speak with Bill. Even if I can't persuade him to work with me, he'll have a lot to say about my plans.'

✤ ✤ ✤

Bill had just come home from another Glasgow run for Shackleton's when Fergus, in shirt sleeves, breeches and sporting a wide grin, called at his home. He was given a welcome pat on the back.

'It's good to see you, Fergus. Come in, sit down. They all miss you at the offices. Are you sure this won't blow over?'

'No, it won't. You must know what happened?'

'Not exactly. Your father sent a memorandum round stating you were no longer in the company's employ. Mr Craggs told us all individually we were not to mention your name in your father's presence. From that, and from those who heard the row at the time, we've all surmised there was a dreadful disagreement and that it might have something to do with Madeira.'

'That's more or less correct. My father gave me the choice of living in Madeira for a year, under the pretext of setting up offices there, or leaving the company. That translates as giving up Becky or resigning. I've chosen Becky and I'm going to set up a company of my own.' He knew he was excited and that his words were tumbling out.

Bill didn't say anything for a moment. 'That's a big step. Here? In Whitehaven?'

'Where else would I do it? You look sceptical. Why wouldn't I start here? It's my home; I know how the town operates.'

Bill sucked in his cheeks. 'It's just that your father has a lot of influence here. By all means start up your own line, but I would caution you against doing it here.'

'I hear what you're saying, but it has to be here. I don't have enough money to move elsewhere. As it is I'm in lodgings in Irish Street.'

'I heard.'

'It must be Whitehaven. I'm hoping Becky will be part of my future now, and I can't ask her to leave.'

'Are you sure about all this? Your father's a difficult man. He might place obstacles in your way.'

'Let's talk no more of him. I've something to ask you.'

'Ask away.'

'My first task is to purchase a brig. Then I need to crew it.'

'You should get crew with the ship.'

'I may, that's true enough, but I need a master I can trust, someone I know. Someone competent, experienced and trustworthy.'

'And you have someone in mind?'

'I know you have a secure job with my father. I know I cannot match the security of a well-established business and I will be hard pressed to match his salary, but –'

'Fergus, you do me a great honour, but, as you say, I have a good position with the company.'

'Has my father asked you to take my place in Madeira?'

'No, although I suspect he may.'

'Will you take it if he does?'

'No. I want a life at sea, not marooned on an island surrounded by agents' bills and tariff notices, however pleasant the climate may prove to be.'

'As I said, I can't offer you a bigger salary, but there *is* something I can offer you he can't, or rather won't.'

Bill's eyes widened slightly.

'I'm using my own money to start up this company. I'm putting everything I've got into it. What I can offer you is a directorship of the company and ten percent of profits at the year's end.'

'And losses?'

'I'll cover those should it be necessary.'

Bill leaned forward. 'I don't know what to say. A directorship? That's some offer if you're successful. I can't say I'm not interested, but if I come in with you and the business fails, your father will make sure I never work in Whitehaven, Liverpool, Cardiff or Dublin again.'

'That's a possibility, I'll admit, but we'll both be driven by the will and need to succeed. We have to make sure we accomplish what we set out to do, otherwise you're right – you'll be blacklisted and I'll lose everything.'

'I know we go back a long way but there's a lot to lose, and Mary and I are hoping for a family.' He rubbed the back of his neck.

'On the other hand, we've also a great deal to gain,' Fergus said. 'We're young and open to new ideas, that must surely be in our favour. You're a master seaman and I'm trained in the business side. We'll start small with a brig, then work our way up to another and then we'll look to steam. That's the way forward. My father still thinks steamships are doomed – because they have no soul and they catch fire!'

Bill considered Fergus's proposition. 'If you're asking me for a definite decision here and now the answer is no. However, talk to me again when you've a ship. Show me something solid, like a seaworthy brig, with a cargo and a place to land it, and then I'll perhaps talk with Mary, but not before.'

'You'll think my proposition over? We can shake hands on it?'

Bill accepted Fergus's outstretched hand.

CHAPTER THIRTEEN

It was Fergus who saw the advertisement in the *Whitehaven News*. The *Eleanor Bell* was offered for public sale, by auction, at the Three Tuns pub the following Friday, the 10th of August. Animated, and with lively eyes, he read out the details to Becky and Dolly as they folded the day's clean laundry.

'All that good brigantine, or vessel, called the Eleanor Bell. With all her materials well found and a full cargo of iron ore as she now lies in the harbour at Whitehaven.'

'How big is she?' asked Dolly.

He turned the paper over to read the bottom half of the advertisement.

'71 tons, carries 196 tons of iron ore at an easy draught of water. Is in good condition and an extremely desirable vessel for the coal, iron ore and coasting trades and may be sent to sea at a trifling expense.'

'They would say that,' said Dolly.

'I'll ask around whether she's been inspected on the gridiron,' said Fergus.

'Wouldn't it say so?'

'Not necessarily. However, if she has, and failed, someone will know. Word gets around.'

'How much, do you reckon?' asked Dolly.

'Depends how old she is and it doesn't say.'

'We can go and look,' said Becky. 'It says she's in the harbour.'

'You can, but I can't. They'll recognise me in a flash.'

'Why don't *you* go, Becky?' said Dolly. 'And take Rory with you. He'll be here in half an hour to collect Charlie. With the boy and the puppy at your side, it'll look as if you're just out for a stroll.'

'I can tell you what to look for,' said Fergus.

'I won't be able to tell much by just looking.'

'You can tell a lot about a ship by its ropes. If they're well-stowed and clean that's a good sign. It's the same with a farmer's hedges. You can tell how well he looks after his fields and animals by the state of his hedges.'

'You can do better than that, Becky. Talk to the crew, see what you can glean. A pretty girl like you growing up in Whitehaven should be able to sweet-talk a sailor by now.'

'Mam! I'm no flirt.'

Dolly raised her hands palms facing outwards. 'All in a good cause, Becky, all in a good cause.'

※ ※ ※

Rory didn't seem surprised when Becky said she would like to accompany him. In fact, he seemed pleased. With

Charlie straining at his leash, wanting to explore every nook and cranny, the two of them set off.

'How's your mam?'

'She sleeps more since she got that new medicine.'

'Still busy with her mending?'

'Aye, she's always doing it. Says it's the money what keeps us together, so I mustn't mind the time she spends on it.'

Approaching the harbour, Becky could see what she thought might be the *Eleanor Bell* out by New Quay. 'Which way do you usually go, Rory?'

'As far as the baths.'

Not quite far enough. 'Do you think we can go out to the Light Boat House today?'

'Aye, we can let Charlie off and give him a bit of a run. I can't do that on my own.'

Becky smiled. *Bless you, Charlie. Perhaps I can encourage you to run off in the direction of the ship. What could be more natural than the two of us chasing a runaway dog?*

As they neared the ship, Becky was relieved when she made out the words *Eleanor Bell*. At her bow was a finely carved figurehead – the top half of a woman in a low-cut bodice, with bright red lips and wide open eyes beneath a mass of tumbling jet black curls. Her shoulders were back, thrusting the rounded curves of her generous breasts forward. A gold painted medallion nestled in the top of her cleavage. She was looking up and to the right, into the distance.

Becky bent down to untie the puppy's leash. 'We can let Charlie off his rope now,' she said. Once free, Charlie shook his head as if to clear it, then, looking around and seeing Becky was blocking his path to return the way they'd come, he set off towards New Quay. Rory didn't notice the little push Charlie had received on his hind quarters to set him on his way. Becky needn't have worried. When they arrived at the *Eleanor Bell* Charlie spotted one of the ship's cats and started barking. The cat's back went up, the dog growled, the cat hissed, the dog barked and an audible battle ensued.

The racket brought a member of the crew to the ship's side. Becky put on her best smile.

'I'm sorry,' she said. 'Our puppy's only a tiddler, but he knows a cat when he sees one.'

The tall blond man, who had a Scandinavian look about him, grinned at her. 'Don't worry, we're used to loud noises on this ship. She's a real "creaker" when we're at sea. When the sails are flapping and the wind's blowing, we've to lip read.' He looked at Rory. 'What's your pup called?' he asked him.

'Charlie.'

'Charlie's a grand name for a pup. And tell me, young sir, what's your sister's name?'

For a moment Rory looked confused, then he laughed. 'That's not my sister. I walk her dog. It's my job.'

Becky wondered if the man would think that strange.

'So, you're working for this young lady? She's your gaffer, is she?'

Rory nodded.

'All right then. What's your gaffer's name?'

'Miss Becky.'

The crewman smiled at her. 'Well, Miss Becky, it's a pleasure to meet you. I would extend my hand to you if you were on the ship, rather than standing on the quay looking up at me. I'm Sven. Sven Nielsen, from Oslo.'

Becky took a deep breath. 'Well, Sven Nielsen, if you invite us onto your ship for a look around, I'll be happy to shake your hand. Rory's never been on one of these, have you?' She turned to the boy and smiled.

Sven looked momentarily disconcerted. Then he said, 'I'm not allowed to let strangers on board, but if the pup was to run up the gangway and you had to follow him, well then, maybe I could show you both around. It would have to be brief though.' He winked. 'Although you'll need to put the pup back on his rope as if he gets close to our cat, Caesar, they'll likely have a grand set-to. He's a good ratter; we don't want to lose him.'

'We'd love to see on board,' said Becky. It took a few minutes to usher Charlie up the gangway then catch him and reattach his leash. At the top, she saw Sven look at Rory's gammy leg, open his mouth as if to mention it, then close it again.

'Rory had an accident. He used to work as a trapper in the mines.'

'A barrel fell off a cart and landed on me,' said Rory, as if it was the most normal thing in the world. He was looking around the ship with a face full of awe.

'Don't worry,' said Sven. 'I'll not be showing you the crow's nest up top, or asking you to man the sails, but be careful. There's ropes aplenty to trip over.'

'Your ropes look tidy,' said Becky.

'The master keeps a tight ship. He's a stickler for everything being in its place or stowed away.'

Sven took Rory under his wing and showed him around the deck. Becky followed, listening intently, with one eye on the cat. It had settled itself in a crouching position on a large water barrel. Its tail, fluffed out, was swishing back and forth. Becky had few doubts the cat would soon have his claws in Charlie's nose, given the chance.

They stopped strolling to look back at the town from the ship's side.

'Where's she going next?' asked Becky.

'I don't know. She's up for sale. That's why there's only me and three others on board. The master's gone ashore to drown his sorrows.'

'Why?'

'It's always hard when an owner sells a ship. It's the uncertainty and the break-up of a team of men.'

'A new broom sweeps clean. Is that it?'

He looked puzzled, then laughed. 'Aye, that's right. You English have some interesting phrases.'

Becky thought he seemed a kindly soul and she felt bad about her subterfuge, although she'd never have gone on board the ship without Rory as chaperone.

'How much does a ship like this cost?'

'There's no fixed price when it's sold at auction.'

Becky was thinking hard about how she could obtain a more definite answer, when Sven added, 'Word is she'll fetch around £2,500 pounds with the cargo.'

'Cargo?'

'We've a full load of iron ore.'

'Then why are you not sailing?' *Too many questions*, Becky thought. *He's going to get suspicious if I go on.*

'Seems the owners are in difficulty and have to sell.'

Becky wanted to ask who the owners were, but instinct told her it was a question too far.

Sven put his head on one side and looked at her. 'Thinking of buying her, then?'

He's flirting with me. She laughed, although to her own ear it sounded hollow and strained. 'Nay, I've enough trouble finding the money to feed the puppy.' She looked across at Rory. 'Which reminds me, if we don't make our way soon, he'll start whimpering for his supper.'

'Must we go now?' he said.

'Aye, we must. Say thank you to Sven.'

Rory pulled a disappointed face, but when he saw Sven's outstretched hand he took it.

'It's been a pleasure to entertain you, Mr Rory, sir. Indeed, it has.' Sven turned to Becky. 'And that handshake you promised me?' He extended his hand, all the while looking into her eyes. To her horror Becky felt herself blush under his gaze and she saw his eyes light up at the spectacle. He held onto her hand a few moments longer than was necessary, before releasing it. He had large rough hands in keeping with his size and occupation, and her small palm seemed lost within his grasp.

When they reached the top of the gangway, Sven, with a gentle touch to her arm, delayed her. 'Where can I find you when I'm ashore?'

'I thank you very much for your tour of the ship. It's meant a great deal to Rory. You've been very kind, but I must tell you I'm spoken for.'

Disappointment registered on his face. 'Now why do I not find that surprising?'

They took their leave. When they reached the Light Boat House, Becky turned and saw Sven was still watching them. He waved and she felt it only polite to ask Rory to wave back with her. As they drew near the Indian King, Becky said, 'There's an extra penny for you today since it was such a long walk.'

He took the penny and, putting it in his pocket, said, 'Thank you, Miss Becky. Mammy'll be pleased with the extra.'

'You've been quiet walking back. Is everything all right? Is your leg paining you?'

'My leg? Oh no. I've had far too grand a time to think about my gammy leg. That was one of the best afternoons ever. D'you think I'll be able to go to sea, Miss Becky? Do they take cripples?'

'I don't see why they can't. Is that what you'd like to do?'

'Right now, more than anything, I want to go to sea.'

Fergus was sitting across from Becky at the kitchen table, pencil in hand, a pile of papers in front of him. '£2,500 including the iron ore cargo? That's quite a sum. Although if she's in as good a condition as she sounds…'

'Does being "creaky" mean anything?' asked Becky.

'No, all ships are creaky. I made some enquiries while you were out. She's one of Brocklebank's, built to order here in 1849 for Captain Bowden. I knew him. Died a few years back. Seems she's been owned by a syndicate since then and one of them wants his money out. Hence the sale. Her reputation is she has "fine lines", which is always good in a brig.'

'So, she's eleven years old. Is that much for a ship?'

'Depends where she's been, who's captained her and whether the owners have kept her in good repair, but she should be in reasonable order. The *Patriot Princess* of our fleet is in her twenty-seventh year.' He frowned. 'I mean my father's fleet.'

'Are you still interested in her? How much do you think you'll need?'

'I make the initial outlay around £2,800. That's £2,500 for the ship, assuming she can be bought for that. Then say another £300 for the auctioneer's commission, insurance, supplies and crew.

'Do you have that?'

'I have £3,000 which, with those figures, leaves me a contingency fund of £200.'

'Agents' fees?'

'I should be able to pay those, and the tariffs, as I go along selling and transporting cargo. Financially it all depends on the auction.'

'What's your next step?'

'I'm sure Bill can find someone to give her a good looking over.'

'Will you ask him to master again?'

'Not yet. He said I could ask when I have a ship and crew to my name.'

'Are you sure you want to put yourself through all this? That it isn't just a way to get back at your father?'

'No, it's nothing to do with that.' Even as the words were coming out of his mouth, Fergus knew he wasn't being completely truthful. It was a lot about proving himself to his father. He reached for her hand. 'I have to do this.' Then, to change the subject, he said, 'What are we going to do about Rory when his mother passes away?'

CHAPTER FOURTEEN

On the day of the *Eleanor Bell* auction, Fergus woke early and lay in bed, watching the dawn break and the room lighten. He told himself if the day went badly there would be other ships and other auctions, but ever since he'd set his mind on buying the *Eleanor Bell*, he'd felt an urgency in his veins to start his new life.

He rose and dressed, choosing a white shirt, his fawn waistcoat with the crossover front that buttoned on the left side, his tailcoat, and his favourite thinly striped trousers for luck. Checking himself over in the looking-glass before he left, he addressed his reflection. *You can do this. You did it for the company, now you can do it for yourself. Keep a level head and all will be well.*

He took out his pocket-watch. He planned to officially inspect the *Eleanor Bell* himself before the auction, then keep an appointment with his solicitor. Out in the street, his agitation over the day's events grew. Because he was distracted, he missed a gap in the pavement and tripped. He told himself to slow down, cursing under his breath. The sale wasn't until mid-afternoon; he'd time enough to do all he had to do. He'd view the *Eleanor Bell* then take coffee in the Waverley Hotel.

* * *

Over at the Indian King, while Fergus was leaving Mrs Williamson's, Becky was feeding Charlie. She turned to her mother.

'Do you think I should go with him?'

'To the auction?'

'Aye.' She'd woken early and lain awake pondering it.

'Has he asked you to go?'

'No.'

'Well, I think that answers your question.'

'But it's so important.'

'Exactly. If it goes wrong, he won't want you there to see it, will he?'

'But if it goes well and he gets the *Eleanor Bell*?'

'I think he'll want to enjoy the public victory and then have the excitement of rushing here to tell us.' She pointed at the old oak door with the shiny brass lock that separated the kitchen from the inn's public rooms. 'When he comes through that door, you'll be able to tell straightaway by his face.'

'Do you like him?'

'As a customer or as a possible son-in-law?'

Becky blushed. 'I mean as a person.'

'Aye, I like him, but I wonder if he's strong enough for

the shipping trade. He's young and maybe a little innocent. Shipping's in his family and he's grown up with it, but it's one thing talking about it by the hearth and another out there batting away the competition. There's a lot of canny people involved with ships. He needs to develop some low cunning and a harder shell.'

'He's kind and thoughtful, not like a businessman at all, and I like that.'

'Yes, but kind and thoughtful is perhaps not right for this new business he's set his sights on. A shipping trader needs to be sharp as a finely honed sword on both edges.'

'Do you think going into shipping on his own will change him?' Becky hoped not; she liked him just as he was, but it was such a thought that had troubled her when she'd woken so early.

'He's bound to change in some ways. He'll be dealing with customers, making important decisions, assessing purchases, chasing up debtors. If you're asking me for advice, I'm saying let's support him as much as we can. If it all goes wrong in the coming months, then he'll need somewhere to lick his wounds. If all goes well, the two of you may end up living somewhere like Queen Street.'

Fergus was delighted with the ship. During the viewing, it had been much easier for him to maintain a low profile than he'd expected, because of all the other people milling around. Several agents had come up from Liverpool, arriving on the early steamship, and there was a great deal of interest from near and far for what he now regarded as 'his' ship.

Retreating to the Waverley Hotel, Fergus found a quiet corner and pulled a handwritten list from his waistcoat pocket. A contact of Bill's had surveyed the ship thoroughly and, finding no major faults, had confirmed she had 'fine lines'. The price was set at £2,500, but Fergus was cautioned to expect it to go for more. He'd spoken to the gridiron attendant, who'd confirmed she'd passed her inspection. His only query was that she might be 'a bit of a lunger' in heavy seas. To counteract that, it was suggested they hire experienced crew with well-tested sea legs.

Since having the money to hand and the motivation, purchasing the *Eleanor* Bell had become almost all Fergus had thought about. He hadn't been able to concentrate on reading, which was something that had never happened to him before. The iron ore, as per the advertisement in the *Whitehaven News*, was of good quality and a buyer was awaiting delivery in Cardiff. It seemed the ship was just what he needed. All he had to do was keep his head. On the assumption he was going to be successful, and based on what he'd seen that morning, he began a pre-sail inventory check as per the ship's sale details. Checking the inventory was usually left to the captain and first mate, but since Fergus didn't have either, the making of the note gave him a sense of potential ownership and control. He wanted everything clear in the forefront of his mind before seeing his solicitor. He'd engaged Edgar Needham of Needham, Baxter & Company on his return from London and had laid out his plans to him. It was just a question of confirming, before attending the auction, that everything was in order.

Arriving at his solicitor's office Fergus was offered refreshment, which he declined, and then directed to Mr Needham's room. His solicitor's desk was a splendid mahogany one, eminently appropriate for a senior partner in a well-respected firm. Clear of paperwork, it sat in the centre of the office and contained just an ostentatious double-ink stand with dip pens and a large green blotter, upon which rested an open ledger with marbled edgings. In front of it were the clients' chairs: a pair of mahogany balloon-backs with seats upholstered in red leather.

Up against the west wall was an oak trestle-table overflowing with files and leather-bound books. The opposite wall was covered, from top to bottom, with shelves on which were stacked black tin deed and executor boxes, each one bearing the client's name stencilled in gold lettering on its side. The boxes – circular, square, and rectangular in shape – all boasted great age and strong locks. Fergus saw at a glance that the great and the good of the town frequented the firm's offices. The room ably demonstrated the trappings and traditions associated with a long-established firm of solicitors in a prosperous town, and the smell of old documents and books underpinned the atmosphere of age and history.

Edgar Needham was in his late fifties and it occurred to Fergus that during most of those years he must have eaten well, for he was affably round in both face and body. His clothes, when purchased, had been top quality, but the impression now was that his current apparel was just as he liked it: comfortable and well-worn. It seemed he must be particularly fond of the red waistcoat with shiny brass buttons. It was unfortunate he also had a beak-shaped nose, for he reminded Fergus of an overfed robin.

He outlined his plans and Mr Needham confirmed the ship deposit monies were available for immediate payment, and further funds were held in their client account with the Savings Bank. When they'd finished discussing the practicalities, the solicitor leaned back in his chair and made a pyramid with his fingers.

'Of course, should you require further funds I have no doubt we could seek financing on attractive terms. Your family has a good name. It's unusual for a ship owner to finance his ship completely from his own deposits.' He was looking at Fergus expectantly, with raised eyebrows.

'Why pay interest on a loan when I have the funds?' Fergus said. 'Perhaps for my next ship.' He stood up. 'Thank you and good day, sir.'

The Three Tuns was crowded and overly smoky when Fergus arrived. He'd hoped to be inconspicuous, but the auctioneer recognised him and called out to him by name. He registered and gave his solicitor's details before settling on a small table which he judged to provide him with a suitable vantage point. He'd already noticed Jeremiah Todhunter, the man he'd christened 'Mr Tweedy' at the previous auction. He was wearing a different tweed jacket, of lighter weight. There were several other bidding agents from out of town whom Fergus hadn't seen that morning.

The *Eleanor Bell* was the third ship up for auction that afternoon. Fergus felt quietly confident as he watched and listened to the other two being presented. Both went for slightly under their estimates, so he was hopeful the *Eleanor Bell* would go the same way. As the auctioneer read out the details of his ship, Fergus's nervousness reached a new level. His stomach began churning, his mouth felt dry and he became light-headed. His hands grew restless and he fiddled with his clothes. He hoped that once the actual bidding began he would feel better, and so it proved.

As before, he waited until the less generously financed bidders fell away. His nervousness changed to excitement as he raised his hand to join at £1,500. Three bidders remained. Him, 'Mr Tweedy' and another man he didn't recognise. The bidding went up in increments of £100. When they reached £2,000, and neither of his fellow bidders had stood down, Fergus felt a surge of competitiveness. He wanted the *Eleanor Bell* more than ever now. He had to have her; all his future plans were fixed on her. Had he paused to think, he would have been unable to recollect anything in his life he'd ever wanted more. It was exhilarating and he felt in complete control. His attention was focused on the auctioneer, who was looking back and forth between him, Todhunter and the stranger, whom the auctioneer referred to as Mr Legg.

'£2,100 to Mr Todhunter,' called the auctioneer.

Fergus nodded.

'£2,200 to Mr Shackleton.'

'£2,300 to Mr Legg.'

Fergus went to raise his hand, but he wasn't quick enough.

'£2,400 to Mr Todhunter.' The auctioneer looked to Mr Legg.

'Mr Legg, do you have a further bid?'

Mr Legg raised his newspaper and waved it ostentatiously.

'£2,500 to Mr Legg. Mr Shackleton are you still in sir?'

Fergus held his breath and waited.

'I have to hurry you, sir.'

Fergus's legs were trembling. It seemed as if time was standing still. He heard himself say, '£2,600.'

'£2,700,' said Mr Legg, coming back quickly.

Fergus heard his name being called, but the voice was distant. *I've used up my contingency. If I bid further, I'll have to borrow.* He was about to withdraw when he remembered Mr Needham's offer of raising further finance.

'£2,800.' His tongue felt too big for his mouth.

Mr Legg countered immediately. '£2,900.'

The next bid is £3,000 and it's likely Legg's limit. If I bid that it might halt him. '£3,000,' said Fergus and waited.

The room was silent. The auctioneer looked at Mr Legg. 'Another bid, sir? I'll take £3,050.'

No, no, don't make it easy for him. Fergus held his breath.

It seemed an age before Mr Legg shook his head and Fergus heard, 'Sold to Mr Shackleton, the *Eleanor Bell*, for £3,000.'

A wave of euphoria swept over him as the other bidders congratulated him. Even Todhunter came up and shook his hand. 'You've a grand brig there, Mr Shackleton. I assume you're setting up on you own. A new Shackleton line, is it?'

'Yes,' said Fergus, 'That's exactly what it is. The new Shackleton Line.'

On his way back from the auction Fergus called at Needham, Baxter & Company to secure an appointment. He was unable to see Mr Needham in person as 'Friday afternoons he represents debtors in court.' There was a lot to do and he had no time for delay. He secured an appointment for Monday and left instructions authorising Mr Needham to release funds to cover the *Eleanor Bell*'s deposit and pay the auctioneer's commission. Then he went to the harbour master's office to settle the harbour fees.

* * *

Contrary to what her mother had told her to expect, when Fergus came into the kitchen after the auction Becky was unable to tell whether he'd been successful or not. He seemed neither agitated nor excited. He turned to Rory, who was about to take Charlie for his walk, and said, 'The next time you go down to the harbour and see that ship you went on, you'll know it's mine.'

'Yours?' Rory's eyes shone with delight.

Becky let out a shriek and clasped her hands together.

'Yes.' He grinned at them both, 'You are now looking at the new owner of the brigantine the *Eleanor Bell*.'

'Does that mean I can go on it again?'

'For sure it does,' said Becky. 'Now, take Charlie out for his walk and I'll talk with Fergus in the kitchen.'

They watched Rory depart, with the puppy jumping up and down at his side, sensing the excitement. Becky plumped up the patchwork cushion on the spindle-backed chair and gestured to Fergus to sit in it, facing her. 'Tell me all. Were there many other bidders?'

'A few, but in the end it came down to three of us: Todhunter, a Mr Legg and myself.'

'Legg's been to auctions here. He'll have been bidding for himself,' said Becky.

'Should I know him?'

'Perhaps not, he's often at sea. Did you pay a good price? Are you pleased?' She wanted to know everything at once.

'Depends what you call a good price.'

'Less than you expected, like when you bought the *Gregory Peat*?'

'No, I bid £3,000.'

'Including commission?'

'No, that goes on top. I overbid by £500.'

Becky quickly ran through the transaction in her head. *His limit was £2,500, yet he's paid £3,000 plus commission. That means he doesn't have the £300 working capital he needs or the £200 contingency fund. At the very least, he's £300 short with no contingency reserve.*

'How will you make up the difference?'

He didn't seem overly worried about suddenly being in debt, although she was sure he'd no further resources to call on. So why was he not showing more concern? She'd never thought of him as reckless, quite the reverse. *Have I misjudged him? Is he a foolhardy risk-taker?*

'Before the sale I saw my solicitor and he advised me he could advance a loan.'

'From his own company?'

'No, he can make arrangements.'

'For a fee?'

'Well, not for nothing. I wouldn't expect that. It will come right, don't fret. I'll see him again on Monday.'

Although Becky did not want to spoil Fergus's good humour by questioning him in greater detail, had it been her she knew she would never have bid over an agreed limit with nothing in reserve.

Early the next morning, to Fergus's surprise and delight, a message arrived for him from Bill. He read it out to Becky and Dolly.

'I hear you are now a ship owner. This is a most excellent piece of news. Mary has no wish to move to Madeira. We must talk business. Noon in the Waverley coffee house?

Yours Truly, Bill.'

'Perhaps I have a master for my ship,' said Fergus, picking Becky up by the waist and twirling her around. 'And a good one.'

＊ ＊ ＊

Bill stood up when Fergus entered the coffee house. 'All goes well?' he asked.

'Well enough. So, has my father offered you the Madeira position?'

'Offer is not quite the correct term. It hasn't been stated, but I get the sense if I don't accept the position I may no longer be employed by Shackleton & Company. It's not just that, though. I hate to say this, but I think the company is losing its focus with setting up an office in Madeira, and with your father at the top, things can only get worse. He's too set in his ways for these times. Does your offer still stand?'

'Indeed. I have a sound ship. There was a lot of interest in her. Are you with me? I'll see you right. Four pounds four shillings a month is the going rate at Shackleton's, but I'll see you five pounds a month and, as I said before, ten percent of year-end profits and a directorship when we're officially incorporated.'

'When do we sail?'

'The 22nd, a week on Wednesday. Eleven days. We'll be away at least five weeks, possibly more. The shamrock triangle – Cardiff, Dublin and home.'

'I'll give notice on Monday. There's much to do and you need crew. Shall you take the same men on?'

'I'll leave that to you, but make sure we have men who are cheerful working in difficult conditions. We've a great deal to discuss. Shall we take luncheon together?'

'Aye, a sound idea, but first we must shake hands on our arrangement.'

Fergus took Bill's outstretched hand. 'I'll have my solicitor draw up the papers. I can't offer you much yet, but together, hopefully, we shall prosper.'

'Let us hope so for all our sakes. What is our shipping line to be called?'

'One ship is hardly a line.'

'We'll not stop at one surely?'

'Not while I'm at the helm.'

CHAPTER FIFTEEN

Mr Needham, after some opening pleasantries, got straight down to business. 'I have supplied monies, as you instructed, via my clerk, for the deposit and the auctioneer's commission. I have also begun making arrangements for your company's incorporation.'

'Bill McRae is to receive ten percent of year end profits.'

'I have made a note of that. Have you decided on your company name?'

'Not yet.'

'We can fulfil that requirement later.'

'I don't think it wise to use Shackleton. It could cause confusion. This is my own venture.'

'Quite so.'

Everything appeared to be in hand. Fergus was relieved. 'The payments for the *Eleanor Bell*, can we go over that once more?' he asked.

'Certainly, I was coming to that. Under the conditions

of sale, you are required to make two further instalments, the first after one month, the second after two months.'

'That is my understanding. I've paid £1,000 deposit, leaving £2,000 outstanding. Two payments of £1,000 yet to be made.'

'There is no problem. You have those funds lodged here as satisfactory security. There is, of course, the additional deduction of the commission at £50, and our own fees and disbursements as listed herein.' He handed Fergus an envelope.

'I need some monies to hand. I have crew to pay, stores, agents' fees, insurance and the like. Can you arrange £400 for me?'

Mr Needham appeared to hesitate, then, after making a pyramid with his hands said, 'I'm afraid that is not going to be possible.'

Fergus's chin shot up. 'Why not?'

'The funds are held in our client account to be paid as and when due. You are receiving a token amount of interest on these. The owners of the ship will not let you take her out on deposit alone without the remaining monies deposited here with us. You could be away at sea when the payments become due and so it is looked to us to act on your behalf. I thought it was clear to you that the monies are to be held by us so total payment can be completed.'

'I didn't realise the terms were quite so non-negotiable.' Fergus thought for a moment. 'Then, as I suspected, I will require a loan. Something you mentioned at our last meeting.'

Mr Needham frowned, adjusted his collar with both hands, then turned to study the deed boxes along the wall before turning back to Fergus. 'Had you asked me last week there would have been no problem.'

'Last week?'

'Yes. How can I put this?'

'Simply?' The back of Fergus's neck was beginning to feel cold.

'Let us say your father has a long reach.'

'My father?'

'Yes. Your father, Hector.'

'What has my father to do with this?'

'It seems he has received word of your recent purchase, and with his influence, particularly within the Gentlemen's Club, has made it clear that anyone aiding you financially will incur his displeasure and likely lose his business. I'm sorry, but there is no one I can approach for a loan on your behalf. All the men of means appear to have taken his side. I anticipated your visit and the request for a loan, and I've been making enquiries everywhere. Some parties have offered funds, but at a rate of interest that it would be impossible to pay. It is their way of saying no, without appearing to do so.'

Fergus was silent. He'd not expected his father to block him financially. He'd not asked for help, but he'd expected to be allowed to find his own way without interference.

'You are saying no one will lend me money for fear of my father?'

Mr Needham picked up his pen as if to write, but instead of dipping it in the ink-well, he rolled it between two fingers. 'Yes, most regrettably that is what I am saying. Many of the people in this town depend on your father's services for transporting their goods and bringing in items they need. People can be fickle when it affects their purses and businesses.'

'No one, not one person, will lend me money?' *I can't believe this, it's ridiculous.*

'I expect you could possibly take out a loan in Carlisle or Lancaster, but the interest rates would be prohibitive and you would never find your feet.'

'So, your previous mention of my having a loan is now nonsense.'

'It wasn't at the time I mentioned it, but now I would say funds are unobtainable within a radius of thirty miles, and perhaps more.'

Fergus's palms began to sweat. *This can't be happening.* He hadn't realised his father had such power within the community. Then, with horror, he remembered Bill was handing in his notice that day. His father would guess Fergus had engaged him; why else would he leave? He wiped his palms on his trousers. He was experiencing his first taste of being responsible for the livelihood of another person and it was unsettling him.

'You are quite definite that you cannot release any of the funds you hold?'

'No, I'm sorry.'

'Then I have a ship sitting in the harbour I can't afford to sail or crew, and people who are dependent upon me for their livelihood who I cannot pay.'

'I'm afraid that would seem to be the case. When are you planning to sail?'

'The 22nd. Ten days. If I can't sail her then I have no way of making any income.'

'All is not lost. Can I suggest you sell the iron ore cargo currently in the hold?'

'And let everyone know I can't afford to sail? That will be my last resort.' Fergus stood up. 'Tell me, sir, did my father send Mr Legg to push up the price of my ship?'

'I have no idea.'

'Really?'

'Genuinely, Mr Shackleton, and if I may make a suggestion, it will do you no good to speak such thoughts aloud to others. They may pass them on. I will continue to make enquiries, but I hold out little hope.'

'My father must have wealthy enemies in this town. He's crossed some, I know that for certain. Perhaps you can find out. Anyone who aids me in this will anger him, and that may be pleasing to them. We can play his game too.' Another thought occurred to him. 'And tell me, what is Needham, Baxter & Company's stance in this matter? I have to ask, are you with me or my father?'

'You are my client and I will do all I possibly can to aid you. Your father's influence does not extend into the offices of the legal profession. His strength is within the business world. I can only apologise for the situation evolving as it has done in a way it never occurred to me it would. For a father to treat...' His voice trailed away.

'And client confidentiality? You, your clerk, and staff can guarantee this?' Fergus sought Mr Needham's eyes and held his gaze. He was gratified to see him appear offended.

'We can and do keep confidentiality. Over all the years the intimate personal and business details of Whitehaven's citizens have made their way across this desk, to my knowledge, at no time have any such private details been divulged, and had they been, even just once, I am sure we would have been out of business years ago. These details are not something this firm has any intention whatsoever of becoming involved in, whether personally, professionally or from a distance. Of that I can assure you.'

Fergus, happy with Mr Needham's explanations and reassurances, took his leave. He'd intended walking to the harbour to look over the *Eleanor Bell*, but he no longer had the heart for it. His prime consideration was to find Bill and advise him of the problem they now faced.

❊ ❊ ❊

'Are you all right?' asked Becky, looking up when she saw Fergus. 'You look pale.'

'It's not surprising if I appear so. I have upsetting news.'

'I can see you're out of sorts. Is there something wrong with the ship?'

'I am unable to secure a loan.'

'Why ever not?'

Fergus related what the solicitor had told him.

She sat down and took his hand. 'What are you going to do?'

'I don't know. I should have taken out a loan before the sale. Not used all my own money to buy the ship. I've made a foolish mistake. It's easy to borrow money when you have it, impossible, it would seem, when you haven't.'

'How much do you need?'

'At least £300. I shouldn't have gone on bidding. I took a calculated risk with the information to hand at the time and it's turned bad on me.'

'You can't change that, and you did think it the right thing at the time.'

'I have an asset, but no cash to work it.'

✿ ✿ ✿

Fergus found Bill at home with a copy of the *Whitehaven News* spread out on the table.

'Have you resigned yet?'

'I have an appointment with Mr Craggs tomorrow. I intend to tell him then. Why?'

'Thank God,' said Fergus. 'I'm in time.'

'In time for what?'

'To tell you not to leave.'

'You don't want me anymore?'

'On the contrary, I need you more than ever. I'm in a hole so deep I can't see the sky.'

Fergus went on to explain his predicament. When he'd finished, Bill was silent for a few moments. Then he said, 'We'll have to sell some of the cargo. That will raise enough to fund Cardiff. We can buy coal there – maybe not a full load, but enough – and head for Dublin, sell that for a profit, then get the agent to find us a cargo we'll receive advance carriage fees for, then back.

'We?'

'You can't do this on your own and I'm definitely not going to Madeira.'

'You mean you'd still come in with me under these circumstances?'

'Yes. It's a chance I'm willing to take and the only opportunity I'm going to get to be a director of a shipping line. Staying with Shackletons in the long run is not going to be worthwhile, unless they go into steam. The *Eleanor Bell* is a sound vessel to start with. We'll have to have a reduced crew, but as it's summer, I don't anticipate any contrary weather.'

'Won't selling some of the cargo let the world and his dog know we're short of funds? The discharging will be plain for everyone to see.'

'It's not something we can keep under cover.'

'I've thirty pounds to hand,' said Fergus. 'It's not much, but it will cover yours and the crew's wages and buy some supplies.'

'Don't worry about that now. You need to think about selling some of that iron ore. If you can do that, we can make a start. There's one thing you could consider.'

'What's that?'

'Insurance. It's a way you could save money. Insure just the ship and not the cargo. It's a risk, but one many take in their early days.'

In his room upstairs the following evening, Fergus lay on top of his bed with his feet outstretched and his hands behind his head, thinking through his day. He'd spent all morning trying to sell the iron ore. There were buyers, but he wasn't prepared to sell at any price –although he knew he may have to. He'd retained three men for security at five shillings a day, and since they'd got wind of his need to sell part of the cargo, he'd had to pay them for a week on the spot. He'd decided not to pay his solicitor; he could wait for his money, and anyway, he had the £2,000 and could divert the interest.

A week passed and Fergus decided to make arrangements for half the iron ore to be discharged the following day and offered for sale. He would sign the papers in the morning. He'd expected it to fetch around six shillings a ton in Cardiff. Instead, even though it pained him to think about it, he knew he might have to accept four shillings a ton as the best offer from the quay. The buyers would assume rightly he was desperate and that he hadn't exhibited much business acumen. He'd got off to a very bad start by managing to accumulate a loss while still tied up. He'd used the money to hand for insurance on the ship's fabric and spent a week of sleepless nights fretting over his uninsured cargo.

Early afternoon, with the threat of rain from the grey clouds hovering over the town, Fergus walked down to the harbour. He had to admit the *Eleanor Bell* rested proudly. As he approached, he saw the tall, well-built figure of the Norwegian, Sven. They'd kept him on, knowing it was wise to have someone who knew the ship's sounds and idiosyncrasies. The three security men Fergus had engaged were on their knees caulking the deck.

Sven came to meet him. 'A man was looking for you, sir,' he said. 'Mr Needham wants to see you without delay.'

'Did he say what it was about?'

'No, just that it was urgent.'

More bad news. As he strode out, he braced himself for what could only be further disaster. Ever since the gavel went down at the auction, everything had started to unravel. It was as if it had been a starting pistol unleashing a downhill race to disaster.

He was ushered straight in to see Mr Needham. As before, the solicitor's desk had been cleared of papers, although this time there was what appeared to be a legal document resting on it.

'Please sit down, Mr Shackleton. I have something that may ease your troubles.'

Fergus sat and waited. Mr Needham's jovial demeanour was in great contrast to his mood of the last visit. He pointed to the document in front of him. 'I have here an offer for you for an advance loan.'

Fergus leaned forward to take a better look. 'Who from?'

'I am not at liberty to say. The lender has made the stipulation that the loan be given anonymously.'

'That's ridiculous. How could I make payment?'

'Our office would take care of all practical matters of that nature.'

'I can't accept this. I could be selling my soul to the devil.'

Mr Needham, as at their last appointment, looked at the deed and probate boxes lining the walls as if seeking inspiration. 'Allow me to set out the details before you come to a decision.'

Fergus nodded.

'The advance loan is for the sum of £400, repayable in full in four years, interest payable quarterly. This means you have three months before you need pay interest. Time to make several transactions and create some profits, I would suggest.'

'What is the rate?'

'One and a half percent. More than reasonable, I am sure you will agree.'

'Too reasonable. What about the initial fee for setting up the loan? What is the catch?'

'There is no set-up fee and no catch, I can assure you of that.'

Fergus sat back and laughed. 'You are expecting me to take out a loan from someone I do not know, who must obviously know me, at a too-good-to-be-true rate of interest and payment structure?'

'Yes, I am. Is this not the answer to your prayers?'

'I'll not deny that, but it's too convenient. Is it something my father could be behind?'

'I can assure you that is most definitely not the case.'

'So, you know the person involved?'

'Yes, I do.'

'He knows me?'

'Yes.'

'Why is he doing this, and in this way?'

'Mr Shackleton, I have no idea. I asked that question myself, but no answer was forthcoming.'

'I cannot do this, despite, as you say, it being the answer to my prayers.'

'Mr Shackleton, as your legal representative, you look to me for advice, do you not?'

Fergus nodded.

'Then let me speak plainly. I advise you strongly to accept this offer. It is a most generous one and could well set you up for life.'

'You've found an enemy of my father's? Is that it?'

'I cannot divulge anything that will reveal the identity of the lender. I have had the papers drawn up in anticipation of your acceptance. You need only sign today and your financial worries are eased.'

'Must I sign today?'

'No, but when you do, funds will be available immediately. I should mention it is all over town you are selling your cargo.'

'All over town?'

'Mr Shackleton, you are very much the talk of the town. It is not every day a Whitehaven family's disagreement spills out onto its streets, and when it does it is lapped up by all and sundry. I'm afraid your business is everybody's business right now, and your affairs are public knowledge.'

Fergus picked up a pen and dipped it in the ink stand. 'I will sign.'

* * *

Fergus went straight to the *Eleanor Bell* and gave instructions the cargo was not to be discharged. He was thankful he hadn't signed any sale documentation.

'We're to sail with a full cargo?' asked Sven.

'Yes.'

'I can't say I'm not relieved.'

Not as relieved as I am, thought Fergus. 'Tell me, is the captain aboard?'

'No, sir, he's at the chandler's. He left half an hour past.'

Fergus wasted no time and was at the chandler's on King Street within ten minutes. Bill was in conversation with the proprietor, Mr Gudgeon.

'I would like to give you credit, Bill, I really would,' Mr Gudgeon was saying. 'But if I give it to *you,* I have to provide it for everyone.'

'I was hoping you might make a goodwill exception this time to set us on our way.'

'I'm sorry.'

Fergus broke into their conversation. 'Captain, a word, please.' He drew Bill to one side. 'We have no need for credit now. I have secured funds at an affordable rate of interest.'

Bill clapped him on the back. 'We sail with a full cargo?'

'We do indeed, all fees paid.'

His friend was laughing and smiling. 'How has this come about?'

'It appears I have a benefactor who has been prepared to give me a loan at very good rates. I think it's one of my father's enemies. It's a personal loan to me so does not affect you in any way.'

'Who?'

'That's of no importance now. Suffice to say we sail as we intended on August the 22nd, fully laden and in fine fettle.'

Bill called Mr Gudgeon over. 'Our situation has changed. We need stores, stacks of them.'

CHAPTER SIXTEEN

'If we had a parlour,' said Dolly, 'we'd be in there now to celebrate, but it was given up long ago for a third guest bedroom.'

'We can celebrate here in the kitchen just as well,' said Fergus, twirling the brandy in his glass, before holding it up to catch the light from the fire, just as his father did.

'Imagine, someone has put up the money for your loan. Do you really not know who?'

'No, truly I do not, but it's my guess Mr Needham found someone with a grudge against my father. There can be no other explanation. Perhaps they still have business with him. People can carry grievances for years.'

'Didn't you see who it was when you signed the papers?'

'No. Mr Needham, acting as agent, placed a paper over the top so I couldn't see.'

'Didn't you worry you were signing a different document?'

'No, I trust Mr Needham, since it would do his company

no good to trick me. And I saw the wording setting out the agreement, so I have no fears.'

'Do you have the agreement?'

'It's in a box in Mr Needham's office.'

'Well, it seems a reet "rum do" to me,' said Dolly, 'but if it's what sets you up, then I'm all for it.' She raised her glass. 'A toast, to the *Eleanor Bell*, her captain and her crew.'

'To the *Eleanor Bell*,' chimed Becky and Fergus, raising their glasses.

Dolly drained then refilled hers. 'On a sadder note, Rory was here to collect Charlie for his walk today. He says his mam has taken to her bed most of the day.'

'Can you go and see her?' Fergus said to Becky.

'She's asked for me. I'm calling tomorrow.'

Arriving at Amy's, Becky found her up and dressed. She'd lost even more weight but seemed more settled in mood. She sent Rory to buy two eggs and, as the door closed behind him, motioned to Becky to sit with her at the table. It was hot and airless in the room, despite scant sunlight entering through the mud-streaked windows. The room had a new smell, one Becky associated with sickness and pain.

'Before you ask, I'm taking my medicine, but my time is running out.'

'Hush, don't say that.'

'T'is true. The time has come to make arrangements for Rory.'

'We'll do whatever we can to help. We can take him in at the Indian King. I've already discussed this with Mam and she's in full agreement. We'll love him as our own, truly we will.'

'I'm more than grateful, I am. I sometimes think his gammy leg has protected him. Through the accident, he's met Mr Shackleton and he knows you, and he's been released from the mine. I pray his good fortune in life'll continue. However, it's the coming months worrying me.'

'Can he not stay here with you?'

'He can, but I don't want him to. With what's to come, I don't want him to see me as I will be.'

'We can take him in now if that's what you want. He can come and visit whenever you like.'

'Nay, you don't understand, I want him well away from me. He must remember me as I am now, not wracked with pain, two staring eyes in a shrunken body, with claws for hands.'

'It may not be like that.'

'But it will be. I've seen it, and not only with my mammy. I've the vision of her in her final days and I don't want Rory to see me like that. He'll never rid himself of it and it'll torment him in the early hours, rise up when he's out walking in the fields, jump into his thoughts unbidden every day, as Mammy does in mine. No. I don't want that. Mr Shackleton must take him on his ship.'

'Are you sure?' Becky gave a small gasp of surprise, but then she remembered how much Rory had enjoyed their covert visit to the *Eleanor Bell*. Perhaps there was something in Amy's request.

'Aye, it's the perfect solution.'

'I'll ask Fergus. I'm sure he'll find a place for him, but that'll mean you don't see him.'

'Nay, it'll mean he doesn't see *me*. Not until we're united in the next world, when I'm restored to health.'

Becky searched Amy's face for any signs of misgiving, but there were none. She appeared completely resolute. 'If it's what you really want?'

'Aye. I'd end it myself if it weren't a sin that might see me in hell for all eternity. I wouldn't like to risk that. I must be in heaven to greet my boy when he joins me and to meet Mammy, who must be waiting for me there. Better to suffer here on earth and ensure my place with the angels and my loved ones. Anyways, I don't think I'm brave enough to do that sort of thing. Since Rory was on Mr Shackleton's ship he's talked of nothing else.' She smiled. 'He wants to visit foreign lands.' She pointed to a blue-and-white bowl with a cracked rim, sitting in the middle of the table. He says he's going to fill that bowl to the brim with the sea shells he brings back from his travels.' Tears dropped from Amy's eyes. 'He has big dreams and I want him to follow those dreams, free of his mammy's ghost.'

'But do you think you're brave enough to have him at sea when it might be the time you most need him near?'

'It's what I want. No deathbed scene. He must remember me as I am now.'

On the way home Becky ran over their conversation, agonising over whether Amy was doing the right thing. *Shouldn't Rory be with his mother at the end? When fully grown, will he feel he'd been robbed of special days with his mother?* Perhaps more importantly, *what can he do on a ship? How will he manage with the wind and the rise and fall of the ship, when he's so unsteady sometimes? Especially as the Eleanor Bell is a pitcher?* There was a solution to the last thought, she was sure of it, if only she could think of something he could do that would not involve heavy lifting or much footwork. She was still engrossed with her thoughts when she saw the baker boy approaching with his loaded basket. She could smell the warm bread as he passed by and then it came to her. *A cook's apprentice, that might work. Sheltered from the wind, inside, not requiring much moving about. That's it. Perfect.*

She ran down to the harbour and was halfway up the *Eleanor Bell's* gangway when a voice rang out.

'Hey, you, stop! You need to be invited on, you can't just board.'

She looked up. It was Sven.

'Oh, it's you again, Miss Becky,' he said, smiling broadly.

'I'm here to see Mr Shackleton. Is he about?'

'He's with the captain. You'll have to wait.'

'I think he'll see me.'

'What's your business?'

'Tell him Becky's found him a cook's apprentice.'

Sven looked puzzled. 'Does he know you?'

'Aye, he does and he'll want to see me.' She was amused by Sven's confusion.

The Norwegian disappeared and reappeared with Fergus and Bill.

'What's all this about a cook's apprentice?' Fergus asked.

'It's Rory.' She looked to Bill. 'Say yes, please, you must say yes. It's the boy you met at the fair. His mother's dying and it's her wish.'

'I remember,' said Bill. 'But isn't he the crippled boy?'

'Yes, that's why he's perfect for it. No running around, stationed in the galley.'

'What do you think, Sven?' asked Bill.

'Is that the boy who came with you when you were here before? The one I thought was your brother?'

Becky felt embarrassed. 'Aye.'

'So you were spying? I never guessed.'

'Can we take on a boy with a bad leg?' asked Bill again.

'He'd not be my first choice,' said Sven. 'And what about pans of boiling water if he's unsteady on his feet?'

'I'm sure you wouldn't expect any young lad to be carrying heavy pots of water in the galley. That's the cook's job, surely?'

Bill didn't look convinced. 'He's too young to be freely associating with the likes of the crew. He's still much of a bairn.'

'Aye, but the cook and apprentice don't keep watch,' said Fergus, who seemed to be coming round to accepting the idea. 'He'll be sheltered from the men and any unseemly talk or jests.'

'Remember he was a pit boy,' said Becky. 'There's not much he won't have already heard and seen down the mine.'

Let's try him,' said Fergus. 'There's no harm and the boy's keen. I know him as trustworthy and reliable.'

'We have several cooks to interview tomorrow,' said Bill.

Fergus looked at him. 'Then let's make sure we employ one who will look kindly on the boy. The least we can do is give him a good start.'

'You'll take him, Bill?' asked Becky

'We'll try him this voyage, that's all I can say. Although we need a letter from his mother. Can she sign her name?'

'Aye, and write. Can he bring the dog?'

'The dog?' asked Bill.

'Aye, Charlie, our dog. They're the best of friends, boy and dog. He'll be a comfort for him and a companion.'

Sven laughed. 'Ah! Charlie the cat challenger. He and Caesar, our fiercest tomcat, had quite a set-to the other day.'

'Aye, that's him.' Becky laughed along with him as the image of the little puppy taking on the big ship's cat came to mind.

'We should take the dog with us, cap'n,' said Sven. 'It'll keep the cats on their toes and will catch the biggest rats, and keep the lad in good spirits.'

'If it's his constant companion, then yes, but it'll have to have sea legs,' said Bill.

'I'm sure if Charlie hasn't got them already, he can grow them,' said Becky.

'I'm glad we've got that settled,' Fergus said to her. 'I'll see you after supper.'

He turned away, leaving Sven to accompany Becky to the gangway.

'Thank you, Sven. You're doing a good thing taking the boy.'

'Happy to oblige, miss. Will you be sailing with us?'

'Me? Nay. I've work to do here, so I'm relying on you to keep a special eye out for Rory. He's a good lad.'

'And an eye out for Mr Shackleton too?'

Becky grinned. 'He can take care of himself, but make sure he returns safe and sound.'

'To you?'

'Aye, to me.'

Dolly and Becky stood on the quay and watched as the last stores were loaded onto the *Eleanor Bell*. She would sail on the early tide the following day. Amy arrived with Rory, whose belongings were tied in a hessian drawstring bag.

Rory looked around. 'Where's Charlie? Is he here?'

Becky raised the top of her wicker basket to reveal the dog curled up inside. He got up on all fours and gave a welcome bark as soon as he saw Rory. 'We thought he'd better have his basket. It'll make him feel more at home.'

'Are you sure you can part with him?' asked Amy. 'He's your dog.'

'He *was* our dog,' said Dolly. 'He's Rory's now.'

Amy brushed the boy's hair back from his eyes. 'I should've cut that fringe shorter.'

'I don't suppose you'll recognise Rory when he gets back,' said Dolly. 'He'll be taller, I bet.'

'He'll not grow that much in five or six weeks,' said Becky. 'More likely grow outwards working in the galley.'

Sven's voice carried onto the quay. He'd lined the crew up on deck and was reeling off a list of offence penalties.

'Smoking below or carrying a sheath knife, loss of

one day's pay. Bringing grog on board for personal use, loss of three days' pay. Anyone bringing contraband on board with intent to sell will forfeit one month's pay. Drunkenness: first offence two days' half-allowance of provisions; second offence as per the master's pleasure.'

'That'll not be you, Rory,' said Amy. 'You'll not be touching any liquor. Neither do I want you smoking. No pipes and no chewing baccy. Do you ken?'

Rory's head bobbed up and down. 'Aye, I ken, but what *can* I do?'

Amy opened her bag and took out an oval tin decorated with red-jacketed soldiers standing to attention, holding rifles. 'There's one barley sugar for each day of the five weeks you're likely to be away. Then five more so you can have two on Sundays, and six more for luck. How many is that?'

'Thirty-five and five and another six, that's forty-six. Two short of four dozen.'

'Aye, you're a clever boy, my Rory. Good with numbers.' She pushed his fringe back again and kissed his forehead. 'Make sure you don't eat them all at once and make yourself sick.' She handed him another bag. 'I've put your soldiers and paints in here. If cook's a spare tin for the sweets you can put your soldiers back in their own tin.'

Rory's eyes lit up when he opened the tin and looked inside. He took a barley sugar out for the others to see. 'Thanks, Mammy.' He gave her a hug.

'Hey, you down there.'

The women looked up. A short, rotund man with a chubby face, framed by thick dark curls that needed a trim, was looking down at them from the ship's rail. 'Will you be Rory Rooke?'

All three women answered for him at the same time. 'Aye.'

'I'm waiting for you. There's 'tates to peel and carrots to chop. Best get yourself and that pup up here, quick sharp.'

A look of hesitation passed over Rory's brow and his lip trembled. He looked to his mother.

'Now get a move on, lad. You've a profession to learn.' Amy kissed Rory again, hugged him tightly for what seemed a long time, then patted him on the back and steered him towards the ship. She watched him go up the gangway, turn and wave to them, then disappear. Tears rolled down her cheeks. 'I'm sorry,' she said. 'He just looks so small next to the ship, and the men are so big compared to him.'

On the way back, Becky and Dolly walked slowly so as not to exert Amy, who was going at a much slower pace than she had been on their outward journey.

'You've been very brave,' said Becky.

'If I don't see Rory again, you will take him in?'

Becky glanced at Dolly and they locked eyes.

'He'll only be gone five, maybe six weeks at the most,' said Dolly. 'He'll be back in no time'

'Mam's right.' Becky tried to sound cheerful, although she was wondering why Amy had chosen that day to make the remark about them looking after him. *I'm sure she has many months yet; she doesn't look that close to death. But maybe death is all a woman with a young child thinks about when she's aware she's terminally ill.*

'God's not ready for you yet.' Becky took Amy's hand. 'You'll be standing next to me on the quay with a big bag of barley sugars when they return.'

Amy gave Becky a strange look, one she couldn't decipher, then turned to Dolly. 'But if I'm not here then you'll take care of him, won't you? There's no one else and he's still really only a bairn.'

'We'll love him as our own,' said Dolly. 'The Indian King, will be his home, don't worry.'

'If he goes in the workhouse, they'll probably set him on with someone cruel and…'

'It won't come to that. I promise,' Dolly replied.

They continued the rest of the way in silence, until Becky and Dolly turned into the Indian King. Becky, glancing out of the window, saw Amy still standing outside, looking at the building. She remained there several minutes, then she traced her fingers over the coloured glass panels set into the top of the door and turned for home, with tears streaming down a face that seemed suddenly to have aged ten years.

Becky jumped up when she heard the soft knock on the kitchen door, even though she was expecting it. She knew Fergus wouldn't leave without saying a private goodbye.

When he'd settled himself by the fire, she took a small embroidered linen bag lying next to her *Forget Me Not* book on the table and gave it to him. 'It's a lock of my hair. I've sprayed it with my scent.'

He took the bag and held it up to his nose. Then he

opened it up. The hair had been gathered together at the bottom and tied tightly with a piece of thin yellow ribbon, so it spread out like a fan. 'That's wonderful, and you've embroidered the bag beautifully. Thank you.'

He leaned forward and kissed her forehead. It was the first time he'd kissed her without asking permission before doing so.

'That's not all, I've decided on the poem.' She picked up the *Forget Me Not* book and removed a piece of paper from it. 'It's a seventeenth-century poem by Giles Fletcher. It's called *The Wooing Song* and it's about love.' She began reading.

'Love is the blossom where there blows
Everything that lives or grows:
Love doth make the Heav'ns to move,
And the Sun doth burn in love:
Love the strong and weak doth yoke,
And makes the ivy climb the oak...'

As she read she saw he was looking at her, clearly enjoying the intimacy of the moment as much as she was. *I hope my message is clear – that I love him as much as I think he loves me.*

'...Only bend thy knee to me,
The wooing shall thy winning be.'

Finishing, she handed him the paper. 'Take this with you, to remind you of me.'

When he took it from her she saw his eyes were moist. 'You think I need reminding, when you've just read me such a beautiful poem about love?'

She laughed. 'Perhaps not.'

'You'll accept the pearl?'

'Yes, I know you well enough now. You'll be back for my birthday. Bring it on that day and I'll wear it.'

He took her hand. 'I can't stay long, there's much to do.'

'I understand, but before you go, I must ask after Rory.' She needed to know he had settled in.

'He was happy and busy when I left. The cook we've engaged seems to like him and is fussing over him. I think the *Eleanor Bell* can make a mariner of him, in time.'

'And in time what will the *Eleanor Bell* make of *you*?' Becky was more conscious of his presence than she had ever been. They'd sat together and walked together many times, but the thought of his leaving the next day, with all the difficulties his departure entailed, somehow made this parting much more poignant.

'I'm hoping this ship will start me off on a new life journey. Not just on the seas, but in my life on land too.' He was looking at her so fixedly, she wondered if he was trying to memorise her features.

'Tell me, will you miss me?' she asked.

'You need to ask? When I'm at sea it will be no different to when I'm here. I'll think of you constantly. I'll wonder where you are and what you are doing. I'll picture you here making lemonade, clearing the table, folding the guest linen. All the things I've seen you do many times. I'll long to hear your laugh and see your smile. And you? Will you think of me?'

'Aye, I'll think of you and worry that a freak wave'll catch you unawares and pitch you into the sea, that your ship'll run aground with all hands lost, that you'll catch a fever with no one to tend you. That you'll slip on wet cobblestones on a quay far from home and break a leg. These are the things I'll dwell on.'

'Those are needless worries, not thoughts. Will you not think of me in sweeter ways, as I think of you? The turn of your head when your hair is caught by the wind, the sound of your tread on the cobbles, the swish of your skirts as you pass by me, the curve of your neck, the laughter in your beautiful grey eyes, the touch of your hand in mine. Will you not think of me in these ways?'

'Not the swish of your skirts, no.'

They both laughed and Fergus, facing her, put his arms around her waist and drew her closer to his chest. She could feel the smoothness of his linen shirt against her cheek and smell his body scent. He bent down and kissed her. A long, deep kiss that forged them together until they both ran out of breath.

If you don't come back, I will not be able to stand it.

As if reading her thoughts, Fergus stepped back and took both her hands in his. 'I want to look you in the eye when I say this. I *will* come back safe and sound. Allow me to prove myself.'

He put his hand up to her face and gently ran his fingers down her cheek, then took her hand and put it up to his lips. 'Until I return,' he murmured. He kissed her hand again, lingered for a moment at the door and was gone.

The dull sound the door made when it closed carried an emptiness that filled Becky's whole being. Her world was silent, and while he was gone it would lose much of its brightness too.

CHAPTER SEVENTEEN

Apart from some unseasonal squally weather that brought unexpected winds and rain on the third day, and some dark damp nights, the *Eleanor Bell* met with little to disrupt her progress. As Cardiff hove into view, Fergus and Bill stood at the rail looking out at the city. He was nervous. They needed a good sale price for the iron ore. Anything over six shillings a ton would be acceptable. However, when they arrived at the broker's office, as soon as he greeted them, his weak smile and failure to meet their eyes told both men instantly he had bad news.

'You can't get six shillings right now. Last month, three weeks ago, maybe two weeks ago you could, but since then there's been an influx. Iron ore prices have fallen. Look.' He gestured towards two other ships. 'Both those are discharging iron ore and already it's piled up.' He pointed at the quay. 'It's a shame you didn't have a firm contract price from your buyer before you sailed.

Although sometimes the price goes up so you're laughing, but not this time.'

'Well, we're not laughing now,' said Bill. 'We've a transferred cargo, so there's no signed contract. What can we expect?'

'I can get five and sevenpence a ton,' said the broker. Then, perhaps feeling uncomfortable with their disappointment, he added, 'Maybe a smidge more.'

'I'd understand if it was common iron ore, but it's best.'

The broker shrugged. 'I'm sorry, but this is the way things are.'

Fergus cursed under his breath. Bill took his elbow and led him out of earshot. 'It's better than the four shillings a ton we'd have got in Whitehaven if we'd discharged it there and auctioned it off on the quay.'

Fergus nodded. 'I hear what you're saying, but it's not a good way to start a business.'

'No, but things are as they are, and we can bring in enough to buy coal for Dublin.'

They came out of the broker's and found a table in a quiet corner of an inn named the Cambrian Lighter.

'We're about even,' said Fergus, writing some figures in a small notebook he'd taken from his jacket pocket. 'We've sold 196 tons of iron ore at five shillings eightpence a ton and we're taking on 185 tons of coal for Dublin at five shillings tenpence. It's going to cost us around £2 10s to discharge the iron ore.'

'What about the broker's bill? How much is that?'

Fergus wrote it down. '£8 5s 9d.'

'We've cook's stores to account for as well.'

'Which are?'

Bill produced a list and Fergus read the contents aloud. 'Potatoes, bread, beef, butter. What's this?' He pointed with his finger. 'Looks like B.S?'

'Barley sugars,' said Bill. 'Cook's put in a special request. Seems young Rory has made unexpected inroads into his stash.'

Fergus laughed. 'He's a good lad. I don't begrudge him a sugar ration in place of a rum one.'

'He's a born sailor, that boy. His tasks are always seen to cheerfully and he can get about when he has to. His only complaint is that his hammock in the galley is too hot.'

'He'll not say that come winter. And the pup sleeps with him?'

'Aye, curled up in his basket beneath him. Two innocent babes.'

✻ ✻ ✻

Four days out of Cardiff, on the way to Dublin, the weather changed, and the captain gave orders for the galley stove to be doused. Fergus, ever mindful of the responsibility of having such a young boy on board, paid one of his regular visits to the galley. He found Rory bending over a large mixing bowl with flour up to his elbows. There were white streaks across his forehead where he'd put his hand up to push his fringe back.

'What are you making?' asked Fergus, looking around for the cook.

'Sultana duff. Cook says there's enough heat left in the stove to cook it, even though he's doused it.'

Fergus turned to go.

'Mr Shackleton, do you think my mammy's all right?' Rory asked.

Fergus hesitated. 'She'll be missing you, I'm sure of that.'

'Do you think she'll get better?'

'Seeing you home and safe will raise her spirits. She'll be happy to see you when we get back. Especially when she sees how much better your hands are now you're no longer a pit boy.'

Rory held his hands out palms up and they both considered them. There were still some dark patches and rough areas where the worst callouses had been, but his hands were clearer.

'Cook's made me put them in salt water. Says it's the best thing for sores.'

'He knows a thing or two.'

'Aye, and there's no rope-pulling, which helps a lot too.'

Fergus looked around the galley and found it all ship-shape. Rory's clothes were stored in two neat piles beside his hammock. Becky had made him a warm jacket and bought some wet-weather boots. She'd insisted Fergus place them with the boy's belongings. The boots were stored neatly under a chair next to the tin soldiers, who had set up camp in an empty butter box.

'I'll be sure to tell your mother how you've kept your things in trim this voyage,' Fergus said. 'You've a tidy mind. She'll be proud of you.' He was aware he'd sidestepped Rory's concerns over his mother's health. The boy was not a fool. He turned to Charlie for diversion. 'I'll bet you don't get any of the cats in here now with Charlie on guard, do you?'

Rory laughed. 'No, they're running away from him now. Even Caesar, the big ginger tom. He hisses, but Charlie only has to bark and he runs off.'

'He's getting bigger every day, a bit like you.' *He's lost his hungry eyes too*, Fergus thought.

'Aye. I've to watch him though. He's always after scraps that fall from the bench. Cook says he's better than a team of sweepers keeping this floor clean. He got a huge rat the other day.'

'He's a working dog now, earning his keep,' said Fergus. 'You get out on deck every day, don't you?'

'I take Charlie out first thing and later in the day. Gives us both exercise.'

'And what do you do when cook gives you time off?'

'Some of the men are teaching me to play cards.'

Fergus was alarmed. 'For money?'

'I haven't got any.'

'No, not on you, but you're earning a wage now and you'll get paid when we get home. If anyone asks you for money when playing cards, or at any other time, tell me. If you need anything you can ask Captain McRae if he's got it in his slop-chest.'

'Barley sugars?'

'Maybe. You'd better ask him.'

Fergus left. He would ask Bill to remind the crew they were to treat the boy well and not lead him into any ill-doing for their own amusement. It wouldn't come amiss to let them know now, quietly, that his mother was dying. They'd respect that.

✳ ✳ ✳

The *Eleanor Bell* had a good run north in the Irish Sea, although for mid-September the weather was dirty. For several days it rained incessantly and the wind was unseasonably cold.

When they reached Messrs Flynn & Brady's offices the following morning it was the same doorman with the gold braid epaulettes. He gave no indication he remembered them. Fergus announced they'd come to see Mr Flynn and expected to be led upstairs. Instead, they were asked to wait. The doorman disappeared.

'Mr Flynn sends his regrets, but he is unable to see you.'

Fergus was surprised. 'Later? Tomorrow?'

'No, he regrets he is unable to represent you.'

Fergus made as if to make for the stairs, but Bill put out an arm and held him back. Addressing the doorman he said, 'I am sure there are other agents who will gladly do business with us.'

Outside Bill said, 'Perhaps we should have anticipated this. Don't worry, it's not as if we're asking for credit; we'll have the coal money. Follow me, I've some contacts in Dublin.'

However, by mid-day it was obvious they'd been blacklisted. The four agents they knew were either unwilling to do business with them or offered them a ridiculously low price for their coal, knowing they couldn't accept it.

'If we can't sell this coal we're done for,' said Fergus.

'There must be someone. Let's find a coffee house and think about it.'

Bill was looking up and down the street when Fergus said, 'Wait, there is someone.' He pulled a commercial token from his pocket. 'We know someone who's not under my father's thumb.'

'Who?'

'Padraig Conran.' He passed the token to Bill. 'Remember? We met him in April. He'd had an argument with my father years ago. He gave me an envelope with a fabric swatch in it. I'm not sure why.'

Bill read the token's inscription. 'PADRAIG CONRAN, BUSINESSMAN & SHIPPING AGENT. IMPORTER OF WHOLESALE AND RETAIL FRENCH & ENGLISH CLOTH – DUBLIN.'

An hour later, Bill and Fergus were sitting in Conran's office. It was a far cry from Flynn's gleaming brass stair-rods and there was no fancy doorman to greet them. Conran welcomed them warmly and, after listening to their predicament without comment, leant back in his chair. 'Sure, I've heard your father's influence is being well-felt here. It's rumoured he'll undercut any costs you charge as a carrier.'

'That assumes we're able to load a cargo to carry,' said Bill.

Fergus nodded. 'And I assume there is also the unspoken threat that agents who deal with us will incur his displeasure.'

''Tis the Holy Truth, no one here wants to fall out with

Hector Shackleton. However, some of us have already fallen foul of him and I'm one, so makes no difference to me.'

'You mentioned that to me in April. What were the circumstances?'

'We'd a disagreement over a cargo from Dublin to Whitehaven. It was due to be forwarded to Carlisle by your father, then he argued onward carriage to Carlisle hadn't been included in the original quotation.'

'Had it?' asked Fergus.

'A verbal contract was made with the ship's captain and this was freely admitted by both parties, but there was nothing in writing. It was a petty matter and could have been dealt with in a flash, but your father blew it up into a major event. He seemed to take the situation as personal criticism and threatened me, as the agent, with legal proceedings.'

'That sounds like him,' said Bill.

As he had done many times before, Fergus gave thanks he'd not inherited his father's volatile personality. 'How did it end?'

'The cargo was held up for two weeks; the owner travelled to Whitehaven and paid to have it transferred to Carlisle. The ship's captain lost his job, I lost a good customer, as did your father. Sure, it was all unfortunate. No one came out of that well.'

'How long ago was that?' Fergus recalled the many occasions when his father had complained about verbal agreements, but could not recall any relating specifically to the name Conran.

'Almost ten years ago.'

'Will *you* do business with us?' asked Bill.

'I'm more than happy to. Apart from seeing you right, your father won't like it if he hears I've helped you, and that will bring not a small amount of satisfaction to me.'

'Can you find us a buyer for our coal?'

'For sure, the coal's not a problem for me.'

'And cargo to return to Whitehaven? As well as a carriage payment we need ballast.'

'I can get you ale. That'll solve your ballast problem, and you'll be able to demand carriage fees in advance. I see no problem with that.'

'This is a lifesaver,' said Bill. 'To set off with an empty hold would not only be financially ruinous, but dangerous.'

'You gave me an envelope with a piece of fabric in it when we first met,' Fergus reminded Conran. 'What was that about?'

'Ah yes, the silk mix,' he replied. 'It's special.'

Bill leaned forward in his chair. 'We couldn't see the significance of it.'

Conran stood up. 'Come with me now and I'll show you. You've time on your hands today, haven't you?'

Bill and Fergus looked at each other. It was true. Now they appeared to have solved the return carriage problem, they *were* are a loose end.

'Come and see the real Dubliners keeping the city turning over.'

CHAPTER EIGHTEEN

Fergus, Bill and Conran were set down from their carriage in Patrick Street by the cathedral, in what appeared to be an artisans' area of Dublin. Signage indicated a network of small workshops housed within old warehouses, their wares spilling onto the street. Grocery and spirit dealers, tallow chandlers, cobblers and repair shops abounded, and outside their premises piles of baskets, brooms, boxes, paint tins, ladders and all manner of artisans' materials were piled high. People were making things, buying and selling them or packaging them up. A familiar smell assaulted their noses, which Fergus associated with the chemical works in Whitehaven. *Sulphur, and maybe a glue works too?*

They entered one of the houses, pushing past several people leaving in a hurry. Conran led the way up some well-trodden stairs to the second floor and knocked on a door that needed a good lick of paint. Without waiting, he went straight in. They found themselves in a room lined with shelves on which were stacked bolts of cloth.

Conran greeted an elderly woman wrapped in a brown woollen shawl who, judging by her wrinkles and weather-beaten skin, was more at home out of doors than in. She was sitting at a pine table clutching a white, long-stemmed clay pipe. She looked momentarily irritated at being interrupted. Then her eyes lit up.

'Ah, Mr Conran, are ye not always welcome here? And ye bring me two travellers.' She looked them up and down. 'English, by the looks of their clothes.'

'Sure, that's so Briony. Come over the sea just to see you.'

She gave a laugh that was perilously close to being a cackle. 'Aye, next I'll hear ye saying they swam over 'specially.'

'We're visiting because they've a ship's hold to fill. I introduce Mr Fergus Shackleton and Captain McRae. The owner and master of the *Eleanor Bell*.'

She looked them over. 'They're young to be important.'

'You'll not hold that against them? 'Tis not a sin to be in the years of youth.'

'Not if they've fine heads on their shoulders.' She sucked hard on her pipe. Fergus wondered at the fire risk in a room full of flammable materials, but when she took the bowl of the pipe and cupped it in her hands, he realised it was cold.

'We're here to see your new stock,' said Conran.

'Aye, I reckoned as much soon as I saw ye.' Briony stood up and pulled the edges of her shawl together, then went to an old chest of drawers and pulled on the second drawer. Having only one handle, the drawer came out at an angle and stuck fast. Conran went to help her and, after some pulling, kicking and swearing, the drawer was released to reveal a large, well-wrapped parcel. Briony asked Conran to lift it out and place it on the table, where she removed several layers of jute. Beneath these was a single layer of thinly woven cotton.

'Here she is.' She spread open the cotton to allow a bolt of the brightest purple cloth Fergus had ever seen fall free from its wrapping onto the table.

'It's dyed silk and wool,' Conran explained. 'Briony's family have been dyeing cloth for generations using madder and other plants, but they fade in the sun, and with washing lose their colour. This cloth has been dyed in a different way, using the new aniline dye – mauveine. As well as its wonderful brightness of colour it'll hold fast in sun and water and drapes beautifully. I was in Lancaster some months ago at the new dye factory and brought some dye back with me. The piece I put in the envelope was an early testing piece. You'll see this is even brighter than that was.'

Briony looked from Fergus to Bill. 'What are ye thinking?'

Fergus was the first to find his voice. 'I've never seen anything like it. The colour is almost brazen in its vitality. May I touch it?'

'Just the selvage.' She pointed to the straight edge, where tiny pinholes showed it had been stretched on the loom.

Fergus put out a hand and took the cloth between his fingers. It was soft and light, and as he moved his fingers it shimmered.

'Liking it, aren't ye?' said Briony,' I can tell by yer faces.'

Fergus nodded and motioned to Bill to touch it for himself.

Conran cleared his throat as if about to make a prepared speech. 'What you are seeing, gentlemen, is something quite magical. I predict this cloth is going to be desired by every woman in the land. Already it's the talk of the London salons, but there it can only be bought as pure silk. That takes it out of the pockets of most women, whereas our Irish wool and silk mix is much more within everyone's reach. We can strike gold with the early shipments while others are still at the starting gate. I need to get this across the water. I've contacts with dressmakers and haberdashers all over the north of England. I see an opportunity to be the first to showcase this colour in wool and silk and, seeing you here today looking for business, I'm thinking this could be the beginning of a useful partnership for us both.'

Bill leaned forward and touched the cloth. 'My wife would love a dress made of this, but fashion is fickle. And won't others follow swiftly if they see you making good profits?'

''Tis true, but being quick off the mark I can make good profits before others know what's happening. The established textile mills are set up for woollen goods and cotton, not the mix of silk and Irish wool I have here. It will be what is termed in the trade "an exotic" and I can exact a premium. We've had to experiment, which has held us up, but we're ready now and you're here at just the right time.'

Bill looked sceptical. 'The textile trade is not something I'm familiar with, although I know many have made fortunes from cloth. My practical worry is we've a hold that's recently carried coal corves. The combination of coal dust and silk in any form is not one I can envisage as sensible.'

Fergus nodded, but he was also processing the ongoing business angle. Conran seemed to know what he was doing and he was prepared to help them, when others were not.

'I'm well aware of what you're saying,' said Conran. 'We'll line the hold with the ale casks, wrap the cloth in tightly woven linen and use sailcloth to seal the parcels.'

'Why us?' asked Fergus. 'You must have other carriers you can use.'

'I do, but I'll be frank. First and foremost, I'm in business and I see a good opportunity here to seal a business bond with you. You're in a bit of a hole, I'm helping you out. You appreciate that, so you're likely to treat me favourably in future. From your point of view, if you serve me well there's future business for you.'

Fergus looked to Bill. 'You're the master of the ship. What do you say?'

'It's water and damp I'm most concerned about. Keeping the cloth dry, although I've experience carrying the Scottish cloth from Glasgow. How much are we talking about?'

'Twenty bolts and passage for myself to Whitehaven.' Conran scrutinised their faces for a reaction. 'That's not a great deal under the circumstances, is it?'

'You're very persuasive,' said Fergus. 'What about carriage?'

'I'm sure we can come to a beneficial arrangement that will suit us both.'

'Tariff fees?' asked Bill.

'I'll see to those.'

'Onward transportation?' asked Fergus.

Conran laughed. 'We'll arrange to have everything collected from the hold. You need only oversee the discharging from ship to quay.'

'You'll be responsible for the wrapping and sealing of the cloth?'

'It's my speciality, transporting cloth over water in dirty holds.'

'And if we meet the biggest storm the Irish Sea has ever seen?'

'Suffice to say carriage payment has to rely on safe delivery to Whitehaven, which is only fair. Your mention of storm is apt. You'll be wanting to get off while the weather is turned fair?'

'As soon as we can dispatch the coal and take on the ale.'

'Well, how about I throw in a little something to cover my board and lodge on the journey?'

'What would that be?' asked Fergus.

'Two dress lengths of the material. One for each of your wives.'

Fergus was about to say he didn't have a wife, then thought no need to mention it.

'Tempting,' said Bill.

'Wait,' said Fergus. 'I've an aunt who would dearly love a shawl of this material. She's a favourite of mine.' *No need to explain she is my only aunt.*

'They drive a hard bargain,' said Briony.

'We can find another piece, can't we?' asked Conran.

'It need not be a long one, a shoulder wrap will suffice.'

'This aunt, is she wedded?' asked Briony.

'No, and opportunities to do so have been discouraged by her brother, my father.'

'There's no loving husband to foot the bill, then?'

'No.'

'I'll see what I can find. There may be a loose single piece somewhere, but I'm not promising. I'm thinking it might help if you're able to offer a little something for my thirst. It's dry work sitting up here in the room all day waiting for custom, not like the old days when I was working the fields.'

Fergus laughed. 'I'll see what I can find for you, but I too am not promising.'

She grinned at him. 'And maybe a bit o' the pipe baccy too? I've a regular cough needs easing.'

'It's you drives a hard bargain,' said Bill.

'Fine-looking men ye both are. I'll wager ye've two pretty colleens waiting at home for your return.'

The three men took their leave and, before hiring a carriage back into the city, Fergus went into one of the grocer's and arranged for baccy and ale to be sent up to Briony.

After agreeing a deal in Conran's office, Fergus and Bill returned to the *Eleanor Bell*. As they approached, they could hear Charlie barking. Once on board they saw he'd cornered his arch enemy, Caesar. The cat's back was up, his tail waving from side to side and he was spitting and hissing. Charlie wasn't brave enough to advance further and Caesar was going to stand firm.

Fergus shouted at Rory. 'Give Charlie something to eat. That'll end this stand-off.'

Rory pulled a bit of biscuit from his pocket. 'Charlie, Charlie, come here, you –' he said, calling out a word he'd clearly learned on board or down the pit. He went forward, holding the biscuit out, but Charlie remained far too interested in Caesar. Rory grabbed him by the tail and pulled on it. The dog swung his head round and Rory held the biscuit out in front of his nose. 'Look, see.'

While Charlie snaffled the biscuit, Caesar took advantage of his momentary diversion to escape, making a long jump landing with a loud thud on the deck before scrabbling about, crashing into Sven's legs and disappearing at speed. Having gobbled up the biscuit, the dog looked round to find his adversary gone.

Rory, with Charlie now tightly clasped in his arms, was making to walk in the direction of the galley when Fergus called him back.

'Now then, young man,' he said. 'What was that you called Charlie?'

Rory's eyes moved upwards and to the left as he thought. Then he repeated the adult word.

'And where did you learn that?'

'It's what cook calls me.'

'Well, listen here, Rory Rooke, I don't want to hear you calling Charlie or anyone else such a thing. I'm asking Sven here to report to me if you do."

'Why?'

'Your mother wouldn't like it, that's why.'

Fergus turned to Bill who was trying unsuccessfully to smother a smile. 'A word from you to the cook, I suggest.'

'I'll see to it.'

❖ ❖ ❖

With the coal dispatched and the hold made ready, there was a morning's wait for the ale. Fergus passed the bolts of cloth, stacked on a wagon waiting to be loaded. *They look like shrouded corpses,* he thought. *No one would ever guess what beauty lies within.*

Mid-afternoon, Conran arrived with a large carpet bag out of which he took three parcels, handing them to Fergus. 'Here you are. Here's your payment for my room and board. Two for you, Fergus, and one for the captain.'

'My thanks. My aunt will be especially pleased. Better than singing for your supper, eh?'

'Believe me, you don't want to hear any of my Irish ditties,' said Conran. 'Are we still expecting to reach Whitehaven on the 8th?'

'God willing.'

Later when they were alone, Conran having retired early, Bill said to Fergus, 'I'm uneasy. So much depends on this trip, although I see nothing untoward with the weather.' He looked up at the sky. 'But it's October now and things can change quickly. I'll be glad to see the candlestick chimney come into view and know we're home and dry.'

'If we can make it without mishap, we'll have made a decent profit.'

'Enough?'

'Enough to pay the interest on the loan and still some. All wages will be secure and bills covered.'

'Do you think your father still holds sway over us in Whitehaven?'

'I don't know, but returning after a successful voyage, having made a profit, may make people think twice about shunning our services.'

'We've been lucky with Conran sourcing us that ale.'

'The good fortune goes back to when he handed me his token in the Green Man in April.'

CHAPTER NINETEEN

Becky was carrying a small basket full of kindling and Dolly was behind the bar when a woman came in holding a blue-and-white bowl.

'Can I help you?' asked Dolly.

'I'm looking for Becky,' said the woman.

'That's me,' said Becky turning to face her.

'You're the one that sees to Amy?'

'Amy Rooke? Yes. What is it?'

'I've a message.'

Becky put the basket down. She wanted to delay the moment, but how could she? There was only one reason a stranger would come to her with a message about Amy, holding the blue-and-white bowl Rory had said he was going to fill with sea shells.

'How is she?' asked Becky.

'She passed o'er in the night.'

Tears pricked Becky's eyes. 'That can't be right. I saw

her yesterday. She was weak, sweaty and in some pain, but no worse than usual. I collected her laudanum for her.'

''Tis a terrible thing. I can hardly bear to tell.' Tears began rolling down the woman's face.

'What?' Dolly stilled in the act of taking the brandy off the shelf behind her.

'They think she killed herself.'

'They?'

'Those that found her. Her neighbours.' The woman pulled a crumpled handkerchief from her jacket pocket and blew her nose.

'How did she die?' asked Dolly.

'She drank the laudanum. Must have been in a lot o' pain to do such a wicked thing.'

'Nay, she said she'd never do that, for fear of being barred from heaven. Maybe it was a mistake?' Thoughts flooded Becky's brain. *Was it the laudanum I collected? It must have been.*

'They're saying she'd a full bottle on the table last evening and when they found her this morning ''twas only above a quarter full.'

'Was there a note?'

'Only one inside this bowl, saying it was for you. Here you are.'

Becky took the bowl, saying, 'That's not the sort of note I meant.'

'No other note as I knows.'

'Well in that case, I think you should think twice before telling people it was a suicide, when you don't have proof. She could have been confused in the night and taken too much.' The woman was irritating her. Becky knew it wasn't her fault she'd to deliver bad news, but even so she didn't have to like her. 'Someone could have helped themselves to some of it.' Even as she said it, she knew that was unlikely. No one would steal laudanum from a dying woman. Not even the most feckless of souls. Becky thought back to the indecipherable look Amy had given her on the quay when she'd asked them again to look after Rory. Perhaps she'd decided all along what she was going to do before Rory returned, despite having said she would never do such a thing.

Dolly poured generous measures of brandy into three glasses and handed one to the woman who, after the shortest of hesitations, put her hand out saying, 'I don't usually partake o' liquor, but seeing as how 'tis for a sudden death, I will just this once.' She hesitated again. 'Although I'm more partial to rum and I likes a bit o' watter in it.'

Dolly said nothing, merely took back the brandy and poured out a rum, putting it next to the woman and setting a water jug beside it. Then she asked, 'Where's Amy now?'

'They've taken her away. Said it wasn't right for a suicide – I mean maybe suicide – to be laid out for folk to come and gawp.'

'Where to?'

'The workhouse mortuary. That's where the last suicide from New Houses went.' Seeing the look on Becky's face, the woman corrected herself again. 'I mean, that's where they take most people from New Houses who die and can't pay.' She drained her glass in one go and looked pointedly at the rum bottle still on the bar.

Dolly ignored the signal. 'Becky, sit down love, bring a seat near the fire. You're white as a sheet.'

Becky did as her mother bade her and sat unmoving, staring into the fire. With so many thoughts scrambling her brain she barely registered it when the woman left and her mother came to her.

'I've asked one of the men to tend the bar for half an hour. Don't fret, lass, it's not your fault and we can't be sure it wasn't an accident. Like you say, she could easily have woken up drowsy and just put the bottle to her lips.'

'Amy was clearly thinking of her death when she was on the quay. It can only be a matter of a few days now until they're back. Although perhaps she looked in the mirror and didn't want Rory to see her looking so poorly. Then again, if she'd wanted to kill herself, why didn't she drink it all? Finish the bottle off?'

'I think I can answer that. If you drink too much it makes you sick.'

'Do you think she'd know that?'

'I think most people are aware of that. You can never be sure what folks are thinking. If I'm honest, my guess is she knew she'd deteriorated. Rory's coming home and, with her way of thinking, it would be better for him if she was gone. You may've thought she didn't look that bad, but I'll wager she looks a lot worse than when Rory last saw her. You've seen her nearly every day, grown used to what she looks like. For Rory it would be frightening for him to see her so ill. She's always said she didn't want him there at the end.'

'Well, she's got her wish all right,' said Becky, suddenly angry with Amy for not waiting until Rory returned. 'Who will tell him? He'll get off that ship looking for her and she won't be there. And it's likely my fault.'

'Stop that. Amy could have sent anyone to collect that laudanum.'

'But she asked me because she said the pharmacist knew me. What difference that made I've no idea. That's just what she said and I was even glad to go.'

'You went because you were helping a dying woman. There's nowt wrong with that, lass.'

'I thought I was helping her to live, not giving her the means to kill herself. We talked about Rory and whether he'd grown much while he'd been away, and how Charlie certainly would've done even if *he* hadn't. I even said, "He'll be home soon.".' Becky's hands shot up to cover her mouth, as if she wished to retract her long-spoken words. 'Do you think that's why she did it? Because I reminded her he'd be home soon?'

'Don't,' said Dolly, in a voice verging on sharp. 'There's nothing you can do now, and we can't be sure it wasn't a tragic accident. If it wasn't, then she wanted to die, and if it hadn't been laudanum, it would have been something else, probably more painful and uglier. If I were a harsh woman, I'd tell you to stop wallowing in self-pity over what's been done.'

Becky burst into tears, unable to speak.

'Now, now lass,' Dolly went on. 'It's a tragedy, but it's what she wished for. There's no reason anyone need hint her death wasn't the Lord's will.'

'We must go to the funeral. Pay our respects.'

Dolly clicked her front tooth with her forefinger. 'We must act fast.'

'Why?'

'If no one steps forward she'll get a pauper's burial, and we can't have Rory come home to one of those.'

'You mean an unmarked grave.'

'I mean in the pauper's grave section of the cemetery.'

The cheap four-foots. Becky remembered when Da had died, they'd paid the extra one and six and laid him in a seven-foot grave. 'Shall I go and see if she's at the workhouse?'

'I'll go, it's no job for a young girl.'

'No, let *me* go. I owe her that and besides, we'll be busy soon. You're needed here.'

'It won't be an easy task. Are you sure?'

'Aye, I'm sure.'

'All right. I'll give you a clean sheet, and take a hairbrush. I'll give you five shillings for initial expenses.'

'What do I want those for?'

'We want her looking nice.'

'Have you done this before?'

'We had a girl rent a room once, several years ago. Afterwards we found out she was expecting a bairn and the father was already married. She tried it twice. That's how I know a full bottle of laudanum makes you sick. Foolishly, the doctor told her she'd made a mistake, so the second time she only drank half the bottle.' Dolly put the brandy and rum bottles back on the shelf. 'Now, if you're going, 'appen best be gone.'

❖ ❖ ❖

At the workhouse, Becky was directed to a lean-to with a tin roof at the back of the main building. The under-matron introduced herself as Cissie. She was a thin, middle-aged woman, with a large mole on her right cheek, untidy hair and black, bird-like eyes. She took a few minutes to find the right key for the padlock.

'She's the only one we've got at the moment. Last week we'd three. With almost 500 inmates we usually have one or two a week, sometimes more. A couple of weeks ago we'd one from a ship, which was unusual.'

There being no windows, Cissie lit a lamp. Becky braced herself, unsure what she would see. Of the several tables, one held a bundle covered in rough jute sacking.

'That's her,' said Cissie. 'Came in this morning. Are you claiming her?'

Becky nodded; she was too nervous to speak. *Maybe Mam should have come, after all.*

'You'd better check it's who you think it is. Don't worry, she's been washed and cleaned up. She'll not jump up and bite you.'

Becky shuddered at the macabre humour.

They walked to the table and Cissie took hold of the cover. 'Are you all right? You look a bit funny.'

'I'm all right.' *I have to do this. I'm doing it for Amy and for Rory.*

Cissie rolled the cover back and Becky saw it was Amy – Amy with a grey face and blue lips and nails; yet it wasn't her, it was just her shell. Although sad tears were rolling down Becky's face, she felt relief inside. Amy was at rest and not in pain.

Cissie replaced the jute cover and Becky opened her bag to take out the sheet and the hairbrush.

'You're going to smarten her up, are you? That's neighbourly.'

Becky nodded. 'Aye, it's Amy Rooke and I claim her. What happens now?'

'I send one of the boys to the undertaker to ask him to collect her. Any particular one you want?'

Becky had never needed an undertaker before; her mother had seen to everything when Da died.

'Where do you live?'

'The Indian King.'

'There's that one top end of Roper Street. He'll do a good job and it won't be far to go if you want to view her laid out.'

Becky nodded. 'Thank you.'

'We mustn't be forgetting our storage and body-washing fee. Can you pay that now?'

'How much is it?'

'Three shillings for the one day and you have to sign the book.' She pointed to a tatty ledger on a stool by the door. 'We don't keep them longer than two days. Just time enough to be claimed. Do you want to sit with her while I send a boy?' She pointed to a long bench partly in shadow.

'Yes, I'll wait.' Becky handed over the three shillings and signed her name in the column next to where someone had written 'Amy Rook'. Without saying anything she added an 'e' to make it 'Rooke'.

Cissie wrote out a black-edged receipt and handed it to her. 'It could be an hour or more before the undertaker comes. You'll be all right, will you?'

'Thank you.' *I can't leave her here in this dreadful place alone.* When Cissie had gone, Becky removed the tatty jute cover, put it on one of the other tables, and replaced it with the clean sheet. After pulling on the sides of the sheet to smooth it down she brushed Amy's hair then sat listening to the everyday sounds of the workhouse. Cissie had closed the door when she left, but Becky found the atmosphere so suffocating she'd opened it. Bells rang, footsteps scurried by and hushed voices filtered in.

When the undertaker arrived with his assistant, Becky was relieved to see he was a regular in the Indian King. She'd always thought he was a carpenter. He greeted her with a smile.

'Sorry to see you here, Miss Becky.' He looked across at the table. 'That's not a workhouse sheet.'

'I brought it with me.'

'Are you taking it now, or shall I drop it off next time I'm round?'

'You can keep it,' she said.

'Shall I use it as a shroud and bury her in it?'

'What do you usually use?'

'Sunday best, nightdress, favourite dress, wedding dress, that sort of thing.'

Becky didn't think Amy had any of those things. Earlier she'd noticed her nightdress and shawl thrown over one of the vacant tables. There was no sign of her clogs; they were probably still by her bed or by now adorning someone else's feet. They'd stripped her to wash her. Better to leave the sad trappings of her life behind.

'Keep the sheet as her shroud.' She thought that would

be what Amy would have wanted, but she picked up the shawl. She'd wash it and keep it for Rory.

She waited until Amy's body had been safely transferred to the undertaker's cart before making her way home. She felt older than when she'd woken that morning. She wondered if she would ever be able to smell medicated soap again without thinking of Amy, and what she was going to say to Rory.

CHAPTER TWENTY

At three in the morning, Fergus was roused by Bill and Sven.

'We've a problem,' said Bill.

'Something wrong with the ship?'

'No, it's the cargo,' said Sven. 'We're carrying whiskey.'

'Whiskey?' Fergus threw back his cot covers, swung his legs round and placed his feet flat on the floor. His heart was sinking fast, and a vision of them all lined up in the dock before the justices at Carlisle Assizes flashed through his brain.

'Definitely whiskey,' Bill confirmed. 'It's likely all the barrels are full of it.'

'Contraband?' Fergus felt his stomach lurch.

'I'm afraid so.'

'I got a faint whiff of whiskey when I was checking the hold half an hour ago,' said Sven. 'I reported it to the captain and asked if we should tap a cask.'

Bill nodded. 'We've just seen to it and he's right, there's whiskey in the cask.'

Fergus looked up at Sven. 'Fetch Conran, we'll see him in the saloon.' After Sven had left, he said, 'This could be our undoing.'

'Let's hear what Conran has to say for himself.'

Fergus stood up and pulled on his jacket. 'I've been an idiot. Conran successfully diverted my attention to the new cloth. The ale was just a sideshow. He knew we were desperate. I'm sorry, Bill, I really am, that I've got you into this mess.'

'We're both to blame. I should have tapped one of the barrels before we took it on. Since I could smell ale I didn't check. Like you, my focus was on the cloth, seeing it was well-wrapped and securely stored.'

'What now?'

'We're in the middle of the Irish Sea. If every barrel really is whiskey, then apart from throwing it all overboard, which we can't as we need it for ballast, I'm not sure what we can do. Let me think on it.'

In the saloon Conran appeared, bleary-eyed and looking grumpy. It was all Fergus could do to hold back from landing a strong punch on the Irishman's jaw.

'Is there whiskey in all those casks?' he asked.

'What whiskey?' Conran rubbed his eyes.

'The whiskey in our hold. That whiskey.'

'What?' Conran turned pale and put a hand out to the table to steady himself. 'Whiskey? I could smell the ale when we were loading the silk mix.'

'They'll have sprayed the casks with ale after they were sealed,' said Sven. 'And now it's started to wear off.'

Conran looked so surprised that Fergus began to doubt any involvement in the substitution. He'd turned a very peculiar colour, not something that could be faked, unless it was because he'd been found out.

'I swear on my mother's life, as the son of my father, as a true Catholic,' he crossed himself, 'believing in God the Father, the Son and the Holy Ghost, I'd no hand in this. None whatsoever.' He put his hand up to his throat. 'I'm sorry. I'll have to sit down. I can taste bile.'

Fergus guided him to a chair.

'Let's assume all the barrels are whiskey,' said Bill. 'It's my responsibility, but we can work together on the solution. The position is we're carrying contraband, and what's worse, it's probably not even branded whiskey.'

'Poteen,' said Conran. 'It comes in from the countryside stills.'

'Aye,' said Bill. 'It's all about lowering the tariff. For ale it's fourpence per 100 gallons, while on whiskey it's a shilling.'

Fergus was beginning to feel a bit sick himself. Talking about the whiskey seemed to be sensitising his response to the ship's pitching.

'Everyone thinks it gets dropped off in caves along the coast,' Bill went on. 'But every now and then they'll try and run one in for ease of unloading. It takes nerve coming in right under the noses of the Excise men. They try it because no one thinks they'll be stupid or brave enough to attempt it. I never thought they'd have tried it with *me*.'

'I can't believe it,' said Conran. 'I used a small supplier so the shipment wouldn't attract attention, being as how your father's put the fear of God into everyone. I thought word might get out, and then they'd maybe try and undercut the order. I did it to avoid trouble.'

'Well, we are where we are,' said Fergus, looking at Bill.

'We've two options – three if we consider pouring it all overboard, but we've already decided we can't do that on safety grounds.'

'What are the other two?'

'We can declare it, or not declare it.'

'Can't we change the manifest?' asked Sven.

'You mean declare it?' said Conran.

'Yes, write out a new one changing the ale to whiskey.'

'No,' said Fergus. 'We left Dublin with ale so we must arrive in Whitehaven with ale. I've spent enough time going over manifests to know Customs and Excise do random checks. If we do that and are found out, even if it's months later, the penalty is most definitely jail for falsifying documents.'

'Even though we're telling them what's really in the hold?' asked Sven.

'Yes.'

'If we declare it and we're fortunate, and they believe we were duped, the Excise men have the power to seize the contents of the hold. Potentially everything, which includes your exotic silk mix, Conran. The whiskey will definitely be poured away, and the silk mix probably sold for next to nothing at a dockside auction.'

'He's right, said Conran. 'Now, do you believe me? Do you really think I'd deliberately carry contraband, when my new silk mix could run the risk of being seized? Is it any wonder I'm fretting so much at the prospect of losing my precious cloth?'

Fergus placed a hand on Conran's arm. 'I believe you for that reason, and you may yet have that high price to pay.'

Bill drummed his fingers on the table. 'However – and it's something I'm hopeful about – if we can convince them we've been duped, they may just seize the whiskey. That will be the best outcome we can hope for, since we were paid in advance to carry the ale.'

Fergus had shrugged off the sluggishness he'd been feeling from being woken mid-sleep, and was now fully alert. 'That doesn't take into account our reputation, though, does it? Word will get around that on my first trip I carried contraband. My trustworthiness and business acumen will be questioned. I may be regarded as innocent of any intentional misdemeanour, but mud sticks. Who will want to use us as carriers when they run the risk of having their goods seized or delayed?'

'I think you could be wrong about that,' said Sven, 'It could work in your favour, indicating you are trustworthy, honest and reliable, and those qualities are of no use to smugglers.'

At that moment Fergus was thinking, *it would have been better if you'd not tapped the barrel, Sven, and we were all in the dark, and the ale was collected with no one the wiser.* Although, when he gave it serious thought, he guessed at some stage someone would find it too good a story not to share that whiskey had been carried in right under Shackleton's nose on his first trip. *The truth will out. Best I release it myself.*

Before Sven and Conran left, Bill said, 'I won't alert the rest of the crew before we dock.'

'I agree. We've all learnt a valuable lesson this evening. Now away and sleep.'

'Sleep?' Bill sighed. 'Just when we thought everything was going right and it's all going wrong?'

CHAPTER TWENTY-ONE

When Mary burst through the door, Becky was down on her knees by the hearth lighting the fire, an untidy pile of logs and crumpled newspaper by her side.

'They're back. I've seen her. The *Eleanor Bell*. Come on, she's closing in.'

Becky looked across at her mother, busy as usual behind the bar. 'Can I go?'

'Aye, I'll send for one of the part-timers. You lasses get yourselves off. Go welcome your menfolk.'

Pausing only to pick up her bag, Becky made for the door. Sergeant Adams, in his usual place, with Molly asleep on his knee, shouted out, 'You'd best not go out without wrapping up, miss. It'll be awful cold down there on the quay.'

Becky laughed. 'I've two mothers now, have I?'

'He's right,' said Mary. 'Fetch your shawl and bonnet. The wind's up and it'll be worse yonder end of the quay.'

The speed at which they sprinted down to the harbour robbed them both of the breath needed for speech. When they arrived, Becky became more and more excited as the ship neared the quay.

'How do I look?' she asked Mary.

'Happy and pretty. How do *I* look?'

'The same.'

'You're happy to see Fergus, I can tell that, but for a minute you looked a bit anxious,' said Mary, her eyes straight ahead, firmly fixed on the incoming ship which was now almost at the quay.

'I've to collect Rory.'

'And tell him about his mam?'

'I'd like to do it somewhere quiet, but he'll be expecting her to be here. My guess is I'll have to tell him right away.'

'Somewhere quiet would be best, although he's bound to wonder why she's not on the quay.'

When the ship's ropes had been secured, Becky saw Sven and waved to him. Her eyes moved to Bill, overseeing operations, and then she saw Fergus on deck. Her heart lit up. She waved furiously to attract his attention. He saw her, but only nodded. Disappointment washed over her. *Is he not pleased to see me?* She'd expected a more welcoming reunion – a big smile, a wave and a shout. Then, as he came more clearly into view, she saw he looked tense. She put it down to the technical operations being carried out around him. Turning her attention to the *Eleanor Bell's* figurehead, she noticed the red paint on her lips seemed less bright, and you could see where the sea water had risen up and the salt had dried, leaving wavy lines and white specks. Otherwise, she looked more or less to Becky's eye as she had done when she departed. *A good omen,* she thought. Then she saw Fergus walking towards the gangway, holding some papers. He looked stiff. Something was wrong.

As he walked to the gangway, with legs like blocks of wood, Fergus's eyes were on the quay, but his thoughts were elsewhere. *Am I doing the right thing putting my reputation at risk? Would it have been better to have turned a blind eye and learned from it?*

The Excise Officer was waiting on the quay to interview him. Almost at the gangway, an excited Rory was looking out over the harbour, a drawstring bag in one hand, the dog basket in the other, and Charlie by his side. Fergus followed Rory's gaze. The Excise man flew from his mind when he realised there was no Amy. Then it hit him: Amy was either dead or seriously ill. He looked back at Rory and instead of the cheerful, happy-go-lucky lad he'd grown so fond of, he now saw an orphan – a boy about to be cast adrift in the world with only his dog for comfort. It didn't take a second for Fergus to make up his mind he was doing the right thing declaring the whiskey. He'd hardly be able to look after Rory if he was in Carlisle jail, but not only that, he was setting a good example for the boy to follow.

Halfway down the gangway, Fergus turned and shouted back to Sven, 'Lockdown the ship.'

The crew stopped what they were doing and watched

in disbelief as Sven sealed the gangway at the top. Fergus's mouth went dry as the Excise Officer walked forward to greet him.

'Good morning,' Fergus said.

The Excise Officer accepted Fergus's hand and introduced himself as Mr Roberts. 'You're in lockdown. Trouble?'

'I'm afraid so.' Fergus explained the situation and handed over the manifest. 'You'll need to inspect the hold.'

'You came straight in from Dublin?'

'Yes, and before that Cardiff.' Fergus's lips were moving and words were coming out of his mouth, but his brain was in turmoil. He finished speaking and, with his mouth clamped tight, took a deep breath though his nose. Every bad smell he'd ever associated with the quay rushed in: dead fish, rotting rubbish, the lichen on the stones, the stale brine in the puddles. His anxiety was heightening his senses by the minute, and not in a good way.

'Liquor and textiles. That's a strange mix,' said Roberts, reading from the manifest.

'It's a new silk-and-wool mix, a special colour.' Taking another deep breath, Fergus said, 'Would you like to see it?'

He managed to deliver a wide smile, although his lips were trembling, and his toes curling in his boots. There was now also a bad taste in the back of his throat, making him nauseous. He knew that soon his palms would begin to itch. If it wasn't all finished in the next few minutes, he might be sick right there on the quay. He took a breath, this time through his mouth. 'I appreciate you have to seize the whiskey, but must you seize the silk mix as well?

That's all laid out correctly in the manifest. There has been no deliberate intention to deceive.'

'As a Shackleton I know your papers will be in order and I accept your explanation about the ale. You're your father's son, after all, even if you've fallen out with him, and you'd hardly have attempted to smuggle on your first voyage. You're no fool. Yes, I would like to see the silk mix, then I'll have to check with my senior about what will be seized. He's new, just transferred from Lancaster, so I can't speak for him.'

Fergus was surprised at the reference to his falling out with his father, then remembered what Mr Needham had said about their business being everyone else's business. He led the way up the gangway onto the deck, where he asked Sven to fetch Conran and also a bale of silk mix.

While they were waiting, Rory came up and tugged on Fergus's jacket. 'Excuse me, Mr Shackleton, when can we leave the ship?'

'We're waiting for this man to finish his inspection.'

Rory looked from Fergus to Roberts and back again. 'Will he be long?'

'Enjoyed your time at sea, have you?' Roberts asked him. 'You're a young'un.'

'Yes, sir, it was a grand trip. I'm the apprentice cook. Charlie and me just wants to get home.' He pointed to the dog.

Roberts appeared to consider something. Then he said to Fergus, 'I see no reason to keep the lad on board. He doesn't look much like a smuggler to me.'

'I can go?'

231

Fergus nodded and watched as Rory set off down the gangway, with Charlie running along beside him.

✽ ✽ ✽

Rory stepped onto the quay and looked around, then made his way to Becky and Mary, picking his way carefully over the uneven surface. Charlie ran around in circles at his side, matching his pace, while investigating all the fresh scents.

'Do you think his walking's any better?' asked Mary as they watched him.

'Aye, he's still slow, but those stones are difficult enough for anybody, never mind a lad with a gammy leg who's been at sea all these weeks.'

They moved forward to meet him, and when they both put their arms around him, he almost disappeared in the fullness of their skirts.

He came up for air, saying, 'Miss Becky, Mrs Mary, we're home.'

'And you've had a good voyage?' asked Mary.

'Aye, it was grand. I wasn't seasick at all – well, only about six times – and Charlie chased Caesar all over the place. He got lots of extra exercise.'

Mary laughed. 'Caesar?'

'The biggest ginger tomcat you've ever seen. And I learnt how to make pea soup and sultana duff and lots of other stuff.'

'Charlie's grown,' said Mary. 'He's no longer a tiny pup.'

'Do you think Mammy'll think *I've* grown?' He looked from Becky to Mary, waiting for an answer, then held up the bag he was carrying. 'I've an Irish linen handkerchief for her with an "A" on it. Mr Shackleton bought it for me in Dublin with some of my wages. An advancement, he said. Where is she? Is she better?'

'That's a lovely present,' said Becky.

'But do you think Mammy'll like it?'

Becky couldn't help it. The tears she'd been holding back since she'd seen Rory walking towards them spilled out and ran down her cheeks. She bent down, enclosed him in her arms and hugged him again. She could see over his shoulder how Mary's eyes were also full of tears.

Rory pulled himself free. 'Why are you both crying? Has Mr Shackleton told you I said that bad word?'

'No, Rory, he hasn't. We're crying because we have sad news.' Becky paused, expecting Rory to say something, but he just stood there looking at her, waiting. She bent down so her face was level with his, took his hands in hers and looked into his eyes. 'Rory, your mammy was sicker than we thought and she'd be here if she could be and –'

Rory cut in. 'Where is she?' He began looking round again, distress registering in his eyes.

'She's with the angels now, Rory,' Becky said.

The boy stared at her. 'Which angels?'

'The angels in heaven.'

'You mean God's taken her, like Nanna when I was a bairn?'

'Yes.' Becky nodded.

Rory pulled his hands free from her grasp. He looked up at them both then, putting his fists to his eyes, began crying, his shoulders moving up and down as he sobbed.

He shunned the women's attempts to comfort him, put his head back and let out a heartbreaking wail, before falling to his knees and curling himself up on the uneven quay stones in a tight ball, like a baby.

Fergus and Mr Roberts turned to look in the direction of the noise. They were both used to the everyday sounds of the quay, but this was the sound of raw grief. In any language it indicated severe distress. Rory was curled up on the stones, beating the quay with his fists, his bad leg twitching against his good one, and Becky and Mary were standing over him, trying to pick him up. He was resisting, almost fighting them off, and all the while the dreadful noise was continuing.

'What's wrong?' asked Mr Roberts, concerned.

'His mother was seriously ill when we left, and I would hazard a guess, since I know him to be not of a nervous disposition, that she must have passed away. She was his only family.'

'Who's that with him?'

'Our captain's wife and my friend.'

Charlie began whimpering in sympathy with Rory's sobs, then barking loudly, and the noise reached an almost unbearable level until, as suddenly as it had begun, Charlie licked Rory's face and it stopped. Boy and dog appeared exhausted by their joint effort. The sudden silence seemed almost as unbearable to Fergus as the wailing had been.

Conran appeared with two crewmen, who came down the gangway carrying one of the textile bales. He boomed out a greeting in joyful tones. 'Good day to you, Mr Excise Officer.' He was all smiles. 'Sure, you must see this. It's brand new to the market, a blessed miracle for the eyes and the haberdashers.'

Instructing the two men to drop the bale, Conran pulled a knife with a short-serrated blade from his pocket and began opening it, all the while explaining how he had sourced the dye, the dyeing process they had tested and refined, and then, in a grand theatrical gesture, peeling back the last covering to reveal his treasure. For Fergus everything seemed to be happening very slowly, as if time had slowed itself down in a bid to extend his anxiety.

Roberts showed interest. 'That *is* bright. And you say it doesn't fade?'

'No, and it can be washed and hardly creases. I tell you, as God and the Virgin Mary are my witnesses, soon every well-dressed woman from Carlisle to Lancaster will be wearing dresses and shawls in this glorious shade.'

Roberts looked at his watch again, then returned to the manifest. 'The number of bales you have here, you're probably right. Very interesting, thank you for showing me. I always like to know what's coming in and out.'

If I try and speak, I will choke, thought Fergus. Conran began repacking the cloth while Mr Roberts looked across at Rory, who was now on his knees holding onto Charlie as if he were the only thing in the world.

'Poor lad. An orphan, you say?

'Yes,' said Fergus, 'so it would seem. But he's a good worker; he'll be well cared for.'

Mr Roberts took his leave, saying, 'I'll be back when I've spoken to the new boss.'

Half an hour passed before he returned. It seemed more like an hour to Fergus as he paced up and down on the deck. He tried to interpret the senior officer's decision by the look on Roberts' face as he approached, but he was giving nothing away.

'We're seizing everything in the hold and there's to be a fine to pay for not having the correct items on the manifest. The new boss wants to see you to give you a talking to.'

It was as Fergus had feared, but perhaps paying the full penalty would work towards keeping his reputation intact. He didn't mind being regarded as foolish and inexperienced, as long as he was seen as honest. 'Thank you. Will he see me now?'

'No. You'll have to make an appointment. We've two ships in from the Orient and their holds are of greater interest than yours, so he's going to be tied up. So busy, in fact, I'd say he's made a convenient snap decision regarding your situation.'

Fergus couldn't bring himself to reply. He was thinking of Conran's loss.

Mr Roberts began walking away. Then he stopped and turned back. 'You do know you can appeal, don't you?'

Fergus nodded and thanked him. He sought out Conran, who was standing watching from the ship's railings, and shook his head. Conran's shoulders drooped. Fergus would speak to him later; the ship was still in lockdown, he wouldn't be going anywhere. He walked over to Rory, who was still clutching Charlie. His cheeks were stained with tears, but he was quiet.

'Mammy's with God's angels,' Rory told him. 'She won't get her hanky with the "A" on it you bought in Dublin.' He began sobbing again, then sniffed and looked up. 'Mr Shackleton, is there anyone to love me now?'

Seeing the despair and loss written all over the boy's face, Fergus felt a sudden new tightness in his throat. It was just all too awful. With the customs threat, and now this, he was having a hard time holding back tears of his own, but he didn't think it appropriate for Rory to see him cry when he was going to be depending on him for support.

'Oh yes, Rory. There's Miss Becky, Mrs Dolly and me, and lots of other people who love you. This is where you have to be brave. I know you can be. Your mother would want it, because she wouldn't want you to be sad.'

Rory appeared to take comfort from Fergus's presence and, releasing his hold on Charlie, allowed himself to be lifted upright.

'I have important business to see to,' Fergus told him. 'But Miss Becky will look after you and I will see you later.'

'We're going home,' said Becky. 'I've told him he's to live with us from now on.'

Fergus nodded. 'I'll call this evening.'

'I'll wait for Bill,' said Mary.

'He's overseeing the cargo.' Fergus had almost said whiskey.

✳ ✳ ✳

Becky tucked Rory up in bed and sat with him until he fell asleep. She put the blue-and-white bowl on a small table underneath the window and let Charlie stay in the room. When she went downstairs, Fergus was sitting at the kitchen table. He told her about the ale being whiskey and briefly referred to 'some fabric of Conran's'.

'You did the right thing. Can you imagine what the town's licensees would have thought when they heard you'd brought in whiskey? You're right, someone would have blabbed. Can they follow it up in Dublin?'

'Conran says he'll report it, but once they hear the whiskey didn't get through, the suppliers will have shut up shop and dispersed into the countryside.'

'You won't do business with Conran again, will you?'

'The businessman in me thinks he could be useful in the future. I've not ruled him out. We've the appeal to lodge for the fabric. He's hopeful, but I'm not sure. Anyway, he's staying in town and we're having a meeting.'

Becky was surprised. It seemed to her Conran had let them down, even if he hadn't meant to. *Fergus is only thinking from the business side, but Conran sounds like he mixes with untrustworthy people.*

Opening a leather bag from the table, Fergus took out a parcel. 'This is for you.'

'For me? What is it?'

'Open it.'

She fetched some scissors. 'Is there really something inside these wrappings?'

'I hope so,' he said.

When the last layer came away and the cloth was revealed, Becky drew in a deep breath. 'This is beautiful. Did you buy it in Dublin? I've never seen a colour like it.' She ran her hand over the material then looked up at him.

'This is the fabric they've confiscated.' He told her about Briony and her unlit clay pipe, and how she'd provided them with the two dress lengths and the shawl in return for the baccy and liquor. 'There being three small separate parcels, we didn't put them in the hold, and I regard these as personal purchases made in Dublin, not imports, so outside of seizure. There should be enough for you to make a dress if you want to.'

Becky held up the panel and turned it. It caught the light from the fire and the sheen changed. 'See how it shimmers. It must be silk.'

Fergus nodded. 'It's Chinese silk and Irish wool.'

She held the material up against herself, all smiles, then put it down and took a step towards him. He placed his hand under her chin, lifted it gently and kissed her.

'Thank you,' she said. 'Thank you a thousand times. It's so pretty. I've never worked with any material like this before. It's exciting.'

After they'd kissed, Becky said, 'I must check on Rory. He went to sleep almost straightaway.' She was gone a few minutes. 'He's still settled. I think he understands this is now his home.'

'Mary told me the circumstances of Amy's passing and the sadness of her funeral.' Fergus folded Becky in his arms again and held her close, breathing in her now familiar scent. The light in the room was dim and the fire's flames cast a golden sheen that flickered across his face. Becky looked up. She could see he was exhausted and ought to go home, but before then she needed reassurance. She indicated to Fergus to sit.

'I just need to say if I hadn't collected the laudanum someone else would've done, but I can't help feeling I played a part in Amy's passing.'

'Amy asked you because you've always supported her so well. You mustn't blame yourself.'

'She thought the accident Rory had with the carter's barrel had turned out to be fortunate in a way, as it saved him from the pit. She thought your paths crossing changed the direction of his life for a better one, despite his injury, and I think she was right.'

'And Dolly? She's happy to take him in?'

'She's being practical about it and saying he can do jobs for us when he's not at sea, but she cares for him as much as we all do.'

'He's a good worker, despite his leg, and he's very good with figures.'

'He asked me this evening if he was to be sent to the workhouse and would they take Charlie from him. Of course I said he need have no fear of that, that Mam and I would see he never got sent there.'

'I will cover his board and lodging.'

'That's very generous of you, but really, we can afford to keep him. As I said, Mam'll make sure he earns his keep. We'll not ruin him with spoiling.'

'I can pay him wages on land, make it so he doesn't realise I'm keeping him,' Fergus insisted. 'That way he can pay his own board and lodging. What about the funeral costs?'

'We were going to cover them all, but there was a small collection up at New Houses. Those folk up there haven't much, so it was generous of them. There were about twenty people gathered at the funeral. In the end, the authorities decided she'd made a mistake and didn't mean to take her own life. Still, folk whisper amongst themselves. But the main thing is Rory has somewhere nice to go and visit his mam. I mean no cemetery is a place you want to spend time in, but there'll be a small headstone and we can plant some flowers. It won't just be a wooden cross that rots and keels over, come the first hard winter. He can take his handkerchief when he goes and I've given him her shawl. I'm sure that'll be a comfort to him in some small way. If only we could help every pit boy and take them all in.'

'We can't and we mustn't try. Like Amy, I've felt our paths crossing that day when the barrel ran over him was more than just a casual chance. He's been a big part of bringing us together too, in looking out for him.'

'Aye, he has and I thank him for it.'

After Fergus had left, Becky, feeling happy and content, went upstairs to check on Rory again. Both he and Charlie were fast asleep. Rory's right hand was resting on Charlie's head and in his other he was holding a corner of Amy's shawl. 'You're a good lad, Rory,' she said softly so as not to wake him. Charlie's ear shot up at the sound of her voice, then just as quickly relaxed.

I wonder what the future holds for us all?

* * *

Later, when Fergus looked back on the evening, he thought of how Becky had held the cloth up against her body. The colour was perfect for her. He couldn't help but register the outline of her breasts pressing against it. Embarrassed at looking at them so directly and possibly seeming to be scrutinising them, he'd looked away, but not before he'd felt a surge of excitement ripple through his body. When he pulled her towards him and kissed her, he'd been so conscious of her body pressing against him. Feelings of love, mingled with heady relief from the anxiety he'd felt earlier in the day, along with respect for her, had combined to bring stirrings within him that he had to fight hard to control.

The Seamen's Haven was quiet when Fergus called with the parcel for Aunt Louisa, most of the men being at the cattle fair. He didn't want to leave the present at Queen Street, even though it was so near, since he ran the risk of running into his father. He'd caught sight of him on the other side of the street the day after they'd returned from Dublin. He was sure his father had seen him, but he gave no indication of having done so. After that chance meeting, feelings of regret and anger combined to disrupt his thoughts, but with business to attend to, he managed to set them aside.

Inside the Seamen's Haven he found the director in his office.

'I'm afraid you've just missed Miss Shackleton, she's been sorting the library books.'

Fergus handed over the parcel he was holding. 'May I leave this for her collection?'

'Certainly. And may I say who's left it?'

'Fergus.'

'Do you have a surname, sir? She may know several by that name.'

'Shackleton,' said Fergus. 'I'm her nephew.'

'Ah, Hector's son?'

'Yes,' he replied sharply. *When will I no longer be my father's son? I'm a Shackleton in my own right, not son of Hector. Will I ever shake off my father's yoke?*

CHAPTER TWENTY-TWO

It was the 12th of October, Becky's nineteenth birthday, and Fergus, all smiles, arrived in plenty of time with the necklace. He waited in the kitchen for her to come down. He was excited at the prospect of finally seeing her wear it. It was coming up four months since his Edinburgh visit in mid-June. A great deal had happened in that time. Becky had been right; he had tried to give it to her too soon. Now, as the closeness of their relationship was blossoming more each day, her birthday was just the right time.

'Keep still,' he said, as he wrestled with the fiddly clasp. 'You're bobbing about like a cork in a pond. This is tricky.'

'I'll stand you a reward when you've done it,' she said, laughing.

'If it's not a kiss then I'm not interested.'

'It might be.' She turned round when she felt the clasp click.

'It looks magnificent,' said Fergus. 'Perfect for you.'

Becky checked herself in the kitchen mirror, putting up her hand to caress the pearl. 'Thank you. Thank you very much. I shall treasure it always.'

'You've forgotten something,' said Fergus, taking a step towards her.

'Your reward?'

'It's a birthday kiss.'

'Aren't you supposed to kiss *me* on my birthday?'

He gave her a teasing smile and took another step. 'Well, as it really *is* your birthday, I think I should kiss you for your birthday and then you can kiss me back for fastening your necklace.'

'But, that's two kisses. That's cheating.'

'I know,' he said. 'I'm no fool.'

He took her in his arms and when their lips met a surge of delight rippled through his senses. His arms took her weight and he felt, touched, smelt, tasted and saw her within one heightened sensual wave. He loved her with a passion that was almost indecent. They separated and looked deep into each other's eyes, then came together again. They were so absorbed in each other and their second kiss that neither noticed the hall door open and Rory's head appear round it. When he saw what they were doing he grimaced before stepping back and pulling the door to.

Later, in the bar, Becky showed her mother the necklace.

Dolly put her hand out to touch the pearl. 'That's a beauty,' she said.

'A beauty for a beautiful girl,' said Fergus.

'It came from Edinburgh,' said Becky.

'A Scottish beauty for an English one,' said Dolly.

Knowing it was Becky's birthday, the regulars came over to congratulate her, raising their glasses and wishing her well.

She's radiant, thought Fergus, *and she's mine.* He couldn't remember ever having been so happy.

An hour later, Fergus looked across the room and saw Bill standing at the door. His face, normally animated and cheery, was sombre, and as soon as Fergus saw him he knew something bad had happened. His first thought was of the contraband whiskey, then of a problem with the *Eleanor Bell,* then perhaps something to do with the appeal. A formal meeting had been arranged for Monday, in two days' time. As Bill approached, all these thoughts flew around Fergus's brain.

'What's wrong?' he asked.

Bill shook his head. 'Not in here. Come outside.'

Placing his tankard down beside the ale muller, where he judged it to be reasonably well camouflaged, Fergus followed Bill through the door.

They were several paces away from the bustling pub when Bill stopped and put his hand on Fergus's arm. 'I've sad news.'

Fergus, who had felt merry and slightly tipsy until Bill appeared, was suddenly sober, with a dry mouth and an awareness of his heart beating in his chest. *Something dreadful has happened. I can see it in Bill's eyes.*

'What is it?' he asked.

'It's your Aunt Louisa. She's had an accident.'

Fergus's first reaction was relief that none of the

scenarios he had envisaged had come to pass. Then the continued sadness in Bill's eyes, and the way he was looking at him, as if he had more to say but didn't want to say it, moved him on to other possibilities. 'What kind of accident?'

'She's fallen down the stairs. They think perhaps the heel of her shoe caught on a stair-rod and she lost her balance, then landed badly. I understand she took a nasty blow to the head, which took the full force of the final impact.' Bill put an arm on Fergus's shoulder. 'I'm really sorry.'

Fergus was hearing the words, but not absorbing them – partly because his thoughts had been so focused on the contraband whiskey and the ship, but mostly because he wanted there to be a mistake. '*My* Aunt Louisa? Are you sure? Is she going to be all right?'

'Yes, it's definitely her. Mr Craggs called and asked me to let you know tomorrow morning.'

'Was she alone? Have they fetched the doctor?'

'I don't know the exact details, but I understand Dr Lennagon's with her now.' Bill swallowed. Fergus could see his friend was nervous; it was always difficult for the bringer of bad news.

Bill continued, 'I know it's Becky's birthday, Mary told me, but I thought you would want to know immediately, rather than tomorrow, because news travels so quickly in this town. I didn't want you to hear about it casually as the latest town gossip, so I thought best to come and tell you straightaway.'

'You did right, thank you. I must go at once to Queen Street.'

'Normally I would say yes, go straightaway. However, there's nothing you can do this evening, and with the way things are within the family, perhaps it's best to wait until the morning. Go back inside and, even if it takes several brandies, be with Becky just as you would have been without this news.'

'What if Aunt Louisa doesn't survive the night?'

'I don't think things are that desperate, or Mr Craggs wouldn't have told me to wait until the morning to tell you. It's Becky's night, so go back in, tell her I wanted to discuss something about the ship that couldn't wait. You can put her right tomorrow. She'll understand. You have to do it or you'll spoil her evening, and I don't think your aunt would want that.'

Fergus drew in a deep breath then let it out slowly through rounded lips. 'You're sure I shouldn't be at home?'

'It's late; you run the risk of a confrontation when everyone's upset, and I don't think that will be useful tonight. Better first thing, when they'll have a firmer idea of her condition.'

'You're right. There's likely nothing I can do and I don't want to ruin Becky's birthday.'

Later, while walking back to his lodgings, Fergus thought back over the evening. It had been difficult after Bill left, but he'd managed it. In his room, though, he experienced an almost overwhelming wave of anxiety. It felt as if something was clutching his insides. He'd not lied in Dublin when he'd described Aunt Louisa as his favourite aunt. Had he had twenty aunts, she would still have been the best; he knew that, and he thought she knew it too.

They were alike in that neither of them had inherited the Shackleton temper, preferring to discuss and negotiate disagreement. They also shared the Shackleton height, the gold-flecked eyes and same sense of humour. He was glad his aunt was an ally in his and Becky's relationship.

The next morning, Saturday, Fergus was shocked to the core when an embarrassed-looking Samuel answered the door and said, 'I'm instructed to say Mr and Mrs Shackleton are not receiving any guests.'

'They will see *me*, surely, under the circumstances?'

Samuel looked down and to one side and then, in a quiet voice, said, 'I've been instructed no one is to enter the house.' He paused. 'Not even you, sir. You were mentioned specifically by name.'

'I see,' said Fergus, biting his lips. *Even in family troubles my father continues with his stupidity and stubbornness.* 'Thank you, Samuel. If you will allow me to pass, I will say I pushed past you and you were unable to stop me.'

Samuel nodded and stepped aside. As Fergus entered the hall, his father came out of the dining room. He frowned when he saw Fergus, then, in a sharp voice, with vestiges of cigar smoke on his breath, turned to Samuel. 'I gave instructions no one was to be admitted.'

Fergus spoke. 'Samuel tried to detain me, but I pushed right past him. How is Aunt Louisa?'

Hector looked away. 'She's comfortable,' he said.

Fergus knew his father well enough to suspect he was lying. 'I'd like to see her.'

'You can't. Dr Lennagon has prescribed total rest, which is why we're not receiving any visitors. Any visitors at all.'

'Well, what can you tell me?'

'She fell down the last few stairs.'

Fergus looked over at the bottom of the stairs, but there was nothing to see. 'I'd like to speak with Mother.'

'No, there's no need, Fergus. Everything is under control.' Hector addressed Samuel again. 'Kindly show Mr Shackleton out. He has his own home to go to.'

Fergus could see he was getting nowhere. The reference to 'his own home' was a remark typical of his father in a difficult mood. 'Father –' he began, but Hector, shoulders hunched, had turned on his heel and was retreating back into the dining room.

Samuel opened the front door. As Fergus passed through, he said softly, in a conspiratorial tone, 'Before you go, sir, if relations continue to be difficult and there is news, I will ensure it is passed on to you if you care to provide me with your current address.'

Fergus took a visiting card from his waistcoat pocket and handed it to him. 'Thank you. I will appreciate that and I respect your shared confidence.'

Samuel looked at the card. 'I heard you'd set up your own company, sir.' He dropped his voice even further. 'May I take the opportunity to wish you good luck with it?'

Samuel had never spoken to him in such an informal manner before. It was as if they were co-conspirators.

Fergus left with his feelings of unease aroused by the way his father had avoided looking at him as he declared his aunt 'comfortable'.

* * *

Early the next morning Fergus received a note delivered to his lodgings. The address was written in a sloping hand he did not immediately recognise. He looked around for his letter opener then, in haste, ripped the note open with his fingers.

Miss Shackleton has been asking for you.

Come between 10 and 11.

The tradesmen's entrance.

Samuel.

Fergus felt instantly better. *My parents will be at Matins. If my aunt has been asking for me, then she must be recovering.* He made a mental note to reward Samuel in some way.

When he arrived at the tradesmen's entrance which was their kitchen back door, Samuel was waiting for him.

'I'm very much relieved you received my message and were able to come, sir. The whole household is at Matins. I alone remain to tend Miss Louisa. Your father insisted on it, in order for everyone to attend and pray for your aunt. He even instructed Cook that Sunday luncheon was to be a cold serving, so she and the kitchen maids could also attend.'

Unease reawakened in Fergus's heart and began to galvanise itself. For his father to do such a thing was unheard of. *The whole household marshalled to attend church to pray?* He followed Samuel through the kitchen, past the open door leading to the scullery and butler's pantry, then up the stone steps, worn down in the centre from constant use. They passed through the servants' door leading into the main entrance hall. With Samuel leading the way, they climbed the main staircase. All the while, Fergus tried not to imagine what it must have been like when his aunt lost her footing. He wondered if she had cried out, whether she had been carrying something, and if the heel really had come off her shoe. She wasn't a person to rush; something external must have caused her fall.

At the top of the staircase, Samuel paused and turned to Fergus. 'Miss Shackleton is not a well woman, sir. Dr Lennagon says she has succumbed to infection.'

Fergus was anxious to reach his aunt's room at the end of the corridor, but Samuel was blocking his way.

'You may find she's unable to thank you herself for your visit. If that is the case, I would like to say, sir, that I am sure your presence will be a great comfort to her and that she will know you are with her.'

Not a well woman? Unable to speak for herself? Everyone praying?

Samuel opened the door and Fergus paused on the threshold. Only when he was sure that Samuel had retreated out of earshot did he enter the room. He took in the details at a glance. As was the household custom during illness, the bedroom fire had been lit. Nursing accoutrements lay on the bedside table: an invalid's drinking cup, a pile of clean white napkins, some medicines and tablet boxes. A glass carafe, engraved with an 'S', had been filled with water, and a tumbler with the same inscription had been placed upside down over it. Someone had put a small vase containing a single rose at one side of the table. He guessed his mother would have seen to that. An upright saloon chair was alongside the bed, presumably placed there for the doctor or a visitor. The only noise was the gentle crackling of the fire.

Aunt Louisa, pale, eyes closed, her hair loose, an intricately embroidered muslin cap resting on her head, was lying on her back, her upper body supported by several large pillows encased in starched, well-ironed pillowcases. The bedcovers appeared fresh and looked as if they'd recently been smoothed down, or perhaps it was that she hadn't moved enough to disturb them. Fergus suspected the latter.

When Fergus sat down the chair creaked. His heart sank when he saw the detail of his aunt's injuries. There was a particularly nasty bruise on the left side of her forehead, with further bruising to her cheek, spreading out around her jawline. She had obviously suffered a terrible impact, and the deeper purple bruises associated with infection which were scattered over her lower arms confirmed Samuel was correct; his aunt was not a well woman.

Fergus reached out and took her hand. Her fingers moved slightly in response, but her eyes remained closed. He would have sat quietly until she woke of her own accord, but his time with her was necessarily limited. He leaned forward and, in a gentle voice, said, 'Aunt Louisa, it's Fergus. I'm here to see you.'

With no response forthcoming he spoke again, in a slightly louder voice, and this time squeezed her hand. 'Aunt Louisa, it's Fergus.' He remembered someone had told him seriously ill people sometimes seem to be able to hear, even if they appear oblivious to all else. 'Do you remember how you used to take me down to the harbour when I was a young boy? We'd look at the ships and you would ask me where I thought they were going or had come from. You used to say if I was a good boy, and spoke politely to the people we met along the way, we could call at the confectioner's on the way home and buy sugared almonds.' He paused. *Am I imagining it? Did her eyelids flutter slightly?*

Encouraged by the possible reaction, he continued, 'You used to read to me. Sometimes you would creep in to see me if Mother and Father were entertaining downstairs and we would choose a book to read together in secret. Then, when I was able to, I would read to you. Do you remember? I'm sure it's those happy moments on your knee and later sitting by your side that gave me my love for books and reading.'

He was going to go on and thank her for enriching his life in that way when her eyes opened.

'Fergus,' she said, in a gentle, wavering voice. 'You've come, I knew you would.' She began a smile then winced, as if the action caused her pain.

'Yes, I'm here.'

'I have something to say to you and then I will die content.'

'Don't say that; you'll get better, I know you will. We'll read together again, I'm sure of it.'

'No, Fergus. It is my time.'

Tears spilled from Fergus's eyes and began rolling down

his face. He brushed them away with his jacket sleeve. 'Don't let it be so. Fight against it.'

'I am at ease with my fate. Father and Mother await me. They were here last night at the foot of my bed; they were young again and happy.'

His tears were now falling so fast, Fergus had to take one of the napkins from the side table and hold it up to his face. He had never sat with a dying person before. A scene he'd only heard others speak of, and one with someone close to death seeing dead relatives, was playing out before his eyes.

Louisa put her right hand over his. 'Ever since I first saw you, I have loved you as my own son, and now you are a man, grown, and able to look after yourself.' She stopped speaking for a while then, with what seemed a great effort, continued, 'You do not need me to look out for you now. Live a good life, Fergus. Trust your instincts. Remember happiness in love is worth far more than any material wealth.' Seeming exhausted, she closed her eyes, and her right hand fell away.

'I thank you for being such a leading light in my life and for all your love and affection,' said Fergus softly. Her eyelids flickered, assuring him she had heard and understood.

Fergus considered remaining and forcing a confrontation with his father so he could stay, then realised it could lead to Samuel's dismissal, and he didn't deserve that. He checked his watch, then raised himself and kissed his aunt on her unblemished cheek, and tried to pull himself together.

In a wavering voice he couldn't control, he said, 'You have a journey to make, dear aunt. I pray it will be a peaceful, uneventful one. You take my love with you.'

As he reached the door to leave, he turned and looked back. His aunt had spread out her hands and she was clasping and unclasping the bedcovers, almost plucking them. That was something else he'd heard about the dying and never wanted to see. He told himself he must accept the inevitable, dreadful though it was going to be.

Fergus reached the bottom of the main staircase to find Samuel across the hall. He handed him the napkin. 'Please can you see to this for me? I had need of it and I cannot leave it by the bedside nor take it away without it being missed.'

'I will see it is taken care of and a replacement put in its place, sir.'

'Thank you, I am greatly indebted to you. You will let me know, won't you?' Fergus could not bring himself to explain further what he meant.

'Yes, sir, I will see word is sent to you immediately.'

✽ ✽ ✽

On Monday the 15th, after coffee at the Waverley Hotel to plot their appeal strategy, Fergus, Bill, and Conran made their way to the Excise Offices. Dark October clouds threatened heavy rain, and the wind was whipping itself up.

'We don't want to be early,' said Fergus.

'We can wait in the Golden Lion,' Conran suggested.

Bill frowned. 'And go in smelling of liquor? I don't think so.'

They decided on a quick walk to pass the time. If Conran was disappointed, he made no attempt to change his companions' decision.

Fergus would have preferred to present their appeal without Conran, but when he'd weighed things up, he realised it would appear weak if the owner of the silk mix stayed away.

When they arrived, exactly on time, 'the new boss', as Mr Roberts the Excise Officer had referred to him, was ready for them. Mr Mathias Pearce, as he introduced himself, was not at all how Fergus had imagined him. He was tall and lanky, with long thin fingers. He had a refined, fine-featured face, and had it not been for his excise uniform he could easily have been mistaken for an educated lawyer or perhaps a priest. He was sitting behind a desk overflowing with what Fergus immediately recognised as mercantile documentation.

Fergus introduced himself and his companions. There was a slight hold-up while another chair had to be found, but when all three were seated Mr Pearce began. 'Gentlemen, I do not need to inform you that serious breaches of the regulations have been carried out by the crew of your ship the *Eleanor Bell*.' He looked at each man in turn. 'You have all been complicit in committing a grave offence, namely the carrying of contraband and the subsequent falsification of your manifest.'

Fergus opened his mouth to protest, but as if he had anticipated it, Mr Pearce held up a hand with the palm facing outwards to silence him. 'You will have an opportunity to put your case, Mr Shackleton. As I was saying, the penalty is confiscation of the contents of the hold, which, as you know, we have already executed. The whiskey has been disposed of according to our rules and regulations. I assume your appeal therefore refers only to the silk mix, which remains in our possession.' He looked at Fergus who nodded, relieved to learn the silk mix was still up for bargaining over.

'Mr Pearce, when we left Dublin we were genuinely of the opinion that we were carrying silk mix fabric and ale. There was no intention whatsoever on our part to travel with false manifest documentation and, contrary to your opening remarks, I must stress that subsequently we made no attempt to falsify the original manifest, choosing instead to report the discrepancy immediately upon arrival.'

Mr Pierce consulted his papers and Fergus could see him checking the manifest document.

'I can assure you we completed all papers in good faith.' Fergus paused for Mr Pearce to respond, but since nothing was forthcoming, he continued, 'Our first mate smelt whiskey, which fuelled suspicion, and so a cask was tapped. As soon as we realised we'd been duped, we made the decision to declare the contraband. At no time did we entertain any thoughts of deliberately deceiving the government of any excise duty.'

Bill raised a hand. 'I would like to confirm we cannot be accused of falsifying the manifest, since when we arrived in Whitehaven it was made out exactly as when we left Dublin.'

'That is correct,' said Fergus. 'We respectfully ask you

to view the silk mix, which was fully declared, as being a separate item.'

Mr Pearce considered Fergus's words. 'I accept the manifest was not interfered with. There is something special about this silk mix, I understand. Which one of you did it belong to?'

Fergus noted the use of 'did', emphasising the silk mix was now regarded as government property.

Conran spoke up immediately. 'It's mine, and if we had some here then I would be able to show you it in all its wonderful glory.'

Mr Pearce sat back in his seat as Conran launched into his marvellous silk mix routine. Fergus had to admit the man could put on a very good show when he was moved to do so. However, it was only when Mr Pearce asked where Conran had obtained the dye that the officer appeared to pay any real attention.

'Lancaster?'

'Yes,' said Conran. 'The big dye works that's opened up there.'

'I know it,' said Mr Pearce. 'It's brought a lot of stable employment to the town.'

Brightly, and quick as a lightning flash in a winter sky, Conran replied, 'Sure, sir, my silk mix can bring a lot of stable employment to Cumberland. Dressmakers and haberdashers will get work, and that can surely only be a good thing, can't it?'

Mr Pearce was giving nothing away. He continued looking at the three men sitting in front of him.

Conran carried on, 'And it really is beautiful, sir. Why

don't you take a wander down to the bonded warehouse? Take a little stroll and get some fresh air at the same time.'

Fergus cringed. Mr Pearce did not seem the sort of man who would take favourably to Irish over-familiarity. He signalled the meeting was at a close by standing up. 'I will give the matter some thought. We will reconvene tomorrow at ten o'clock, when I will deliver my decision.'

Fergus spent the rest of the morning with Bill, planning the next shamrock run. After the meeting Conran had left them for the Waverley Hotel to 'refresh his spirits', and Fergus doubted they would see him again that day. After calling in to the Indian King to report to Becky and Dolly on the morning's proceedings, Fergus, unable to concentrate and feeling in need of exercise and fresh air, climbed up the cliff where the Wellington Mine's candlestick chimney stood tall, like a monumental tower. From there he could see the whole town spread out in the valley below. The chimney was the town's landmark, the physical entity all returning sailors looked for: a symbol of the physical sanctuary of homecoming and of the financial security provided by the town's main industry – coal.

Sanctuary and security, he thought. *That's what this candlestick represents.* Then, in an attempt to keep hold of the idea, he said the words aloud: 'Sanctuary and security.' *That's what I should work for; not to prove anything, but to provide for those dependent on me and those I love.*

From his high vantage point Fergus looked down at the *Eleanor Bell*, where her crew were busy with their tasks.

From the harbour his gaze moved through Market Place to the bottom of Roper Street. As his attention travelled up from there he could make out the roof of the Indian King, and past that Queen Street, where his aunt lay close to death. He decided he would visit her again the next day, after the appeal result, come what may.

As they arrived for Mr Pearce's decision, Fergus wished Conran would be quiet. He had had a bad night thinking about Aunt Louisa and didn't need Conran's continual chirping to interrupt his thoughts. It was unfortunate the man reacted to nervousness with a desire to chatter for Ireland and the colonies. Fergus caught Bill's eye and pulled a face.

Although he had no financial interest in the silk mix, Fergus wanted the decision to go well for them. This would vindicate his actions and go some way to rectifying any damage done to his reputation. The story had gone round town, but so far nothing too detrimental had been reported back to him other than that he'd been a bit of a fool, and he could live with that, since it was true.

'Conran,' said Fergus, 'as the owner of the *Eleanor Bell* I will be the spokesman today. The decision is final and we must abide by it. If it goes against us and we complain and make a fuss, it will only serve to go against us with the Excise Officers in any future dealings.'

Conran shrugged. 'If you say so. Although I do want to know if he actually went and looked at the silk mix. I mean, if he did then we're home and dry, of that I'm sure.'

Once they were in his office, Mr Pearce wasted no time in getting down to business. 'I have given serious thought to your appeal and taken into account the various different aspects. It is true that no attempt was made to falsify the manifest after departure from Dublin and that no attempt was made to hide the contents of the *Eleanor Bell's* hold. However, you did bring in contraband in the form of Irish whiskey, for which the penalty is confiscation of the contents of your hold in its entirety.' He paused.

Fergus braced himself for bad news. He hoped Conran could control his disappointment, as he had been bidden to do.

'That is, unless there are mitigating circumstances.' Pearce went on, 'I found time to inspect the bonded material and there is no denying it is of fine quality and most decorative. I have also received further information as to your background and family business, Mr Shackleton, and I do find it hard to believe that a man such as yourself would knowingly aim to deceive the appropriate authorities – especially on the maiden voyage of a new company. However, I am required to set an example to others that any form of smuggling is unacceptable, whether intentional or not. As such I have decided, Mr Shackleton, to fine your company a lenient penalty of twenty pounds for carrying whiskey not recorded on the manifest, plus the excise duty on the whiskey. If you are prepared to swear and sign an affidavit that this was unintentional on your part, then a note to this effect can be entered in the records.'

Fergus agreed. He was having his wrists well and truly slapped for his foolishness. It was a stiff fine, but he told himself it could have been a lot more, and to have the sworn entry placed alongside the record was a welcome addition.

Conran wriggled in his chair, unable to contain himself. 'And the silk mix?' he asked.

'If I release the silk mix to you, Mr Conran, you will personally derive a considerable profit from its sale. However, your comments about potential employment within the county have resonated with me, and it is because of this prospect that I intend to release the silk mix upon payment from you personally of ten pounds. I would have made it more, but I fear that would serve only to raise the resale price of the silk mix to a level that could impact on the potential employment prospects heretofore referred to.'

'You mean I can take the silk?' asked Conran, looking confused.

'Yes, but it will cost you ten pounds,' said Mr Pearce, abandoning his official Excise Officer manner.

Conran's enthusiastic thanks went on for so long, Fergus was obliged to curtail it by giving him a quick kick on the shins.

Mr Pearce stood up. 'It just remains for me to remind you that this is a first offence and that further irregularities will not be dealt with so leniently.'

All three men thanked Mr Pearce individually again before taking their leave.

When they were outside and out of earshot, Conran said, 'Thirty pounds earned for the government by an official sitting behind a desk. That can't be bad now, can it?'

'We've been exceedingly fortunate,' said Bill. 'He could have fined us a lot more *and* kept the silk mix.'

'I agree with you,' said Fergus. 'Although I'm not sure I would place a twenty pound fine in the 'lenient' category. And he charged us the duty on the whiskey, which seems a bit unfair.'

'Twenty pounds is the equivalent of four month's wages for a well-paid sea captain,' said Bill.

'And a lot more for carpenters, caulkers and blacksmiths,' added Fergus. He was about to suggest they hold a small celebration when he saw Samuel walking towards him.

'Here's our butler,' he said.

Bill looked at Samuel then turned to Conran. 'Conran, you and I have some arrangements to make for collecting your silk mix. Let's see to it now. You can catch up with Fergus later.'

Before Conran could protest, Bill had taken him by the arm and was steering him away.

Thank you for your thoughtfulness, Bill. Fergus didn't want to receive what he anticipated was going to be very bad news with Conran by his side.

✻ ✻ ✻

Even though Fergus was expecting it, the news of Aunt Louisa's death was a terrible shock. Contrary to how he'd expected to feel, he needed company, and he went straight round to the Indian King.

When he told Becky his aunt had passed away, her eyes filled with tears. She opened her arms and hugged him, and they both sobbed quietly.

'I can't believe she's gone,' Fergus said. 'It's so final.'

'I understand. I felt like that when Da passed away.'

'I keep thinking about her; my mind won't settle.'

'That's only natural, and with time that will ease. You'll find having the funeral comforting, because it's a way of saying a public goodbye.'

'You mean it draws a line under it?'

'Not exactly. It's more that it's a public recognition of the family's loss. I found that helpful. Mam wonders if you'd like to stay here this evening. We've an empty guest room you're welcome to use.'

'Please thank her for me. It's a kindly offer, but I anticipate I will not sleep well, and I'd prefer to be in familiar surroundings.'

He anticipated correctly, for the next morning his eyes were bloodshot and heavy after weathering a fitful night tossing and turning. Each time he'd woken it had been to an unfamiliar sensation of sadness, until he remembered what had happened to make him feel that way.

CHAPTER TWENTY-THREE

Fergus arrived at St Nicholas' Church for the funeral consumed with grief, but in a spirit of reconciliation towards his parents. The sun was doing its best to break through the clouds, and he knew Aunt Louisa would not have wanted them to quarrel on the day she was laid to rest. He arrived at eleven o'clock, just after his parents, who had accompanied the horse-drawn carriage transporting the hearse to the church. Those closely connected with the funeral were dressed in mourning black, and his mother, as a chief mourner, was heavily veiled.

As it was a Shackleton funeral, many of the townsfolk had gathered to pay their respects and witness the event. The black plumes on the horses' heads bobbed up and down as they moved, and the family's flowers could be seen through the glass sides of the hearse. As the coffin was drawn out, Fergus stepped forward and placed three red roses upon it. He was conscious of his father's eyes boring into him and of his mother's quiet sobs. Fergus thought how much she was going to miss her quibbling sister-in-law. They'd had differences over the years, but there had always been a shared respect for each other's good works, their bickering always superficial and soon mended. His mother was going to be lonely.

Although he'd been to other funerals, this was Fergus's first for someone he loved. It passed far too quickly, and during the service a jumble of past remembrances entered and left his consciousness. It seemed no time before they were all standing outside the cemetery gates. The procession from carriage to graveside became a blurred walk alongside well-intentioned people who were all speaking at him rather than to him, expressing condolences, wanting to shake his hand. Fergus was sure he was related to some of them, but they were trespassing on his grief, and he didn't feel guilty about giving them short shrift. As he took a place across from his parents at the graveside, he felt as though he and his father were on show, and that the people were there watching to see whether they would acknowledge one another.

When the interment was over, Hector shook hands with the rector, apparently expressing his thanks. He then sought out Fergus with his gaze and indicated he should approach.

'Have you been instructed you're required at the reading of the will?' he asked.

'Yes. I will be there. Four o'clock.'

'We shall proceed there directly after the wake at the Lonsdale, which we expect you to attend out of respect for your aunt's memory. No doubt you can make your own way.' It was not a question; it was a statement. Fergus was still *persona non grata* as far as his father was concerned, as he had expected he would be.

Fergus was relieved to say goodbye to the mourners at the wake and arrive at Cartwright, Lockhart & Company for the reading of the will. He was ushered into the partners' meeting room. His parents and three other people were already seated around a highly polished rectangular table. Mr Cartwright was standing at one end of the table and in front of him was a black tin deed box with LOUISA MAY SHACKLETON printed in blocked gold letters on the side. The solicitor announced they were waiting for Mr Needham to join them before beginning the reading of the will.

Fergus wondered idly why it was necessary for *his* solicitor, Mr Needham, to be there, but it was his first will reading, so he wasn't sure of the procedure. He sat down on the opposite side of the table to his parents, next to a man he recognised as the director of the Seamen's Haven.

The director turned to him. 'A terrible loss. Dreadful.'

Fergus nodded, but didn't reply. He wasn't surprised to see the director at the reading, since Seamen's Haven had been one of his aunt's favourite charities. She must have left something to them. He assumed she must have had some money, but he had no idea of her actual circumstances. His personal expectations were limited to a small keepsake or bequest, and that was only because his presence had been requested. The two others present were Samuel, their butler, and Annie Forsyth, his aunt's personal maid.

His mother turned back her veil. Her eyes were looking sore and the skin around them swollen. She kept fiddling with the black lace fichu around her neck as if it was scratchy. Several times she glanced across at him. His father was drumming his fingers on the table, looking bored by the proceedings and anxious to get away.

Mr Needham entered, apologised for being a few minutes late, and took his place beside Mr Cartwright who opened the deed box.

'Those whom the deceased requested to be present are gathered, so we may commence,' he said, taking out a parchment document. He began reading, '"This is the last will and testament dated the twenty seventh day of August eighteen hundred and sixty, made by me, Louisa May Shackleton of Queen Street, Whitehaven, in the County of Cumberland".'

Mr Cartwright named himself and another partner in the firm as executors and, if his father was surprised at not being so appointed, he did not show it. He stopped drumming his fingers on the table and took to examining his fingernails.

'Now we come to the bequests,' said Mr Cartwright. 'I give and bequeath to my loyal servant, our butler, Mr Samuel Sykes, and to my personal maid, Annie Forsyth, the sum of one hundred pounds each.'

Hector, in a quiet voice, but not quite quiet enough, was heard to say, 'My goodness, that's over-generous. I hope they make good use of it.'

Fergus smiled at Samuel and Annie. 'Well deserved,' he said. 'You both looked after her admirably.'

Various other small bequests were read out in support of local charities before Mr Cartwright coughed loudly, put his shoulders back and lifted his chin. 'We come now to the main section of Miss Shackleton's will. "From my shareholding in Shackleton & Company I leave five percent of this to the Seamen's Haven, in trust, that they may receive the dividend payments therefrom to support their good work".'

The director drew in his breath. 'Bless her. God bless her.' He raised his hands as if to begin clapping, then, perhaps remembering the gravity of the situation, stopped himself.

'And the remaining shares to me, as we agreed,' said Hector in an overloud, satisfied voice.

Mr Cartwright's head shot up. He looked taken aback. 'Mr Shackleton, kindly allow me to finish the reading of the will, sir.'

Hector frowned. Fergus knew his father hated it when he wasn't in charge of a meeting. Having previously appeared bored by the proceedings, he now seemed alert and was looking up and down the table, moving from face to face. Fergus wondered at his behaviour. His father would surely receive the rest of the shares, and the dividend income from the five percent in trust for the Haven was not a threat to him or the company.

'"I bequeath the remainder of my estate to my nephew, Fergus Patrick Shackleton, to include the remainder of my shareholding in Shackleton & Company, the two cottages on Coates Lane for his own use and benefit absolutely, my jewellery, including my mother's necklaces, her diamond and other rings (apart from the ruby ring and brooch, which I bequeath to my sister-in-law Elizabeth Shackleton), and any other chattels in my possession in my rooms at the time of my death, as heretofore stated, to my dear nephew, Fergus".'

Upon the mention of the ruby ring, Fergus's mother broke down.

Hector's jaw dropped. 'What? All to Fergus?' His eyes widened and he banged his right fist on the table. 'No, that's not right, it's not what we agreed. She cannot have been of sound mind. This cannot be the right will.'

'Mr Shackleton, I must ask you again to refrain from speaking whilst I am reading the remainder of this document.' The solicitor waved the will in Hector's direction. 'If you cannot remain silent then I shall have to ask one of our clerks to escort you from the building.'

'I'm one of your best clients. How dare you –?'

'Mr Shackleton, please, sir,' said Mr Cartwright.

Hector, his lower lip protruding and a vein in his forehead beginning to twitch erratically, banged again on the table and looked directly at Fergus for the first time. 'You've tainted her mind,' he said. 'Don't think I don't know you called and saw her on Sunday. How you entered I do not know, but she told me you'd been.' He looked across at Samuel, then back to Fergus. 'You put her up to this, didn't you, Fergus? I know you did.' His face was bright red and his breathing had become laboured. He struck one of his closed fists against his chest, as if to clear his lungs.

Before Fergus could defend himself, Mr Cartwright intervened. 'Hector, this will was executed on the 17th of August. It is now the 19th of October. I was not summoned to see Miss Shackleton for further instruction. The will stands.'

Hector made no comment, but his eyes continued to bore into Fergus.

While all this was going on, Fergus's mind was spinning. His aunt had left him her shares in the company and he was delighted. Not particularly because of any pecuniary advantage this might involve, but because she'd recognised him as someone important to her. At the same time he realised he was in a state of shock. He made a conscious effort to take deeper, longer breaths. Mr Cartwright began speaking about discharging debts and funeral expenses, but all Fergus could do was clasp the underside of his chair. *Shares. Shackleton shares? How many?*

After the reading had ended, Mr Cartwright thanked the director of the Seamen's Haven and the two servants for coming and dismissed them, saying he would be in touch. He then took the key from the lock of the deedbox and handed it to Mr Needham.

'Please accept this key as the official transference of Louisa Shackleton's deedbox and contents to you, as Mr Fergus Shackleton's solicitor.'

Mr Needham looked to Fergus who, still in a daze, nodded. He then accepted the key, 'on behalf of my client.'

'May I speak now?' asked Hector, using his most sarcastic voice.

Mr Needham raised an open hand. 'If I may ask you

to indulge in a little more patience, then I will be most grateful. We have further business to attend to relating to your late sister's will.'

Hector, fidgeting and now as red as Fergus was pale, put his elbows on the table, clasped his hands together and closed his eyes.

'I think I am correct in saying, Fergus, that since your aunt owned thirty percent of Shackleton's shares, after those to be placed in trust for the Seamen's Haven are deducted, that you have inherited twenty-five percent of Shackleton & Company, which is a sizeable –'

'No!' Hector shouted. 'Everything was to go to me, and to Fergus upon my death.'

'That is not what the will states, Mr Shackleton,' said Mr Needham.

'For goodness' sake, man, call me Hector. You've known me for thirty years.'

'As you wish, Hector, but you're not making this any easier with your constant interruptions.' Mr Needham held up a document. 'This may explain everything. It is a statement your late sister asked to be read out after the reading of the will to yourself, your wife Elizabeth and Fergus. If you will allow me to continue, then I shall read it.' He unfolded the letter, which Fergus saw was written in his aunt's hand.

It has always been impressed upon me that upon my death I should pass my company shares and effects to my younger brother, Hector. He would then pass all these to Fergus upon his own demise. My brother actively dissuaded me from entering into marriage. He discouraged suitors and impressed upon me that my duty was to look after our widowed father. I now realise there was more to this; he was aware that upon marriage the ownership of my shares would pass to a husband, and thus out of his reach. On many occasions my brother has asked me to transfer my shares to him, but I have always refused, stating our father left them to me personally, and must have done so for good purpose. My refusal in transferring the shares has now been proven to have been most expedient.

Recently I have had to stand by and watch as my brother has denied Fergus the right to pursue personal happiness. He has also made it impossible for my nephew to remain under his parents' roof and effectively denied him his birthright of employment within Shackleton & Company. I trust that my bequest to Fergus will enable him to have the financial means to stand up to his father. I already know he has the resilience and determination this requires. It is my wish that father and son can work together in the future to achieve some measure of familial cooperation within the business, and that scars in their relationship, so recently created, will, as a result, be healed and forgotten.

Written by my own hand
Louisa May Shackleton.
Dated this day 27th August 1860.'

Hector stood up. 'This is a nonsense. She must have been unbalanced.' He pushed his chair back and walked up to Mr Cartwright. 'You stood by and let her write this shocking statement?'

'It was handed to me as a sealed document.'

'Is it witnessed?'

'No, but as a statement it does not need to be.'

'That's as may be, but you drew up the will, did you not?' Hector's fists were clenched by his side, but whilst Mr Cartwright was looking uncomfortable with his client's proximity, he was standing his ground.

'If you are asking did I act upon my client's instructions, as I would yours, then yes, you are correct.'

Hector stepped back. Fixing his eyes upon his wife, he said, 'Elizabeth, we are departing.'

Fergus watched his parents leave, his father in a terrible temper, his mother following behind meekly. As she passed, he caught her eye and smiled. At first, she appeared not to register it, then at the last moment, when Hector could not see, she glanced back and returned a sad smile with tearful eyes.

Fergus, still in a state of shock, thanked both solicitors for the reading.

Mr Needham spoke first. 'This must be quite a surprise, albeit a pleasant one. My advice is to take some time to digest today's news before making any decisions.'

'I didn't expect this.'

'No, I can see that. There are more papers in your aunt's box. Deeds for the cottages, personal letters, that sort of thing. Shall I transfer the items to your own deed box? In fact, I think you will need a bigger box now. Shall I order one for you? Or perhaps we could change the name on your aunt's box?'

'I'd like to keep her box. I don't think I can deal with much more right now.'

'In that case I will arrange it and transfer everything, but there is one item you ought to read today.' Mr Needham handed him a parchment document.

Fergus opened it out and scanned the first page. 'It's the loan document.'

'Yes.'

'It was Aunt Louisa?'

Mr Needham nodded.

'But you said "he" when we were talking about the lender.'

'I must correct you. I was most careful not to give any indication of the lender's sex. You referred to the lender as "he", not I. I chose not to correct you.'

Fergus thought back, but he couldn't remember the exact conversation. 'How did she know I was in difficulties?'

'She told me she'd heard via the Seamen's Haven. The fact you were making plans to discharge your cargo was as sure a sign as anything that you were light on funds. As you know, the shipping fraternity in Whitehaven is a close-knit one. Triumphs and disasters are readily shared on the dockside and within the taverns. She gave me instructions I was to offer the loan and do my utmost to persuade you to take it on, but under no circumstances was I to reveal she was behind it.'

'You are now in the enviable position of owing money to yourself,' added Mr Cartwright.

Fergus found himself unable to speak, so raw were his emotions. Tears pricked his eyes and he turned his face away from the two other men. He took out his handkerchief, for he knew the tears were going to spill out onto his cheeks. He thought of the shawl he'd left at the Seamen's Haven and wondered if his aunt had received it. Then he thought of Becky. Nothing stood in their way now because he could offer her a solid future. The words 'sanctuary and security' entered his thoughts. And Rory, his future was assured too. He would see the boy was well supported in whatever he chose to do.

I'm now a man of property. Fergus wiped his falling tears away and turned back to face the solicitors. It was surely not weak for a man to shed tears of grief for a close loved one.

'There's much to consider. I need fresh air.'

Mr Needham picked up his pen. 'Shall we make an appointment for Tuesday next?

'Yes. Thank you. What time?'

'We shall need all morning. There is a great deal to discuss. Perhaps afterwards you will join us both for luncheon at the Gentlemen's?'

'As Mr Fergus Shackleton, or as Hector Shackleton's son?'

Both men looked confused. 'As Mr Fergus Shackleton, of course,' said Mr Needham.

'Then in that case I accept.'

As he stepped out into the street it occurred to Fergus that nothing was going to be the same, and clearly things could only be for the better. Could they not?

CHAPTER TWENTY-FOUR

The next day Becky was listening to Rory read in his bedroom when she heard Fergus's voice through the open window. She raised the sash and stuck her head out. Fergus was in the street below, talking to some passers-by. He had a black band around his arm.

She shouted out and waved to attract his attention. 'Fergus, you're early. I'll be twenty minutes.'

'In that case I'll wander down to the Golden Lion and have an ale there while I wait.'

She pulled a face. 'Don't you dare. I'll tell Mam if you start taking your business elsewhere.'

He laughed. 'Now there's a threat!' He pulled a silly face. 'I'll wait inside for you; then we need to talk.'

Talk? About what? Anxious to hear what he had to say, Becky left Rory to practise his letters and hurried downstairs, tripping over Charlie on his way up. She knew he was going to whimper at Rory's door until he was allowed in, and usually she shooed him back downstairs, but she was in a hurry.

Fergus was standing at the bar talking to Dolly. Becky pretended to slap his hand. 'He threatened to go drinking in the Golden Lion. What shall we do with him?'

'I don't believe you. The ale there's not half as refreshing as ours. Why don't you two take a stroll? It's a lovely afternoon, if a bit chilly.'

'Then a brandy at the Three Tuns?' said Fergus, laughing.

'You'll find them far more expensive than here. Now get off, the two of you.' With a smile on her face, Dolly made a shooing motion with her hands.

Outside, Becky shivered. What little warmth the air had held during the morning had disappeared with the thick cloud rolling in from the sea. Fergus offered her his arm. They walked along Roper Street in step, then turned right into Chapel Street, while Fergus told her about the funeral and shared his grief.

'How was the will reading?' Becky asked.

'I'll tell you when I can sit opposite you and see your face.'

'Where are we going?'

'Just along here. I want to show you something.'

They walked on a little way until they were standing outside a three-storey stone warehouse. 'What do you think?' He motioned in the direction of the building.

'About what?'

'About this warehouse?'

'It's a fine-looking one. Well positioned for the harbour.'

She wasn't sure what Fergus wanted her to say. He was looking at her with eager eyes. 'I should think it can store a lot.'

'Exactly. There's six loading bays, and the lifting-gear hanging from the top on both sides looks in good shape. The bays are well positioned, three on each side. That door in the centre leads to an office area, so visitors can be received in private away from the stores. So what do you think?' he asked again.

'I can see it's a warehouse, but I can't say I know much about them.'

'I'm not expecting you to, it's just that I want you to see it before I tell you about the will. It needs a lick of paint.'

Becky pulled her jacket tighter around herself.

'The wind's freshening,' said Fergus.

'There's a tearoom close by that sells excellent seed cake and lemonade. Let's go there and you can tell me what you've to say. You're behaving mysteriously.'

They found a corner table and Fergus waited until they'd been served.

'I hope you like the warehouse because it's going to be our headquarters.'

'Headquarters? Are you going to rent it?'

'No, I'm thinking of buying it and having our offices there.'

'Buying it?'

'Yes, buying it as a headquarters for the business.'

'I understand that part, it's just what are you going to buy it with? How are you going to pay for it?'

'This is what I want to tell you. Things have changed

for the better. Aunt Louisa has left almost everything she owned to me.' He searched her face, gauging her reaction.

'Enough to buy the warehouse?'

'Yes, and much more than that.' So anxious was he to share his good fortune that words began flowing from him as quickly as water escaping through a crack in a dam.

Becky put a finger to his lips. 'Slow down. You're excited, you're talking too quickly. She looked around. 'And rather loudly.'

'Well, don't you see? I'm trying to tell you I'm rich.' He was looking at her, willing her to share in his excitement.

'Very rich?' *What do I mean by very rich?*

'Some would say so. Certainly I have no money worries now.'

'That's wonderful.' *Look happy, for Fergus's sake, look happy.*

'You don't look very pleased about it,' said Fergus. 'Your brow is lined.'

'I *am* happy, it's just a shock, that's all.' *Why do I suddenly have this pit in my stomach and the feeling a dark cloud is passing over us?*

'A good shock, I hope?'

'I think so, but any shock needs time to sink in.' *What's wrong with me? Why do I feel this way?*

As they walked back to the Indian King, Fergus continued to talk excitedly about company shares, how his prospects had changed and how good it was going to be for them and his company, but Becky wasn't listening. The voice in her head was monopolising all her attention. *You thought the two of you were going to work as a team, gradually building the business up. Success was going to be something you both worked for and shared together. Now it's all just there for the taking and so everything is different.*

When Becky arrived home Dolly was busy seeing to one of their resident guests. She would have to tell her mother in the morning. Anyway, maybe things would look different then. All she wanted at that moment was to be alone.

❖ ❖ ❖

'Well, I'll certainly agree with you things have changed, but why so sure it's not for the better?' asked Dolly, as she and Becky made their way to church.

'It's stupid of me, but I'm afraid.'

'Of what?'

'That Fergus will change. That he will lose his gentle nature and turn into a hard businessman.'

'Like his father?'

'Aye.'

'Fergus like Hector Shackleton? I doubt it.'

'How can you say that? You've never met his father.'

'Nay, but his reputation travels before him. I can't imagine Fergus being as ruthless as his father. See how he cares for Rory, and he's not even his own flesh and blood.'

'I realise that, but if I marry him now so much will be expected of me. I'll have to change. To become a rich man's wife.'

'I don't think that's so hard,' said Dolly, laughing. 'And there's plenty would like to try it.'

'Please don't laugh. I don't mean the money, or the security of not having to want. I mean it's one thing to oversee an ale-drinking competition, but quite another to host a company garden party.'

'And you think a daughter of mine, meeting and dealing with all sorts of people every day, is not up to that sort of thing? Don't be daft. The first question you've to answer is, do you love him? The second is, do you want to marry him if he asks for your hand?'

'There's no doubt about either of those questions. I do love him and I do want to marry him, but I love this Fergus: the caring, bookish man who loves me for what I am – a publican's daughter.'

'Don't fret yourself over your background. Shackleton's are just shippers, when all's said and done. It almost seems as if you'd be prepared to lose the man you love just because you weren't brought up surrounded by family silver.'

'That sounds foolish.'

'That's what my ears are hearing.'

'He'll change, I just know he will.'

'Why so certain he'll change for the worse? What if business is the making of him?'

'I hadn't thought of that.'

'What's to say you won't both grow and change together? That you'll become closer? Do you think you have to strive and live through hardship for a marriage to be a success?'

'Questions, questions. It's answers I need.'

'Well, you're in the right place to pray for them,' said Dolly, as they arrived at the church door.

* * *

A few days later, Fergus and Bill agreed they were of one mind that the Chapel Street warehouse was exactly what they needed, providing spacious office and storage space.

'This will do us well,' Fergus said. 'We can purchase and hold non-perishable stock and wait for the right price. That's the beauty of having solid financial backing – being able to sit and wait for rising prices. I don't want to delay and, as it's too big, we can rent out space to small companies on short-term leases.'

'No mortgage to pay either.' Bill stepped back and closed the warehouse doors. 'Your ship certainly has come in, Fergus.'

'Although why use our own money when we can use someone else's? I've learnt that lesson. Soon we can look towards a second ship.'

'Now you're interesting me,' said Bill. 'Sail or steam?'

'We can discuss this at length another time, but I'm thinking a second brig while we look into steam. It's early days; we want to make sure we buy tried-and-tested equipment.'

'You realise when we have two ships we'll be a shipping line?'

'I suppose we will.'

'We need a name.'

'We can't use Shackleton, it will cause confusion.'

'May I make a suggestion?' asked Bill.

'What are you thinking of?'

'The Louisa Line?'

Fergus's face lit up. 'Would you agree to that?'

'I suggested it, didn't I?'

'Yes, I know, but I thought you might like your name incorporated in the title, and she was a Shackleton.'

'No, I think we should seriously consider the Louisa Line. In some ways it *is* her line, and it has a lovely ring to it.'

'I think it's perfect, and more than generous of you.'

'We're agreed?'

'Indeed, we are,' said Fergus. 'The Louisa Line.' *I wonder if Becky will like the name? I'm so thankful she met Aunt Louisa, if only briefly.*

Recently, Fergus had been so busy he hadn't given Becky the time she deserved. He knew sometimes he talked about ships and shipping far more than was probably interesting to her. He'd known her for well over six months, studied her expressions, shared her emotions, both happy and sad. Lately he'd felt she wasn't happy. She was sometimes quiet in his presence, but he didn't know why and she wouldn't say.

Bill brought him out of his reverie. 'If downstairs is going to be the main office, let's discuss our business there.'

'I know you have questions to ask.'

They made their way from the warehouse to the office room, which was bare apart from a chair and an old sea chest chained to the wall. Fergus took the chair and Bill perched on the chest.

'You've already settled my first question,' Bill began, 'which is am I working with you or are we all part of Shackleton & Company now. As you know, my standing with your father's company –' He corrected himself. 'With yours and your father's company is not good. I doubt your father will consider employing me again.'

'The Louisa Line is totally separate from Shackleton's. We've set this all up; it's our company. Why should we give it up? Although I have my aunt's shares, this doesn't give me control of the company or mean I have to work for it. My aunt Louisa rarely set foot in the office.'

'Surely you have one advantage, though?'

'What's that?'

'That the directors will have to inform you of company business?'

'Only as a shareholder. They don't have to make me a director.'

'You won't be called to the board meetings?'

'Not if I'm not a director.'

'So, we'll still be in competition with Shackleton & Company, despite you being a shareholder? How will that work?'

'There may be a solution. I can sell my shares and forego my association with the company, or I can persuade my father to step down. We could then merge both companies.'

'We?'

'Why not? Wouldn't you like to be a part of it?'

'Certainly, but your father will never step down.'

'It's early days. Let's continue as we planned and build up the Louisa Line.'

As he spoke, Aunt Louisa's letter came to mind. *It is my wish that father and son can work together in the future to achieve some measure of familial cooperation within the business…*

CHAPTER TWENTY-FIVE

'You are a wealthy young man, Fergus,' Mr Needham said as they sat in his office. 'Word has flown around Whitehaven and already I've been approached by several people regarding your shares. It seems your father has not kept his own counsel, and everyone knows about your inheritance.'

'They want to buy my Shackleton shares?'

'Yes. A number of the town's prominent businessmen have approached me.'

'All my shares, or just some of them?'

'Should you wish, you could sell all the shares and raise a considerable sum. Do you require my advice on this matter?'

'It's a strange feeling suddenly being courted by Whitehaven's "great and good". It's too early to make any decisions.'

'That would indeed be my advice to you.'

'Do you think my father is behind these advances? That he wants my shares?'

'I have no idea, but there is the possibility he might approach any purchaser and offer a higher price, in order to gather them in. This may be the intention of the prospective purchasers – that they buy from you then immediately sell to your father, making a quick profit.'

'Who are these people?'

'I am not at liberty to divulge this information.' Mr Needham shuffled the papers on his desk. 'You have twenty-five percent of the shareholding, your father has seventy percent, and five percent is in trust for the Seamen's Haven. I think it of the utmost importance that you are granted a seat on the board.'

'I would rather my father stepped down, but he will never agree to that. My aunt never sat on the board.'

'The fact your aunt was a woman made it easy for him to argue her presence was of no value to the business. However, you, as a man who has actively worked for the firm and as a descendant of the firm's founder, Norman Shackleton...well, this makes it a totally different matter.'

'What can we do?'

'I will write to the company on your behalf requesting an invitation to join the board. My records note that the current members are your father, Jonathon Craggs, the company secretary, and Joseph Rudd, the company accountant. Your father is the only shareholder represented on the board, and has been since his father's death.'

'Surely the others will vote as he instructs them?'

'Yes, but there is a moral aspect here that may be to

our advantage. The "great and good" of Whitehaven, as you referred to them earlier, will find it peculiar you are not on the board. It may be thought that your father is not running the company in an efficient way; that he is making a bad business decision in not taking you in. I am sure the last thing your father wants is for such talk to be passing around the town.'

'You think that may work in my favour?'

'It won't change his mind, but in combination with other pressures we can bring to bear, it is something for him to ponder. Word travels. People gossip. Whitehaven's businesses are not just of interest to the people of Whitehaven. The "great and good" of Liverpool, Hull, Cardiff, Dublin and beyond, to mention a few, keep their eye on our town. I may be wrong, but certainly it is an aspect worth being aware of.'

Fergus felt as if he was being initiated into the confidential transactions of a secret society. 'In the last few months, I've learnt a lot about the intricate links that connect the shipping brethren,' he said, thinking of his father's power to effectively blacklist him in Dublin.

'Let us move on.' Mr Needham handed Fergus a piece of paper on which were written columns of figures. 'The bottom figure is the one you will be interested in. It confirms you have funds available to purchase both the warehouse you are interested in and another ship.'

'I never knew Aunt Louisa was so wealthy.'

'She banked most of her dividend payments and they have come to quite a sum, although if you look at the last few payments the amounts have been decreasing year on year. They are still a tidy amount, however.'

'And the cottages?'

'They are interesting. They're on Coates Lane, she bought them some years ago. One is currently leased to the Seamen's Haven at a low rent to shelter crewmen overnight. The other is tenanted on a short lease at a higher rent.'

'She always said if they could keep a man away from the crimps for twenty-four hours after picking up his wages, he had a much better chance of passing some of them on to his wife and family.'

'Shall I make arrangements for you to take the cottages back in hand?'

'Not the Seamen's Haven one,' said Fergus. 'That will not be necessary. I intend to continue funding them.'

'They did receive a very generous bequest from your aunt.'

'Even so, for the time being I will continue to support them. The other cottage I may have a use for in due course, but only when the lease has run its course. I shouldn't want to force an eviction.'

When all the business was concluded, Fergus and Mr Needham made their way to the Lonsdale. In the Gentlemen's Club, the table his father had wanted to occupy for their meeting with Bill had been reserved for them. Fergus scanned the room. There were many familiar faces: men his father had entertained at home and some he recognised as visitors to the company offices. To his relief, there was no sign of his father.

It seemed, at first, as if they would never be able to order. A steady stream of Whitehaven's business community approached their table intent on shaking Fergus's hand, presenting their business cards, offering services from caulking ships' decks to new topcoats. Several members expressed their condolences, despite Fergus being quite sure most had never actually met his aunt.

Luncheon proved to be a substantial meal of veal pie, assorted vegetables and mashed potato, washed down with several glasses of excellent Madeira. The conversation passed from local news to international and they spent a considerable time discussing the merits and demerits of steamships. At two o'clock Mr Needham bade him farewell. Fergus, suddenly drowsy from the food and wine, stood up and made his way over to the newspapers to glance at the *Liverpool Mercantile Gazette*. As he was leaning over the table, studying the list of ship arrivals, a man approached.

'Mr Shackleton, pray forgive my intrusion. My name is Robert Curwen. Allow me to introduce myself as the club secretary.'

Fergus smiled. Another hand to shake. 'Mr Curwen.'

'I hope it is convenient to have a word with you in this moment? The committee have asked me to invite you to join us as a full member. Would that be of interest to you?'

It hadn't occurred to Fergus he would ever join the club; it had always seemed full of his father's generation.

The secretary seemed to take his deliberation as a sign of misgiving. 'I shall be happy to prepare the nomination forms if you will consider joining, and I can assure you a proposer and seconder will be no problem.'

Fergus was about to turn the offer down, but that would have been the old Fergus – the Fergus who always had his head in a book. That Fergus was still there, he knew that, but the new Fergus was now astute enough to realise the contacts he would make in the club would be very useful to the Louisa Line.

'Thank you, I would be delighted,' he said.

'Excellent. I will inform the committee. Where shall I send the papers? You will need to sign the nomination form and return it to me.'

Fergus was momentarily nonplussed. He couldn't use the Queen Street family address anymore so he gave his Irish Street lodgings. If Mr Curwen was surprised at him using a lodging house as his *poste restante*, it was not apparent. It was at that moment that Fergus realised he needed to make appropriate arrangements for a permanent address of his own, and that he must ask Becky to marry him at the first opportunity.

❖ ❖ ❖

Sorting through the post, Dolly held up a black-edged letter and waved it at Becky. 'It's for you. Looks important. Expensive paper.'

Becky took the letter and turned it over in her hands. She didn't recognise the imprint in the wax, which was black for mourning. She broke the seal, opened it and went straight to the signature at the bottom of the page.

'It's from Elizabeth Shackleton.'

Dolly stopped sorting the post and looked up. 'Fergus's mam?'

'Yes.'

'What does it say?'

'It's an invitation for afternoon tea, today. What can she want with me?'

'I've no idea. Fergus may tell you.'

'He's away to Workington to look at steamship plans.'

'I thought she wasn't speaking to Fergus.'

'As far as I know, she isn't. What shall I do?'

'Perhaps she wants to build bridges and is hoping to use you as a go-between. Everything is different now. You must go. Not least to find out what she wants.'

Becky handed the invitation back to her mother. 'It's very formal. Like an official summons.'

'I'm surprised she's sending invitations.' Dolly held it up. 'Look, it's black-edged inside too. The house is in mourning. I didn't think they'd be receiving visitors yet. Like I say, it must be important.'

'What shall I wear?'

'Nothing bright, or it will look disrespectful. There's your tartan with the brown bodice. I'll brush it down for you.'

'And the black boots?'

'Yes, but mind they're freshly polished.'

'Do you think anyone else will be there?'

'You'd best be prepared for anything.'

❋ ❋ ❋

Before he left for Workington, Fergus was at the warehouse with Bill, where they'd now set up an office. There was a knock on the door.

'Mr Craggs,' said Bill. 'This is a surprise.'

'May I have a word in your ear, Fergus?'

'Certainly. Please come in.'

Bill tactfully picked up his coat. 'I have matters to attend to,' he said, and disappeared out into the street.

'You will appreciate I am here without your father's knowledge,' said Mr Craggs.

'He's not sent you?'

'No, quite the reverse. I am here because I think it advantageous for your father and your good self to mend your relations for the sake of Shackleton & Company. I will candidly admit I have a vested interest in the firm. It has, after all, provided me with my livelihood over the past thirty-five years, and I have been able to maintain a more than satisfactory living. However, that is not the only reason I am here. I truly believe that with you and your father at loggerheads, nothing good can come of it.'

'In confidence, I'm in agreement with you, Mr Craggs. Yet my father is so stubborn and hot-headed I cannot see him backing down.'

'That is true. Your father received a letter from your solicitor which I understand requested that you be given a seat on the board. It pains me to inform you that your father went into a frightful temper. His words were he would never allow you to sit on the board, that he would never let you in the premises and that he would never speak to you again. He became very agitated and breathless. In fact I feared for the health of both his mind and body. All of this was within earshot of the other employees. You can see I am justified in saying this feud is bad for the company. There is also talk that you are now a competitor who may have access to our confidential business details. It is unsettling for everybody.'

Fergus sighed. 'It is worse than I feared. That he should bring our troubles out into the open is monstrous.'

'I would add that such a rift in the firm does not bode well for the company's reputation with the business community, both here and abroad.'

'My solicitor has voiced the same opinion. Do you have any suggestions as to how we can rectify this trouble?'

'The only solution I can see is for you and your father to settle the matter face to face.'

'He will never agree to a meeting. You just said he didn't want to see me.'

'I agree, but can we not engineer a meeting in a neutral place?'

'We can try, but where?'

'I would suggest the Gentlemen's Club at the Lonsdale.'

'In such a public place?'

'Exactly. Your father may feel constrained within its confines. It is my opinion you will at least be able to talk things through, which, I can tell you in confidence, both myself and Mr Rudd are in favour of. The company needs young blood on the board. Times are changing, even I can see that.'

'Steamships?'

'Not just that – wood-and-iron combination ships. Our rivals have branched out and set up repair contracts with steam-tugs and dredgers.'

'You are in favour of steamships, then?'

'My view is that my time for overseeing innovation has passed. It's not my place to work towards bringing the company up to date. My job is to keep the company on an even keel while it journeys into the future. We need new blood and ideas to bring in the steamships, minds that are sharp and open to all these new inventions. Minds such as yours. You've shown beneath your calm exterior there is a competent businessman.'

'You mean I am my father's son?'

'No, you are more like your grandfather. He took the risks when he founded and built up the business, but he had the same gift you have.'

'Which is?'

'The ability to feel empathy. You care about others.'

'And my father does not?'

Mr Craggs looked uncomfortable. 'It's not my wish to speak ill of your father. He has expanded the business beyond your grandfather's dreams and done good by me. It's just that ways of doing business are changing. His dictatorial ways are not as useful to the company as they once were. If I may say so, the most obvious solution is for your father to step down and for you to take over.'

'Despite my having set up a rival firm?'

'The answer to that is quite clear to me, and I'm sure you've thought of it yourself.'

A merger. He's suggesting a merger. Fergus was impressed. He'd always thought of Mr Craggs as having a conservative disposition. He'd been wrong – or perhaps more likely Mr Craggs' views had changed.

'I have an appointment in Workington today,' Fergus told him, 'but I'm prepared to meet with my father tomorrow. I'll report to Mr Needham to let him know my father's response to his letter.'

'Will you be here this evening?'

'No, I have something important planned.'

'Then early tomorrow morning?'

'Yes.'

'I will send word. I have an acquaintance I can trust to invite your father to the club, who will ask no questions.'

After he'd gone, Fergus called at Mr Needham's office, advised him of developments and asked for his deed box. Alone with the box, he removed his aunt's jewellery box. Within it were three rings: an emerald, a diamond and a sapphire. He placed them on the table side by side, then held each one up to the light in turn.

Which one? The diamond looks bigger, but the sapphire is brighter. Which one did Aunt Louisa wear? It was the diamond. Then he remembered. His aunt always reserved the emerald for special occasions. *The emerald. It has to be that one.* He put the ring in the black velvet drawstring bag that had held the diamond and placed it in his inside waistcoat pocket. There were some letters in the box he kept meaning to read properly. He'd glanced at one briefly, but the time had never seemed quite right to give them his full attention. So it was then. It was sufficient he knew they were still there and safe.

CHAPTER TWENTY-SIX

In Becky's opinion, the Shackleton residence on Queen Street was one of Whitehaven's most handsome. It was perfectly proportioned. Five windows looked out from the first floor and the front door was placed directly beneath the middle one, marking the centre of the building. Small white columns rose either side of the shiny black front door to support a porch roof. The door itself, with its gleaming brass knocker and letterbox, was approached via four well-worn stone steps. A low stone wall topped with railings, set back several feet from the house, separated it from the pavement. Incorporated into the left-hand side of the house was the carriage entrance.

Becky, in her nervousness, lifted the knocker higher than was necessary; when she let it go it banged so loudly it made her jump. Samuel opened the door. To her horror, she realised she was shaking.

'I'm Becky Moss to see Mrs Shackleton.'

'You are expected. Please come in, Miss Moss.'

Should I have said I was Miss Moss and not Becky Moss?

Entering the hall, Becky saw the main staircase immediately in front of her. *Those must be the stairs Fergus's aunt fell down.* The tiles were black and white, reminding her of a chess board. As she followed the butler, she was conscious of the noise her boots made on them. They mounted the stairs to the drawing room.

'Miss Moss to see you, ma'am,' Samuel said.

Elizabeth Shackleton, dressed entirely in black mourning crêpe, was sitting in the middle of a large sofa. She remained sitting when Becky entered and motioned her to a small upright chair on her left. A fierce fire was burning in the grate, but even so the room felt cold.

Mrs Shackleton addressed Samuel in a mistress-of-the-house voice. 'We will have tea served now.' He bowed and left.

Ever since she'd received the invitation, Becky had tried to imagine what it was going to be like inside the Shackleton home. Nothing had prepared her for its grandeur. The silver gleamed and the upholstery was of the finest quality. Everything sparkled and screamed wealth. The fireplace had two sets of irons: a well-polished brass set for show and a blacked set for use.

Mrs Shackleton spoke first. 'May I call you Becky?'

'Yes, of course.'

'Short for Rebecca?'

'No, just Becky.'

Mrs Shackleton raised her eyebrows. 'That's unusual. Becky is usually a diminutive of Rebecca.'

Diminutive? Shortened? 'I was christened Becky.'

'Which church?'

She wants to know if I'm a Catholic. 'St James. On the hill.'

Mrs Shackleton looked relieved and smiled. 'Yes, I know it. We are communicants at St Nicholas' Church. Some of our forebears are buried there.'

What does she want? 'Thank you for the invitation, Mrs Shackleton, especially at this difficult time for the family.'

'Thank you, my dear.' She smiled at Becky. It wasn't an unkind smile, but it stopped before it reached her eyes. 'Let us be honest with each other. You are no doubt aware of Fergus's rift with his family and of his recent good fortune.'

There was a knock on the door and a maid came in carrying an oval tray containing not only tea, but also two slices of cake and some linen napkins. She placed it on a kidney-shaped table with ornate legs.

'Becky, would you mind pouring?' Mrs Shackleton looked down at her hands. 'I know it is unusual for the guest to be asked to perform this little task, but since my sister-in-law's sudden passing, I have felt weak in body and I've developed a slight tremor.'

Becky went over to the table. The crockery was bone china and the teapot was silver, as were all the accoutrements. The cups had been stacked and there wasn't enough room on the tray to set two cups out side by side. That wouldn't have mattered if the table had been wider. The only thing she could do was put one cup and saucer on another table. She looked around and decided she would put her own cup on the table closest to where she'd been sitting. Having poured in the milk she picked up the strainer, but as she poured tea into Mrs Shackleton's cup the shaking in her hand betrayed her nervousness. She passed the cup over and was about to offer the sugar bowl when Mrs Shackleton shook her head. Becky then took her own cup, placed it on the tray, added the milk and poured in the tea.

'You will take cake, won't you?' Mrs Shackleton said. 'I ordered it from below stairs especially.'

'Thank you.' *I don't want any, but I can hardly refuse.* She placed a slice on one of the small plates and handed it with a napkin to Mrs Shackleton, then helped herself to a piece and sat down.

For a few minutes they sat in awkward silence. Becky sipped some of her tea and ate her cake. She had a feeling that now the tea had been served Mrs Shackleton would reveal the reason for the invitation. She looked around the room again and waited.

'Tell me, Becky, how is Fergus?'

'He seems well enough and busy.'

'I hear he has rented a warehouse from the Earl of Lonsdale.'

'He has taken a warehouse for his company, but I think he's buying it. At least they're working from there now.'

'Really? I heard differently, but then he does have access to funds since our dear Louisa passed away.' Mrs Shackleton looked into the distance, put a handkerchief to her eyes, and dabbed them. 'I am wondering what my son's intentions are towards you. Has he said anything to you?'

Becky was shocked at her forthrightness. 'His intentions are honourable towards me, I'm sure.'

'Has he asked for your hand?'

'No, he has not.'

'Do you think he will?'

'I cannot say.'

'And should he, what would your answer be?'

'I think that is between him and me.' She wanted to say 'It's none of your business,' but knew it would be a terrible mistake.

'Since he has not yet asked for your hand, perhaps you may wish to consider a few things should he do so. I have no doubt, one way or another, Fergus will make a success of business. He may act rashly sometimes, but in general he has the calm head of his grandfather on his shoulders, a trait his father lacks. You should consider what being the wife of a successful businessman will require from you.'

'From me?'

'Yes. If I seem a little harsh in what I am about to say it is my intention to be helpful to you, my dear, with my own experience of the role. It is for this reason I have invited you here, even though the household is in mourning. Fergus is my only child, and I want the best for him. Relations may be difficult right now, but eventually I have faith things will resolve themselves, and I pray for that every evening. My intention is to do all I can to ensure Fergus is happy.'

'And you think I can't make him happy?'

'Initially I am sure you can. Should you marry I have no doubts that the first few years will prove to be as happy as those of Hector and myself. However, I found as

Hector became more successful, I was called upon more and more to support him socially. I think the question you need to ask yourself is could you fulfil such a role? Could you plan the required menus? Instruct the servants?' She looked around. 'Could you decorate and furnish rooms as befits a Shackleton household?' She paused to regard Becky expectantly.

She says 'household', not 'home'. 'You're saying I'm not good enough for him? That I'm beneath him in station?'

'I'm saying it will be your duty as his wife to protect him from dreary domestic details. For example, the cook's foibles, the servants' rota, the cleaning of the silver, the menu lists. After all, men do not discuss their office work with their wives, do they? It will be your place to oversee important dinners, to entertain important clients in a social setting, to hold afternoon tea parties for their wives.'

'Mrs Shackleton, every day I meet people and engage with them. I'm not afraid of meeting new people.'

'How can I make this clearer? The people who attend your establishment are working people, are they not?'

Becky nodded.

'People who would not notice if you put milk in a teacup before the hot tea?'

'I'm sorry?'

'The point I'm making is that in the society you will find yourself, the tiniest matters of etiquette are of great importance. No one in polite society would put milk in a teacup before adding the tea. It is well-known that within the working classes it is necessary for the milk to be poured in first, so the rough clay cups do not crack when

303

the hot tea is added. With fine china teacups such as this,' she held up her own, 'the quality of manufacture is such that the cups will not crack. If the tea is poured before the milk, the strength of the tea can then be judged, as well as the amount of milk required. It is by such nuances that people will judge you and, more to the point, they will judge Fergus through you.'

'You asked me to pour the tea so you could judge me?'

'That is a rather unrefined way of putting it, but it is for your own benefit that I am giving you this advice. Similarly, when eating cake, it is expected that a small pastry fork will be used or, if one is not provided, such as this afternoon, then small pieces should be broken off discreetly as needed. On no account should the whole piece be picked up and a bite taken out of it. By such things will Fergus's household be judged.'

Again, the use of 'household'. 'Mrs Shackleton, these things may be important to you in the circles you move in, but I can assure you there are more important things in life that Fergus and I will be concerned with should we marry. For example, making a home.' *I don't care, I'm going to say it.* 'Not a household.'

Mrs Shackleton's jaw dropped slightly and her eyes grew wider. *She understands what I mean.* There was an almost unbearable silence and, although quite warm, Becky shivered.

'You're cold? I have a shawl you may borrow while you are here.' Mrs Shackleton stood up and went over to a tallboy and, with her back to Becky, opened a drawer. It was only when she turned round that Becky saw she was holding a shawl that was the same brilliant purple colour as the material Fergus had brought her from Dublin. It had to be Aunt Louisa's shawl. *She's taken it for herself. What will Fergus say?*

The shock was so great and so sudden, Becky upset her teacup and watched in horror as the warm liquid fell first upon her own skirt, then rolled down onto the expensive, intricately patterned carpet where it began to form a small brown puddle. She leapt up, grabbed hold of her linen napkin and fell to her knees, where she began mopping up the mess. As soon as she did so she realised her mistake. To Mrs Shackleton she would look just like a servant. Wasn't that what she had been saying? That she was just a servant and Fergus was a gentleman? She'd just shown she couldn't even conduct herself appropriately for an afternoon tea, never mind host a dinner for important customers.

Mrs Shackleton's expression, which had initially been one of pity for Becky, turned to one of horror when she looked down at her carpet. Becky stood up, the damp napkin clutched tightly in her hand, and looked at the door.

Mrs Shackleton rose, went over to the fireplace and pressed a button in the wall. Everything seemed to stop. Neither Becky nor Mrs Shackleton spoke or looked at the other. They both stood stock still, waiting for the bell to be answered.

After a few minutes Samuel appeared.

'I think Miss Moss is ready to leave.'

Samuel looked at her sympathetically and put his hand out for the damp napkin. Becky stumbled to the door, her vision blurry from held-back tears and her face and neck so red, she thought she must surely have caught fire.

✤ ✤ ✤

On his return from Workington, Fergus called into his lodgings to change. He told Mrs Williamson he would not be dining in.

'Make sure you eat,' she said.' You don't eat enough. That's why there's nothing to you.'

'I'm too excited to eat this evening. I have an important task.' For the tenth time that day he put his hand to his waistcoat and felt for the velvet bag. *Tonight. It's going to be tonight.* He had everything planned. He'd wait until Rory was in bed and Dolly safely out of the way. Then he would take Becky's left hand and say something like, 'This was my Aunt Louisa's ring. Will you marry me and wear it?' Then he wondered if, 'Will you marry me, be my wife and wear this ring? It was my Aunt Louisa's' sounded better. He practised various versions all the way to the Indian King.

On arrival he found Rory in the kitchen playing jacks on the floor, with Charlie stretched out beside him. The dog's head bobbed up and down as he watched the rise and fall of the ball.

'Where's Miss Becky?' Fergus asked him.

'She's in her room.'

'Would you like to run up and ask her to come down?' Fergus could have bitten his tongue off. The boy couldn't run anywhere. 'I'm sorry,' he said.

'What for?' asked Rory.

'Never mind.' If Rory hadn't seen the irony in asking him to run upstairs there was no reason to point it out. 'Can you ask Miss Becky to come down, please?'

'I can try, but after she came in from tea with your mammy, she rushed off upstairs, and she's been up there ever since.'

'Tea with my mother?'

'Mrs Shackleton's your mammy, isn't she?'

'Yes, but…'

The door leading from the bar opened and Dolly came in. 'There's been an upset,' she said.

'My mother?'

'Reet enough. She invited Becky for tea this afternoon.'

'Why didn't she tell me? I'd have warned her not to go or else gone with her.'

'You'd left for Workington.'

'What happened?'

'She didn't say much, except that your mam had your aunt's shawl. The one you got in Dublin. She said you'd be upset about that.'

'She'll come down if she knows I'm here, won't she?'

''Appen. Whatever went on it's upset her dreadfully. Rory, go upstairs and tell Miss Becky Mr Shackleton's here and wants to see her. Then get yourself ready for bed, there's a good lad.'

Rory gathered up his jacks and ball and put them in his pocket. 'Goodnight, Mr Shackleton. Goodnight, Mrs Dolly.'

After he'd gone, Dolly returned to the bar while Fergus waited. He heard Rory knock on Becky's door. A few minutes later she came into the kitchen. Fergus was shocked. She was very pale, almost ghostly, and it was obvious she'd been crying over a long period of time. He opened his arms and embraced her, whereupon she burst into loud sobs. He held her close and waited for her distress to subside, all the while his mind in turmoil. This was nothing like the romantic evening he'd planned and practised for.

When Becky eventually grew quiet, Fergus loosened his embrace, and she took a few steps back. He picked up the spindle-back chair and placed it nearer the hearth, then added more coal to the range.

'Sit here in the warmth and tell me what happened,' he said. After fetching her a glass of water, he brought up another chair for himself, sat down and reached for her left hand. As he did so, he looked at the wedding finger and felt an immense surge of disappointment; tonight was not the night for a proposal of marriage.

She took a sip of her water. 'I don't want to talk about it,' she said.

'But you must. You can't be in such a state and not tell me what's happened to make you so. It causes me pain to see you so distressed. It's my mother, isn't it? What did she say?'

'Please, Fergus, not so many questions. Give me a moment to settle my thoughts.'

Fergus looked into the hearth at the jumping flames and listened to the wood crackling, all the while holding Becky's hand, thinking of what might have been that evening.

'Your mam invited me for tea. I went and she confirmed my worries that the gulf between us is too great to be bridged.'

'What do you mean? What gulf? I think we're perfectly matched. Don't you think so, too? We are kindred spirits.' He reached out and ran his finger gently down her cheek. 'I love you, Becky, and you love me. That's true, isn't it?'

'Yes, but...'

'But what? What else matters?'

'Oh, Fergus, you are such an innocent sometimes and that's the part about you I love the most.'

'I'm not sure that's a compliment.'

'It is, truly, believe me. What your mam said is that the Fergus I love is not always going to be as you are now. You're going to rise up in society. Already you've told me about being invited to join the Gentlemen's Club, and you're becoming more business-driven each day. Your conversation now is always about another ship, or steamships, and how you're going to fill the warehouse with goods to sell. Don't you see?'

'See what? That I've proved myself competent? That I can grasp the circumstances fate has dealt me and work towards making a success of my life? For us?'

'You're going to be an important businessman, just like your father, presiding over an empire made up of ships and shipping. If not your own business, then Shackleton & Company, now you've got all those shares. You've entered a different world. It's as if your aunt has unintentionally handed us one of those cups. Like in church, only poison.'

Fergus thought for a moment. 'A chalice?'

'Yes, that's it, a poisoned chalice. You've said yourself people view you differently now, and it's no wonder, because you *are* different.'

'I'm not different inside. I'm still the Fergus I was when we first met.'

'No, you're not. Fergus, the thoughtful lover of books and poetry, has been swallowed up by different books: day books, wage books and cash books. My guess is it can only get worse.'

'Yes, lately I've been somewhat overrun with business affairs. They've been pushed upon me and, as you rightly say, I have in some ways been handed a poisoned chalice. I don't have time to read like I used to; I have fewer calm moments in which to do so, that's all, but it won't always be like that.'

Becky looked as if she was going to break down again. 'You say that now, but how can you know what you'll want or how you'll be as you become more successful?'

Fergus sighed. 'We're talking in circles. You've had a bad day. I'll leave now, and tomorrow I'll call on my mother and sort this out.'

❃ ❃ ❃

When Fergus arrived early at the warehouse, after a night during which sleep had successfully evaded him for most of it, there was already a message from Mr Craggs. His father would be at the club at eleven o'clock that morning expecting to meet a man who wanted to reserve cargo space. Fergus had planned to see his mother at that time; now it would have to be later in the day.

He settled down to look through some invoices, but his mind returned continually to Becky. He felt helpless. How could he predict what he was going to be like in five, ten or even twenty years' time? Becky clearly thought she could see into the future, and it was fast becoming one she didn't seem to want to share with him. His mind was muddled, and lying awake the previous night thinking about it and tossing and turning hadn't helped. Fresh air, that's what he needed. He'd wander up to Lowther Street and collect the boots he'd left for repair. It would take half an hour, and by then perhaps his thoughts would have cleared, and he'd have a better idea of how things stood and what he was going to do.

It proved to be a wise decision. Walking back, with the sun on his back casting his long shadow on the stone pavement in front of him, he felt invigorated. He would put his anguish over Becky to one side while he dealt with his father. Then he pulled himself up short.

Here I am, immersing myself in business, putting Becky to one side while I prepare to stand up and fight my corner. Perhaps Becky's right. The old Fergus would have shied away from such a confrontation and buried himself in a book. Am I deceiving myself? Have I perhaps changed as much as she says I have? He stopped and looked skywards. *Aunt Louisa, your attempt at bringing the family together may result in my losing the love of my life. You surely didn't want that, did you?*

✳ ✳ ✳

Becky too had passed an uncomfortable night. She'd been unable to rid herself of the memory of Mrs Shackleton's expression – pity then horror. She'd shown herself up. Just thinking about it made her cheeks burn again.

At breakfast she confided in her mother about the pouring of the tea and the subsequent spillage. As she'd expected, Dolly reacted furiously.

'I shouldn't have let you go on your own. We should have waited until you'd discussed it with Fergus. He should have been with you.'

'No. Don't say that. We thought it was right I should go. It really wouldn't matter, but I've thought about it and I think she thought she was doing the right thing. She's already lost him from Queen Street. She loves her son and wants him to be happy; it's just that she doesn't think I'll make him happy. She thinks Fergus wants the same things she wants for him herself, and she can't see he doesn't.'

'Fiddlesticks. A daughter of mine is good enough for the Prince of Wales, never mind a shipper's son.'

'I've no idea what to do.'

'Remember, "When in doubt, do nowt." There's plenty of truth in that old saying. You've said Fergus is going to see his mam. Wait and see how things are after that.'

'Do you think I'm making a mountain out of a molehill?'

'No. He's changed, it's true, but in my opinion for the better. He's become a man. He's had to go out into the world and fight his corner, and he's built a protective shell around himself. I'm sure if you scratch the surface you'll find the same Fergus underneath. You only have to see the way he is with Rory.'

CHAPTER TWENTY-SEVEN

Entering the Club, Fergus saw his father sitting at a table for two by a window. He was twirling a glass of brandy, watching the liquid rise and fall. When he saw Fergus approaching, he frowned and looked away.

The Club secretary approached. 'Will you take a table, Mr Shackleton?'

'I will sit with my father and take coffee,' said Fergus, just loud enough for his father to hear. He sat down at the table before Hector had time to move.

'What do you want?' Hector asked, in the voice that, when Fergus was a child, had always reminded him of a growling dog.

'We must talk, Father.'

'I've nothing to say to you.'

'In that case I'll talk and you can listen.'

Hector glanced towards the entrance. 'I have an appointment and am waiting for a client to arrive.'

'I am your appointment. No one else is coming.'

His father was about to speak when a server arrived with Fergus's coffee. They both waited until it was poured and the server had moved away, Hector all the while looking out of the window.

'You are aware it is bad form to discuss business here?' said Hector.

'As a new member up for election, having recently been provided with a set of the club's rules, I am more than aware of that, but I'm also aware it is a rule no one ever enforces, and that much of the town's shipping business takes place within this room. However, let's stop this posturing and move on to what really needs to be discussed.'

'It *is* business then, not a personal matter?'

'Business. My solicitor sent you a letter requesting a seat on the board. You received it?'

'I may have done.'

'He tells me you haven't had the courtesy to reply.'

Hector sucked in his cheeks and pushed out his lower lip. 'It is not incumbent upon me to grant you a seat on the board, despite your shareholding. Neither is it incumbent upon me to admit you to the company's premises, especially now you have set yourself up as a competitor.'

'Father, I am hardly a challenge with one ship, although ever since I bought the *Eleanor Bell* you've gone out of your way to impede me in business.'

'But thanks to Louisa you have the means now to become a serious competitor.'

'Wouldn't the solution be for you to step down and let me take over the running of the business? Shackleton's could incorporate my ship. There are lots of ways this can be resolved.'

Hector spluttered. 'I cannot believe you have the audacity to suggest such a thing.'

'Can I at least ask you to consider it? Not even when I remind you Aunt Louisa left me her shares in the hope it would heal our current rift?'

Hector, lips now clasped tightly together, shook his head and glared at Fergus.

'You're your own worst enemy, Father. You leave me no choice but to take further legal advice regarding a seat on the board.'

Hector stood up, a vein pulsing in his head, his eyes bulging and his fists clenched tight by his sides. He looked clammy and short of breath. 'You're threatening me? Your own father?' his voice boomed out.

The room went quiet, all eyes feasting on the two Shackletons with their locked horns.

Fergus's voice, in contrast to his father's, was calm and steady. 'You dismissed your son from employment in his own family's business.'

'You showed disloyalty. No true son is disloyal to his father.'

'No loving father would have put his son in the situation you placed me in.'

For an overweight man just turned fifty Hector could move very quickly when he wanted to. He was out of the door in an instant leaving Fergus to apologise to the server for the disturbance. He signed for both men's accounts then left the club and went straight to see Mr Needham, who received him at once. Fergus told him what had happened.

'I am not surprised. Your father, if I may speak out of turn, is an extremely stubborn man. Whilst he is correct in that you have no right to a seat on the board or to be allowed on the premises, and that you are a competitor, albeit a minnow in the field, any right-minded person can see the answer is for him to take you back into the business. I would suggest we pursue a seat on the board with this aim in mind. We may, with persistence, bring him round to see what is obvious to all.'

'What happens now?'

'It is a question of continually knocking on the door. Having anticipated the need, I have drawn up a second letter in stronger terms that, with your approval, I will send to your father later today.'

He handed over a piece of paper headed 'DRAFT' and Fergus began reading.

Dear Sir,

Further to our correspondence of the 26th inst., we reiterate that your son, Mr Fergus Shackleton, is now a significant shareholder in Shackleton & Company.

As such Mr Fergus Shackleton desires to have a seat upon the board of Shackleton & Company and hopes your agreement will be forthcoming expeditiously.

However, if your agreement is not obtained within the next ten days, our client will be

calling a meeting of the shareholders to
expedite this matter.

We look forward to your early reply.

We remain, dear Sir,

Yours faithfully,

Needham, Baxter & Company,
Solicitors,
Lowther St.,
Whitehaven.

Fergus handed the letter back to Mr Needham. 'Send it
and let's see if we can bring him to his senses.'

✳ ✳ ✳

Having settled things with Mr Needham on the morning's
events, Fergus prepared to sit tight and await developments.
His next step was to call on his mother. When Samuel
opened the door, he didn't wait to be invited inside but
strode straight past him upstairs to the drawing room.
His mother, in mourning dress, stood up when he entered.
Fergus saw immediately that the shawl he'd brought back
from Dublin for Aunt Louisa was draped around her
shoulders.

She was smiling. 'Fergus. This *is* a welcome surprise.'

'You can hardly say that, Mother. You must surely
have been expecting me after what happened yesterday.'

'Yesterday?'

'You invited Becky for tea and humiliated and upset her.
As far as I can gather, you filled her head with nonsense

about whether she was competent enough to support me as my wife.'

'I did *not* mean to upset her. I was trying to advise her. In fact, if anything was upset it was her cup of tea.' She looked down at the carpet. 'Thankfully, downstairs have managed to erase the stain. I have to say I was somewhat taken aback when Miss Moss took one of our best linen napkins and started mopping up the mess. It was not very ladylike.'

Fergus sat down. 'I've come this afternoon for two reasons. Firstly, to tell you I have every confidence in Becky's competence to support me as my wife in the life I wish to lead and that I have every intention of asking her to marry me. Secondly, I see you have something that belongs to me.'

'You make your intentions perfectly clear. I would, however, repeat, I was only trying to help, and it was not my fault the tea was spilt. However, as to my having something of yours, you will have to enlighten me.'

'The shawl you're wearing is the one I brought back from Dublin for Aunt Louisa. Since it's one of her chattels, and those were left to me in her will, I claim it. I left it for her at the Seamen's Haven the day before she fell. I imagine they delivered it here when they heard she'd passed away.'

Elizabeth stood up, removed the shawl from her shoulders and handed it to him. 'It's true it was delivered here. However, I did not realise a lady's shawl would be of such importance to you. Did you not bring one for Miss Moss herself?'

'I brought her a full crinoline length, and this shawl

will match the dress she's making for herself. She is a competent needlewoman.'

Elizabeth returned to the sofa and as she did so the sun, shining directly through the window, fell upon her face. Suddenly she looked much older than her forty-eight years. The wrinkles around her mouth, once finely etched, now seemed deeper and more permanent. The lines around her eyes, too, were more noticeable and there was a general weariness about her. Grief was aging her. Fergus remembered how quickly Louisa had been taken from them. Such an accident or disease could befall his mother too. If he'd learnt one thing in the last few weeks, it was that death could be instant. It was like scissors cutting through a thread, the separation brought about always final and impossible to put right. Not everyone had the dubious privilege of a death scene played out surrounded by family.

Then suddenly he thought, *are you the old Fergus or the new one? This cannot go on. She's your mother; you love her despite her faults. She's in mourning. Nothing is going to be gained by continuing all this upset.* He smiled inwardly with relief. He knew then without a doubt that bookish, gentle Fergus still existed. He'd just taken cover to avoid the current chaos and was waiting patiently for it all to subside.

He held out the shawl. 'Keep it, Mother. Please. I'm sure Aunt Louisa would have wanted you to have it.'

Elizabeth began sobbing and Fergus walked over, sat beside her on the sofa, and put his arms around her.

'Fergus, what has become of us? We are all of us changed. Where are your books and poems? Where is my heart? I've been so lonely since Louisa passed away and now I've become a foolish old woman, trying to hold on to her son. Instead, I'm driving you away. In my loneliness and fear of losing you, I have become unkind.'

'Everything is different for us all now. I know my life is not turning out as you thought it would, and that my love for Becky is difficult for you to come to terms with. Can I ask you to love the son you have, rather than the son you would like to have?'

Elizabeth looked into the fire, appearing to be considering his words. When she spoke it was to say, 'There is much sense in what you say. You have a wiser head than I upon your shoulders. You cannot doubt I love you, Fergus, and I know your father does too. It is his stubbornness that makes him so difficult. You have no idea how much your snubbing the offer of being made a company director shocked and upset him. In his own way, he was distraught. He was offering you something he valued and thought you would too. He never thought for one moment you would stand up to him over the Madeira position, and now he can't see a way to back down. If only you could both call a truce and start again.'

'I can only do that when he allows me to lead the life *I* want to lead, not the one he has mapped out for me. The price for the directorship, a year or more in Madeira away from Becky, was too high. I'm not asking you to change your beliefs, I'm asking you both to accept the woman I love, who makes me happy, and to let me tread my own path. Isn't that what you've said since I was a boy – that you just want me to be happy?'

'I just want you to be absolutely sure this girl really will make you happy, and yesterday I wanted her to know what it is like to be married to a successful Shackleton. It just all went dreadfully wrong and I'm sorry.'

'She *will* make me happy. As for her being married to a successful Shackleton, I'm not like my father. It won't be for her as it has been for you.'

'Then when will you ask her for her hand? I would like notice so I can be prepared. Your father will not take it lightly.'

'As soon as the right moment comes, although after the tea yesterday, she may need some persuading to join our family. I have the ring ready. One of Aunt Louisa's.'

'Which one?' Elizabeth dried her eyes with a lace handkerchief she'd withdrawn from her sleeve. 'I think her diamond is the prettiest.'

Fergus took the velvet bag from his waistcoat pocket and withdrew the ring. 'I've chosen the emerald. It was Aunt Louisa's favourite.' He looked down at the ring.

'Yes, well, Dr Fincham gave it to her when they were betrothed.'

Fergus's head shot up. 'She was betrothed?'

'Oh yes, she was quite beautiful when she was young, and he was very handsome, particularly when mounted on his horse. He was tall and statesmanlike and they made a splendid-looking couple, for she was tall too as you are. He became a ship's surgeon. However, now is not the time for speaking of this. We should be looking to the future, not the past, especially an unhappy past. It all happened such a long time ago and she never referred to it. I'm sure she was well over it.'

'That seals it. It has to be the emerald. As it was so special for her I know Aunt Louisa would have wanted Becky to have this ring to seal our engagement.'

'I will write to her,' said Elizabeth, 'and try to mend things. She will receive my note this afternoon.'

'Thank you.'

As he left, Fergus apologised to Samuel for having pushed past him. It was the sort of behaviour his father sometimes exhibited and he was embarrassed. It wouldn't happen again.

CHAPTER TWENTY-EIGHT

'What do you make of this? It's from Fergus's mam.'
'More etiquette advice I'll warrant.' Dolly put out a hand to take the letter.

'Nay, it's an apology.'

Her mother began reading.

Dear Miss Moss,

I write in the hope that you will look upon me kindly as a mother who loves her son. I was remiss in not making you more welcome in our home yesterday, and by humiliating you I made you nervous. My motivation was a selfish one – to keep Fergus close. However, I realise now I have only succeeded in driving him further away. Having heard from his own mouth how much he cares for you, I must step back. He is a man now, not my child. Fergus's happiness is all that matters to me, and I think you are of like mind.

Relations between father and son can often be difficult, and affairs between Fergus and his father are very much strained at this present time. There is history in this family of thwarted love and we should have learnt that it causes great unhappiness. Fergus may be his father's son, but he is not like him and I am sure never will be. He has always shown a kindly Christian heart. I think it is too late for his father to change, but I hope Fergus and Hector will find a path through life they can travel together with less animosity.

Please accept this sincere apology for humiliating you yesterday and I hope for a more convivial meeting in the future.

Yours sincerely,

Elizabeth Shackleton.'

'Well, she's changed her tune. I wonder what she means by thwarted love?' said Dolly. 'That's a strange thing to write.'

'Something in the past. Fergus's past?'

'He can probably tell you what it means.'

'Should I show him the letter?'

'Why wouldn't you? I expect she'll have told him she was going to write, won't she? They've talked about *you*, that much is clear.'

'Why this sudden change of heart?'

'Again, you'll have to ask Fergus.'

'Do I need to reply?'

'I don't think so. She specifically says Fergus is not like his father. It's as if she knows what's troubling you.'

'I see she writes about "our home". She really does know the difference between a household and a home.'

Dolly picked up a clean apron and wrapped it around her waist, tying a bow at the front. 'You've never met Hector Shackleton, have you?'

'No, but his reputation goes before him. Fergus has talked about him, and look how he's treated his son.'

'True, but perhaps you should meet him. You're on the verge of deciding not to marry the man you say you love because he may turn into someone you've never met.'

'What do you mean I *say* I love him?'

'Well, this is what it sounds like to me. Take account of what you know and see, not what might be. You love Fergus, he loves you. Most people would say that was a sound base for a marriage.'

❊ ❊ ❊

After a short meeting at the warehouse with Bill to discuss shipping agents, Fergus settled down to some paperwork while Bill left for the bank. Fergus had sorted outstanding invoices into two piles: those for immediate payment and those he could defer. He was just thinking they would soon have to take on a bookkeeper, especially now they'd rented out the top two floors, when there was a loud rap on the door. It was Mr Craggs again.

'I won't keep you, Fergus,' he said. 'I just want to report the receipt of your second solicitor's letter to Mr Shackleton senior.'

Fergus invited him in, offering refreshment.

'No, thank you. I have further visits and we are busy.'

'Business is good, then?'

Mr Craggs pulled a face. 'Suffice to say you know I cannot discuss Shackleton & Company financial business outside the office.'

'So my father received the letter?'

'He did indeed and there was another almighty explosion. He sent word for his solicitor, Mr Cartwright, to attend him in person at the office immediately. He's never done that before. I was invited to join them. While we waited, your father paced the floor, muttering and making quite a "to-do". In fact, I almost feared for his safety, he was so angry, throwing his arms around.'

Fergus sighed. 'I can hardly say I'm surprised.'

'Mr Cartwright confirmed what Mr Rudd and I have been telling your father, that you could cause quite considerable disruption. It was pointed out by us that should you wish, you could call a shareholders' meeting not just once a quarter, or a month, but every week or, God forbid, every day. Upon hearing this your father paled, and Mr Cartwright urged him to accept you on the board.'

'And he still said no.'

'That is correct. However, an hour later, when he had calmed down, he asked me to call and invite you to a meeting. He wants to see you to, as he said, "settle everything once and for all.".'

'Do you know what he's going to say?'

'No, but you'll come to the offices tomorrow?'

'What time?'

'Four o'clock.'

❊ ❊ ❊

Fergus met Rory in the street, with Charlie in tow.

'Is Miss Becky at home?' Fergus asked.

'Aye, but she's still not happy.'

'Why is that?'

'I don't know. She looks sad all the time. Will you cheer her up?'

'I'm on my way to do just that. Will you come back with me?'

Rory considered the invitation, then shook his head. 'No, Charlie needs his walk and so do I.'

Fergus gave him a penny for some barley sugars, patted the boy's head and continued on his way. Arriving at the Indian King he saw business was slow; that meant Becky would be in the kitchen seeing to chores. He knocked on the interconnecting door.

Becky called out, 'Come in.'

She looked up when he entered, then returned to her task of making pies.

Fergus undid his coat and was about to speak when Becky said, 'I've had a letter from your mam. An apology.'

He nodded. 'She told me she would write. In her own way, she means well for me.'

Becky ruffled through a pile of papers, pulled out a piece of cream notepaper edged in black, and handed it to him. Fergus recognised both the notepaper and the writing. He read it then returned it to Becky and took her hand. 'It's a heartfelt letter. When I saw her yesterday we talked, and I think now she accepts she must let me find my own way in all matters, both business and the heart. Do you feel more at ease now?'

'Perhaps, but I would like to meet your father.'

'Why?'

'I want to meet this Hector people talk about. I want to see if he is the ogre everyone paints him.'

'He's not an ogre, he's just a difficult man. Obstinate, pompous, set in his ways, used to having his own way. Then when's he wrong, even though he knows it, he cannot bear to admit it.'

'You're hesitating.'

'I have a meeting with him tomorrow. Let me see what happens.'

Becky tossed her head. 'That means nay, doesn't it? You're batting me away with "let me see" aren't you?'

'No, it does not mean nay. It means things may be different after the meeting tomorrow. There's nothing I want more than to settle your needless worries. I will say it once more, when you do meet my father, you will see I am nothing like him and never will be.' Fergus was suddenly irritated and frustrated, but he knew to show it would make a nonsense of his claim not to be like his father. He reined himself in, willing his irritation to dissolve. 'Do you love me?' he asked.

'You know I do. It's just that it's much harder for me than you. You're the Shackleton, I'm just plain Becky Moss, the publican's lass.'

'And I want to be Fergus Shackleton the shipper's lad, if only other people will allow me to be.' *It's Becky Moss, the publican's lass, I love and want to marry.*

Out in the street again, Fergus shook his head. Ever since Aunt Louisa died, nothing seemed to have gone smoothly regarding Becky. Thinking of his aunt reminded him of her unread letters. He would call and collect them.

CHAPTER TWENTY-NINE

The next morning Fergus rose early. A sea fret had pushed its way in overnight and everything was grey and wrapped in mist. After a quick bowl of over-salted porridge, he ventured out, turning his jacket collar up. The town was opening up for the day; people were rushing to their places of work, goods were being set out on the pavements.

Just after half past nine he called in at his solicitors to collect his aunt's correspondence from his deed box. When he arrived at the warehouse, he remembered Bill was to settle the final crew list, so he was alone. The *Eleanor Bell* was leaving on November 6th for another shamrock run to Cardiff and Dublin. How different things were this time from previously. Valid contractual arrangements were in place for discharging and loading; they had reliable suppliers and buyers, and plans afoot for another ship. Fergus pulled himself up. It was not true nothing had gone right since Aunt Louisa's death; it was just that there had been a reversal. When business was precarious, affairs of the heart prospered, and when business prospered, affairs of the heart were uncertain.

His aunt had left three letters. The first was one her father had written on her twenty-first birthday, wishing her health and happiness in the years to come. It was this one Fergus had glanced at when the letters first came into his possession. The second was also from her father. This was a letter he'd left to accompany his will. He thanked her for all she'd done for him, especially in his later years, and said how much her features had reminded him of her mother, which had been both painful and soothing. He mentioned the sacrifices she'd made in order to benefit his comfort. He realised she'd given up much that many women valued in life – a husband and children – and he thanked her for that which had eased his final years.

The third letter was in a different hand and the creases were worn. It appeared to have been read many times.

My Dearest Louisa,

You cannot know the pain I am feeling since receiving your letter. The way ahead for me is now eternally bleak. I foresee only sadness. I know this pain in my heart will forever plague me and I will bear it deep within me to my death. On the sunniest of days, when the sky is the deepest blue and others around me are joyous and happy, I will smile along with them, but my heart will be sad, for I will be thinking of you.

Your devotion to your father is exemplary. A truer, more loyal daughter can surely not be found in all Christendom. I know you would have been devoted to me too, for you have expressed your love for me, as I have for you. We are in love, but your familial obligations mean we will never be lovers. I take some comfort from knowing you do still love me and that you say you always will. I will hold that in my heart too. Wear your emerald on special occasions and think of me.

I cannot remain here knowing that at any moment our paths may cross, so I will make arrangements to travel. My medical skills give me that option. I had hoped we might travel the journey of life together, but it seems fate has other plans for us.

Remember, my dearest, I will always love you.

Hold me in your heart forever.

Nicholas.

After he'd read the letter, Fergus sat quietly, staring out the window. He had no doubt his aunt, whatever his mother might think, had carried the pain of this lost love throughout her adult life. That she had kept the letter was testament to that. His grandfather's letter indicated he too felt regret, or perhaps guilt, over her sacrifice, and this was perhaps why he had provided so well for her on his death. However, whatever her father had felt, it had not been enough for him to release her from the obligation of looking after him.

Fergus wasn't going to let his family stand in the way of him and Becky. All he had to do was persuade her they could be happy together.

❊ ❊ ❊

Fergus felt out of place going back into Shackleton & Company's offices. The atmosphere was palpably tense. The staff looked up as he passed their desks, and on seeing it was him, looked away quickly. It was almost as if they were nervous on his behalf. Only Mr Craggs, waiting for him in the entrance vestibule, had shown any welcome, but he too looked strained.

As he made his way towards the stairs leading to his father's office, Fergus glanced over at his old desk. It was still there, empty, vacant. He wondered if his father had ordered it to be left like that as a warning to the rest of the staff. 'Disobey me and you are dismissed.' It was the sort of thing he would do.

Fergus knocked and waited for his father's 'Enter'. There was the sound of a drawer being closed and papers being tidied. When the summons came, Fergus was relieved to find he felt calm and that the nervousness he'd experienced on arrival was under control. He sat down and looked his father straight in the eye. If not being afraid of his father anymore meant he'd changed, then Becky was right: he *had* changed. But wasn't that for the better?

Hector rested his elbows on his desk and looked at Fergus over tightly clasped hands.

'You wanted to see me?' asked Fergus.

'It is time to put an end to this directorship business. You cannot be on Shackleton's board whilst you are in competition against us.'

'I agree it is impossible.'

'Good.' Hector smiled in a way that suggested he had just played his trump card. 'Then you will withdraw this foolish plan?'

'No. Firstly, because it's not a foolish plan. I own twenty-five percent of the business. You're a businessman;

if you had a quarter shareholding in a company, would you sit back and let someone else manage, with no input whatsoever? Wouldn't you fight for a seat on the board?'

Hector looked startled, as if it had never occurred to him to place himself in Fergus's position.

Fergus continued. 'Secondly, Shackleton's needs to move forward, and with you at the helm the company is standing still. Look to Thompson's in Maryport. They've invested in steamships and they're stealing your contracts. Soon the business will be moving in reverse. Let me come in and take over. I'm a modern man with fresh ideas.'

Hector laughed. 'I should work side by side with a son with whom I am in direct conflict?'

'This conflict is of your own making. No, you should step down. Resign, let me take hold of the reins.'

'You? A mere boy? I was well into my thirties when I took over from your grandfather.'

'Age has nothing to do with it and I am no longer a boy. It's about competence.' *Is he going to mention the whiskey? Does he know?*

Hector took out a handkerchief and mopped his brow. 'What do you suggest I do?'

'Take Mother on a tour of the Continent, visit Venice and Paris. Come back with news of their docks, their ships. Bring back a business report that will be useful for the company.'

'Put me out to grass, would you?'

'It doesn't have to be like that.'

'Well, it sounds like it to me. You've missed the boat in more ways than one. I offered you the directorship and you chose not to take it.'

'I chose not to be banished to Madeira and be separated from the girl I love. Tell me, when I returned would you not have found some excuse to delay making me a director? Would you have said I was "too young", "not experienced enough", or perhaps "we need you to stay another year"?'

Hector's cheeks and neck flushed.

Frustration overcoming him, Fergus swore. 'I'm right, aren't I? It was all just a ruse to get me out of the way.'

Hector lowered his eyes to the floor and Fergus knew then that his arrow had found its mark.

His father swallowed. 'What happened in the past is over. I made you an offer, you made your choice and declined. Let me tell you how the future is going to be. It is the reason I have called this meeting.'

Hector's brow was covered in sweat and he'd turned a peculiar colour. The expectant atmosphere in the room was tainted with animosity and Fergus thought it would choke him if he didn't get away soon. He waited with foreboding for his father to continue.

'The company will no longer be paying dividends. Instead, I will take an appropriate wage. That means your shares will, in effect, be worthless unless the business is sold. So, your worries about not having any control over how the business is run are not worth a button.'

Fergus was stunned. It took a moment for the repercussions to sink in. No dividends meant no annual distribution, no monies being paid out to shareholders, just a wage for his father. He was horrified. It was something he never thought his father would stoop to do and the consequences would not only affect him.

He leaned forward and, in a calm, steady voice, said, 'You are living up to your reputation of being a heartless, vindictive old fool. I am ashamed to have your blood in my veins.'

Hector, his forehead wrinkled, looked taken aback. He mopped his brow with the crumpled handkerchief he pulled out of his pocket. 'You dare say such a thing to my face?'

'Yes, I do, when you would stoop to letting customers and competitors think the company does not have the funds to support such a distribution. Apart from the effect that would have on the business in the long term, your reputation as a businessman would disappear overnight. Worst of all is that you would do such a terrible thing out of spite and deprive the Seamen's Haven of their main source of income – Aunt Louisa's charity, which she built up and supported for years. That you would so go against her wishes is an appalling stain on your character and illustrative of your inability to make appropriate decisions, both within and outside the business. It's no wonder that the dividends have grown thinner each year with you at the helm. Yes, I know about that. I've seen the payments made to Aunt Louisa going down each year. Even *she* thought you should step down and I should take your place.'

Fergus, just getting into his indignant stride, would have gone on, but Hector wasn't paying attention. He was leaning forward, resting against his desk with his hands on his chest. Whereas a few minutes previously he'd only looked off-colour in an unfamiliar way, he was now very grey. He began to make a strange noise.

Fergus stood up. 'What's wrong?'

Hector tried to speak, but was only able to manage a strangulated gurgle.

Alarm flooded Fergus's brain and body. He ran out of the office and shouted down the stairs, 'Fetch the doctor. I need help, immediately. My father has taken ill.'

He heard Mr Craggs issuing instructions in a rapid, authoritative voice and rushed back to his father.

'Help is coming.' He looked into his father's face and instead of the confident, brash bully he saw the eyes of a terrified man – a man who couldn't speak, a man short of breath and in pain – and immediately all the talk about dividends and shares became irrelevant. The only thing that mattered was that his father should not die. Never before had Fergus had such mingled sensations. He hadn't known that anger felt towards someone could turn to compassion for them with so little warning.

❖ ❖ ❖

After Hector had been taken to the Infirmary and Fergus had been to see his mother and comforted her, his next port of call was the Indian King. Becky was tidying up when he entered and Rory, overseen as usual by Charlie, was setting out his soldiers on an upturned box, preparing them for a skirmish. Becky saw the expression on Fergus's face and sent Rory up to get ready for bed.

Fergus outlined briefly what had happened. 'I think I brought the attack on. I wasn't shouting, I was very calm, but I was furious and I know it showed.'

Becky took Fergus's hand. 'Don't think that.' She

thought back to Amy's laudanum overdose and how difficult it had been for her not to blame herself.

'Although I was so angry with him only moments earlier, when I realised he was really ill and we were waiting for the doctor, I was praying for him to live.'

'He's your father and he's lost his way. It may seem a strange thing to say, but your reaction to his heart attack has simplified things for me. It's shown me that the old Fergus is the real Fergus.' She took his hand. 'There's something I need to say.'

'What?'

'I know now that you're nothing like your father. His blood may run in your veins, but your heart is your own.'

'Well, that's a huge relief. What's changed for you to think this?'

'A hard-hearted businessman would see this as a blessing, a way of moving in and taking control, but it's obvious to me your thoughts first and foremost were and are for his recovery.'

'I just wanted desperately to come to his aid, to help the frightened man in front of me. The terrified look in his eyes – it was dreadful, as if he were looking at hell, and the noises he was making.' He shuddered and Becky put her arm around him.

'When can you see him at the Infirmary?'

'I'm meeting Mother tomorrow morning and we're going together. You'll come with us?'

'Is that wise? Won't it be a shock to him if I'm there?'

'Whatever the outcome things have changed, and we must start now as we mean to go on. I would like you by my side.'

'I want to meet him, but not under these circumstances. And your mother will probably think, rightly, I'm intruding on a family visit to a sick man.'

'If it's easier, will you come with me and wait in the vestibule? Then I can see how things are, and at least you'll be there when we leave.'

CHAPTER THIRTY

The Whitehaven and West Cumberland Infirmary in Howgill Street was an impressive building and the freshly cut stone walls of the new fever ward complemented its grandeur. Fergus escorted Becky to a bench just inside the entrance. His mother was waiting by the main staircase under a mahogany wall-board listing the Infirmary's original benefactors. As Fergus approached he scanned the names and was not surprised to see that beneath 'Hector Shackleton' was inscribed 'Louisa Shackleton'. He looked again, a little lower down and saw the name 'Nicholas Fincham', who he now knew was Louisa's lost love.

His father, seeming shrunken in size in the Infirmary bed, was looking tired and sallow. He raised himself slightly on one elbow when they entered.

After exchanging greetings, Elizabeth said, 'Dr Lennagon called to see me last evening. He told me you had a case of violent palpitations and associated dissolution, and had it not been for the rapid application of a very hot pedilavium and the blood-letting, things could have gone very differently.'

'Yes, they put my legs in an extremely hot bath to draw the blood down and then added several leeches. Pesky things, but they must have done the trick, as I felt much better after it.'

'You're a very lucky man, Hector. The doctor has prescribed rest and a light diet to avoid a recurrence and, more importantly, a change in your approach to life.'

'A change in my approach to life? What the devil does that mean?'

'A more even-tempered attitude is what it means. You are forever getting heated about things of little importance. He suggests a mellowing of your manner. He went on to tell me the feeling of approaching dissolution accompanying violent palpitations is common in those with unbalanced bile. It is connected with irritation and ill temper. I told him you had been having these attacks more recently and that you had regularly been short of breath, yet you refused to consult a doctor.' Elizabeth paused and looked at her husband.

He put his hand up to his chest as if reliving the discomfort. 'It is true I thought I was going to meet my Maker and that I was about to be judged in the courts of heaven before my time.'

'I'm sure it was very frightening.' said Fergus. He found it an emotional relief to be able to talk to his father without their recent animosity.

'It was terrifying. In the night I had the wildest dreams and I thought I was going to die. Alone.' He shuddered.

'I had some dreadful visions. I was in hell, there were flames everywhere. Devils with knives and hot metal rods were taunting me, saying I had earned my money on water and where was it when I needed it to douse hell's flames? Another devil, laughing and sneering at me, gave me water to drink, but it was sea water and aggravated my thirst even more. Flames were licking at my feet and I couldn't breathe.' He trembled. 'You know, Elizabeth, I've always been terrified of fire since I was a child and saw that charred body on the quayside in Newcastle.'

Suddenly everything slotted into place. *The steamship boilers. That's why he won't sanction them. It's his own fear of fire that's holding him back.* 'I don't think you will be judged too harshly,' said Fergus, hoping to cheer his father's sombre mood.

Hector's face brightened. 'Do you not think so? Perhaps I am fearing needlessly.' He looked at the laudanum bottle beside his bed. 'Is it the medicine giving me these visions?'

Elizabeth took her husband's hand in hers. 'No. It is your conscience speaking to you. It takes more than going to church to be sure of a place in God's house.'

Hector looked thoughtful.

'It's about how you live your life and treat people,' she went on. 'How you help or hinder them. It's also about having a clear conscience that you have treated people fairly, so you can face divine judgement without fear when it comes. For example, subscribing to charitable works.'

'I've supported charitable works,' Hector said. 'I've been giving ten guineas every year for twenty-five years to this Infirmary.'

'From your own pocket?'

Hector turned from Elizabeth's steely gaze and looked down at his bedclothes.

'I thought not. You withdrew money from the company and donated it as your own. When the time comes for you to answer for your life, I must remind you it is on the day-to-day things you will be judged. The way you treat your staff in the office.' Elizabeth looked at Fergus then back at Hector. 'The way you treat your son and...' She paused. '...And even the Seamen's Haven.'

No one said anything for several minutes. The tension in the room was so great, Fergus thought you could have put it in packets and sold it. It was only the thought that he didn't want to leave his mother alone after she'd taken such a stand that was keeping him there.

Elizabeth picked up her bag and turned to the door. 'Reflect on what I've said, Hector. Doing the right thing means one sleeps at night. A clear conscience is worth any number of pills and potions prescribed by the doctor. Yes, you are a lucky man. You've been given a second chance. Those demons were warning you.'

Elizabeth and Fergus left him open-mouthed and thoughtful.

Outside, away from Hector's hearing, Fergus's mother turned to him. 'I too have had a sleepless night wondering how I could persuade your father to see sense. Perhaps these palpitations, which have given him a fright, will prove providential if we can persuade him to mend his ways. He's not a foolish man; he knows he is his own worst enemy. It's all about losing face.'

Fergus hugged his mother. 'You were brave just now. Father wasn't expecting you to speak to him as you did.'

'Sometimes a mother has to fight for what she thinks is right for her child. You may be a man, Fergus, but you will always be my son, and it's you who should be running Shackleton & Company. Now, was that Becky I saw when I arrived?'

'Yes, she's waiting for me.'

'Go to her. Dr Lennagon says your father will be home in a few days.'

'I really didn't mean to upset him when we quarrelled. I feel responsible.'

'You have had every reason to be angry, Fergus, and I suspect you were telling him the truth. The difference between you and your father is you know when to be angry. It seems as if your father is angry all the time and often over the slightest things. Through his bull-headedness and refusal to seek medical help he has brought this on himself. As he's grown older his ability to put up with life's annoyances has become weaker and weaker. If I didn't think it a blasphemy then I would say God sent this latest episode to warn him.'

❖ ❖ ❖

Three days later Fergus left the warehouse office at the end of the working day, having divided his time between occupying himself with business matters and supporting his mother, Arriving at the Indian King the first thing he did was have a quiet word with Dolly in the kitchen.

'I'll be happy to help,' she said, smiling conspiratorially. She turned to Rory. 'Come along, mister, we've jobs upstairs.'

Rory picked up his soldiers and made to follow, but just before he reached the door he turned and said, 'Now you've kissed Miss Becky are you going to marry her, Mr Shackleton?'

'Have I kissed her?' said Fergus, pretending to look shocked.

'I saw you, just the once, when you put that necklace around her neck,' he said. ''Cos if you do, can I come too, with Charlie?'

Fergus locked eyes with the boy. 'I can't answer that question for you right now, but I may be able to later.'

Rory left, whistling a sea shanty. A few minutes later Becky came in.

'I've something for you to read,' said Fergus. 'There are people who say I'm a lot like Aunt Louisa was, not just in height and build, but in temperament too. I take pride in that, as she was a much-respected person with a kind heart. It's one of my lasting regrets that you never got to know her properly.' He handed Becky Nicholas Fincham's letter. 'This letter was in her deed box. It explains a lot about her life's pathway.'

Becky sat down and began reading. As she neared the end her eyes filled with tears, and when she'd finished, she continued to look at it.

'This is so sad. Is it why she never married?' A tear rolled down her cheek and Fergus leaned forward to brush it away with his thumb.

'Yes, and Fincham never married either. What I'm trying to say is, we are in love like them, but we have the chance of happiness. Trust me that we will be happy. I love you, Becky Moss, the publican's lass, with all my heart.'

'I love you too, Fergus. You don't doubt that?'

By way of answering he took the emerald ring out of the velvet bag and held it in his palm. 'Let me read something from the letter that is pertinent now. "Wear your emerald on special occasions and think of me." This is the same ring, and this is a special occasion. Will you marry me, Becky Moss, and wear this ring and think of me?'

Becky's face lit up, her eyes full of excitement and her smile the widest he'd ever seen on her. 'Yes, I will, and it will be an honour to wear your Aunt Louisa's ring,'

'Shall we seal it with a kiss?' he said, taking her in his arms. It was a long kiss that ended only when they both ran out of breath.

'There's something we must do now,' said Fergus.

'Tell your mam?'

'Yes, and...?'

'Rory?'

'Yes. Can we tell him he and Charlie can come and live with us?'

'Aye, I never thought he wouldn't live with us, although Mam'll be upset to lose him.'

'We'll make a home close by.'

'And we've to tell your mam and da.'

'We can speak to my mother right away.'

'You go and tell her. She'll appreciate time with you by herself. Trust me, and I've chores to see to.'

'Are you sure?'

'Aye, I'm sure.'

CHAPTER THIRTY-ONE

Hector was reclining on the chaise-longue in the drawing room when Becky and Fergus arrived the next morning. Elizabeth walked forward to greet them and, after introducing Becky to Hector, turned to him and said, 'Fergus has an announcement to make.'

Hector looked confused. He glanced from Becky then back to Fergus and said, 'And what is this announcement?'

'I'm happy to announce Becky has agreed to be my wife.'

A silence followed – a silence of anticipation as they all looked at Hector.

'Did you know about this, Elizabeth?' he asked, still seeming somewhat nonplussed.

'Yes. Fergus called to see me yesterday evening with the news. You were resting and I thought it would be a nice surprise for you today.'

Fergus thought Becky looked as if she was about to faint. He took her hand and squeezed it. They were all still looking at Hector, who seemed to be undecided as to how to react. He removed his spectacles and wiped them with a handkerchief.

'This is most irregular,' he said. 'A *fait accompli.*'

'Remember, Hector,' said Elizabeth. 'You are the new Hector now; the one that's turned over a new leaf.'

'Yes, of course, it's just, as you say, a surprise. There is a proper way of marking such an occasion and I do intend to follow that path. I just need to compose myself. Fergus, kindly fetch me a brandy, a large one.'

Elizabeth began to speak, 'Hector, I don't think you should –'

'Not now, Elizabeth, dear.' He cleared his throat. 'Pour yourself one too, Fergus. The best brandy.'

When Hector and Fergus had their brandies to hand, Hector raised his glass and, addressing Becky directly, said, 'Welcome to the Shackleton family, Becky Moss of the Indian King.'

Becky and Fergus smiled at each other as Hector raised his glass and almost drained it.

'You'll be needing a wedding present.' He fumbled in his jacket pocket. 'Here, make sound use of this.'

Fergus gasped. His father was holding out the office safe key.

'Go on, bo –' He stopped mid-word and corrected himself. 'Go on, son, take it. It's yours now. We'll make an official announcement later. Your mother's sound advice and the prospect of death has given me an opportunity to reassess things. Take your seat on the board and you can represent my interests too. I'm taking your mama on a tour of European capitals and ports.'

Fergus caught his mother's eye. She gave a slight nod in response to his gaze. She was right. The previous evening when they'd met, she'd said she thought Hector might be persuaded to see the palpitations as giving him the excuse he needed to step down without losing face, and she would guide him gently towards such thoughts.

Fergus looked down at the key. He was familiar with it but had never held it in his hands before. So many emotions were running through his head. His father doing the 'right' thing for once, Becky agreeing to marry him, being able to move the company forward, securing Bill's employment, giving Rory a secure family home. *Rory!*

'And there's young Rory,' he said.

Hector and Elizabeth looked at each other. 'Who is Rory?' they asked in unison.

'There's a child?' spluttered Elizabeth, looking at Hector as if expecting him to have known, her eyes opening wide, and her hand leaping up to cover her mouth.

'He's a little boy we're going to adopt and take care of,' said Becky. 'He's eleven and he used to be a pit boy, then he'd an accident and Fergus tended to him. His mam died recently.'

Elizabeth recovered quickly. 'You must introduce us.'

'We will,' said Fergus. 'There's plenty of time to tell Rory's story another day. Right now, I'm raising a toast to calmer, happier times ahead.' He put his arm around Becky's waist and, raising his glass while looking directly at his father, he said, 'Calmer and happier times for the Shackletons of Whitehaven. For us all.'

THE END

ACKNOWLEDGEMENTS

When this story was in its infancy, my first port of call was the Cumbrian Archives in Whitehaven and I would like to thank the archivists there for their help and expertise during my visit. Some months later I realised I'd omitted to uncover a vital piece of information and I thank them also for going the extra mile and searching for it on my behalf when I was 237 miles away.

I would like to thank my four beta readers for providing valuable feedback: Mike Bird encouraged me to expand some important scenes and increase the tension which added much greater depth, Emma Chatterton made some excellent observations and I thank her for the chopping board of "one thousand cuts", Pat Langridge kindly shared her library of books on Ireland and her knowledge of Dublin, and Dr Christopher Roberts, casting his legal eye over my manuscript, pointed out a crucial omission.

David Preston FRCP, who lectures on Regency medicine, helped me with the history of laudanum in the 19th century and shared pictures of laudanum bottles from his collection of apothecary boxes.

I would also like to thank Peter and Michael Moon of Michael Moon Books for, over more years than I care to remember, being the source of the many interesting books, maps and pamphlets that make up my personal library on 19th century Whitehaven.

Three of my author chums have been wonderfully supportive: Lizzie Lamb, Ros Rendle, and Adrienne Vaughan. Thank you, ladies, for sharing the ups and the downs of it all and giving me the benefit of your collective experience. I am fortunate in having an excellent production team: My editor Helena Fairfax, My proofreader Julia Gibbs and my publisher Sarah Houldcroft of Goldcrest Books. They all encourage and support me. My cover is designed by Tim Barber of Dissect Designs who seems to understand instinctively what I am describing then improves it.

My family not only support me in the writing of my books, but also read them which I see as a great compliment. My husband, Jim, travels the journey with me and many a productive hour has been spent discussing the characters and plot around the kitchen table with a glass of red.

ALSO BY LORNA HUNTING

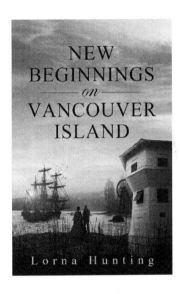

The year is 1854 and Stag Liddell, a young collier from Liverpool, signs up to work in Vancouver Island's new coal mines. Whilst waiting for his ship to Canada, he meets ambitious school teacher Kate McAvoy who is also making the trip.

As the ship nears its destination, Stag and Kate's relationship begins to blossom, but damning information comes to light and a pact made years before comes into play.

Will their budding romance survive these devastating revelations? And will they both achieve their dreams in this new land?

Available from Amazon

ABOUT THE AUTHOR

Lorna was born and brought up in the UK. Her forebears on her mother's side fled the Irish famine in the 19th century to settle in Parton, near Whitehaven in Cumberland. In the mid-1850s they emigrated to Vancouver Island, Canada, to open up the new coal mines. Coal was also important to Lorna's father's side of the family as they were involved in the coal-trading business with Coote and Warren, covering East Anglia and the north London suburbs.

After teaching the piano and raising a family, Lorna exhibited and lectured on antique Chinese textiles in the UK, New York, China and Hong Kong. Following on from that she studied and taught at the School of Oriental and African Studies (SOAS) in London gaining a doctorate in Chinese history. She now writes historical fiction full time and lives in Stamford in a very old house with stone walls and lots of beams. Just the place for a historian. She is very fond of rabbits.

Contact Lorna

www.lornahunting.com
Twitter: @lornahunting
Facebook: @huntinglorna
Instagram: lornahunting

If you've read and enjoyed this book, please leave a review on Amazon or Goodreads.

Printed in Great Britain
by Amazon

86509925R00203